ONE IF BY LAND

THE REGULATOR SERIES, BOOK 4

ONE IF BY LAND

ETHAN J. WOLFE

FIVE STAR
A part of Gale, a Cengage Company

GALE
A Cengage Company

Farmington Hills, Mich • San Francisco • New York • Waterville, Maine
Meriden, Conn • Mason, Ohio • Chicago

LIBRARY OF CONGRESS CATALOGING-IN-PUBLICATION DATA

Names: Wolfe, Ethan J., author.
Title: One if by land / Ethan J. Wolfe.
Description: First edition. | Waterville, Maine : Five Star Publishing, 2017. |
   Series: The regulator series ; 4
Identifiers: LCCN 2017013512 | ISBN 9781432837334 (hardcover) | ISBN
   1432837338 (hardcover) | ISBN 9781432840198 (ebook) | 1432840193
   (ebook) | 9781432840181 (ebook) | 1432840185 (ebook)
Subjects: LCSH: United States—History—Civil War, 1861–1865—Veterans—
   Fiction. | Retired military personnel—United States—Fiction. | Murder—
   Investigation—Fiction. | BISAC: FICTION / Action & Adventure. | FICTION /
   Westerns. | GSAFD: Western stories. | Mystery fiction.
Classification: LCC PS3612.A5433 O54 2017 | DDC 813/.6—dc23
LC record available at https://lccn.loc.gov/2017013512

First Edition. First Printing: September 2017
Find us on Facebook–https://www.facebook.com/FiveStarCengage
Visit our website–http://www.gale.cengage.com/fivestar/
Contact Five Star™ Publishing at FiveStar@cengage.com

Printed in the United States of America
1 2 3 4 5 6 7 21 20 19 18 17

ONE IF BY LAND

CHAPTER ONE

William Burke, Special Assistant to President Chester Arthur, rode a rented buggy along a narrow dirt road to the Tennessee farm of the senior Murphy. John Michael Murphy grew corn and tobacco on a thousand acres of prime bottomland. The corn was used to distill the excellent whiskey Murphy produced in a large warehouse-type barn on the property. The tobacco was harvested into cigars and for pipes.

On his right were fields of corn. On the left were tall fields of tobacco. Workers mingled in the fields, checking crops for harvest.

Burke had visited the farm before, usually when, as was the case today, the younger Murphy wasn't home at his farm adjacent to his father. After an hour's ride in the buggy, Burke finally arrived at the large home of John Michael Murphy.

Besides the home, there was a large corral and the barn used to distill the whiskey. Burke parked the buggy beside the corral where a dozen horses grazed from bales of hay.

He stepped down and stretched his back for a few seconds. The house was quiet, but he could hear activity coming from the barn several hundred feet to his left. He walked to the barn's open doors and peered inside.

The barn was at least thirty feet high with four tiers that housed barrels of whiskey. Men were in the tiers rotating barrels of whiskey as part of the aging process. John Michael Murphy shouted orders to his men on the location and ages of the barrels.

Burke came up behind John Michael and said, "Mr. Murphy, a word please."

John Michael turned and looked at Burke. Not as tall or as broad as his son, John Michael was still an imposing figure for a man in his sixties.

"Do you remember me, Mr. Murphy?" Burke asked.

John Michael sighed. "I remember you, Mr. Burke," he said.

"Can we talk privately for a moment?"

"Come over to the house," John Michael said. "We'll have us a drink."

Seated in chairs on the porch, John Michael and Burke sipped from tall glasses filled with ice and two ounces of whiskey aged, as John Michael put it, three full years in a barrel.

There was a box of cigars on the table between them, and John Michael opened the lid and removed two cigars and gave one to Burke. John Michael picked up a wood match from the small tinderbox next to the cigar box and struck the match. He lit Burke's cigar, then his own, and discarded the match.

"Now suppose you tell me why you're here," John Michael said.

"I stopped by your son's place first and he wasn't there," Burke said. "Some hands in the fields told me he rode here early this morning."

"I meant why did you travel all the way from Washington to see my son?" John Michael said.

Burke took a sip of whiskey, then said, "Because he's needed."

John Michael puffed on his cigar and blew a cloud of hazy smoke. "Why can't you people leave my son alone?" he said. "There must be others you can call upon in that Godforsaken city?"

"Not like your son, Mr. Murphy," Burke said. "Please tell me where he is."

"Waging war on some stumps that need clearing in the west field," John Michael said. "I don't expect him until dark, so if you want to talk to him now, I'll take you to him. Can you ride a horse?"

"I have a buggy," Burke said.

John Michael looked at Burke.

"I can ride a horse," Burke said.

Shirtless, sweat dripping from his face and torso, Murphy braced his hands against the massive stump and pushed with all of his weight behind it. A thick rope was looped around the stump and tied to the saddle horn on his massive horse he called Boyle.

"Pull," Murphy said and Boyle inched forward as Murphy pushed.

The stump rocked slightly.

"Come on, you son of a bitch," Murphy yelled and the stump rocked a bit more.

For many long seconds, neither Murphy nor stump moved, and then Boyle snorted loudly and strained every muscle in his being, and the stump started to break from the ground.

"That's it, damn you," Murphy yelled as the stump broke free from its roots and upended.

Murphy fell forward onto the stump and sucked wind. Boyle turned and walked to him and nudged him gently.

"Well, that wasn't so bad, now was it?" Murphy said.

Behind Murphy, seated on horses, Burke and John Michael watched the scene unfold.

"Why don't you hitch an entire team and let the beasts do the work?" Burke asked.

"Now that would make sense," John Michael said. "But my

son doesn't always do what make sense."

Murphy stood up and looked at Burke.

"Lucky for you I'm not wearing my gun," Murphy said.

Burke dismounted and walked to Murphy. Burke was always surprised at the sheer size and width of Murphy whenever they stood next to each other. At five foot eleven, Burke was four inches taller than the average man and Murphy made him feel like a child.

Burke extended his right hand and it all but disappeared inside Murphy's bear-claw fist.

"We need to talk," Burke said.

"Where's Ma?" Murphy asked as he took a chair on the front porch.

"Went to visit with her sister," John Michael said. "Be back tomorrow sometime."

Murphy had a glass of whiskey and his pipe. He sipped and then lit a wood match and held it to his pipe.

"Now why don't you tell me why you're here?" Murphy asked Burke.

"The President . . ." Burke said.

"Arthur is a sniveling pipsqueak," Murphy said.

"Your opinion aside, he is the President," Burke said.

"Not elected," Burke said.

Burke sighed. "Are you going to listen to what I have to say, please?"

Murphy blew clouds of smoke and nodded.

"In one month, representatives from the United Kingdom, Germany, Japan, France, Spain, and Austria will meet in New York City with President Arthur to discuss economic and trade agreements," Burke said. "There is, for loss of a better word, a killer roaming the streets of New York, causing fear and disruption in commerce, and the President would like this killer apprehended or killed before the meetings commence."

"How many victims?" Murphy asked.

"Fourteen so far. All of them women."

"What are the city police doing?"

"All that they can."

"Then let them deal with it," Murphy said. "I don't see how this is a job for the Secret Service."

"Maybe not, but it is a job for a regulator, and there is none better than you," Burke said. "The President feels that with your skill and knowledge of modern forensics and police techniques, your assistance to the New York police will be invaluable."

"The only place I dislike more than Washington is New York," Murphy said.

"You don't have to like it to do the job," Burke said. "The President of the United States is hosting the six major powers in the world besides us, and how is it going to look if the host city is besieged with the murders of women on the streets?"

Murphy took a sip from his glass and then set it on the table. "I'm going to take a hot bath," he said.

"For God's sake, Murphy," Burke said. "Is that all you can say?"

"Will you stay for supper?" Murphy asked.

"Yes."

"Then I'll say more then," Murphy said. He stood up, took his pipe with him, and entered the house.

Burke looked at John Michael.

"The secret to dealing with my son is not to tell him what to do," John Michael said. "Let him come around gradual to thinking it's his idea."

Burke sighed.

"How about a fresh cigar?" John Murphy said.

★ ★ ★ ★ ★

Murphy soaked in a hot tub of salts and some of his mother's bubble bath. At his mother's insistence, his father had the private room built for the large tub, complete with a gravity-fed tank on the roof and a fireplace for heating hot water.

He soaked a washcloth in the hot water, rested his head against the rim, and placed the facecloth over his eyes.

The hot water penetrated deep into his muscles to the bone, and he felt some of the weariness melt away.

There was a knock on the door; it opened and his father walked in with a mug of coffee and set it on the table beside the tub.

Murphy removed the washcloth and looked at his father.

"Rufus made a roast for supper," John Michael said.

Rufus, the man his mother took in fifteen years ago, was a master chef in the kitchen.

"That man Burke, exactly what does he do for the President?" John Michael asked.

Murphy reached for his pipe on the table and tobacco pouch. "He's in charge of taking out the trash," he said as he stuffed the pipe.

"Trash?" John Michael said.

"Never mind, Pop," Murphy said as he lit the pipe with a wood match.

"Son, listen to me now," John Michael said. "The war's been over for eighteen years now. Your wife and child have been gone for close to twenty. Sally left more than a year ago. You can't carry around all this bitterness inside you like this. I believe God put each and every one of us on this earth for a purpose, no matter what that purpose is. You're bored working your land, hated being a congressman, and you can pull all the stumps out of the ground until not one is standing. It won't do you one bit of good. And do you know why? Because you're wasting the

12

talents God gave you. It's your decision, of course, to stay or go, and your mother will understand if you go, but a man can only stand so much boredom in his life if you ask me. There, I've said my piece. Do you want another bucket of hot water?"

Dressed in a suit, Murphy met his father and Burke at the table in the main dining room off the parlor.

Rufus had a full spread on the table consisting of pot roast, potatoes, corn, salad, bread, and wine, with freshly churned ice cream and coffee for dessert.

Murphy took a chair and looked at Burke.

"So, when do we leave?" Murphy asked.

Burke looked at John Michael and the senior Murphy shrugged.

"First thing in the morning," Burke said.

Murphy nodded.

"I won't ride in a buggy," he said.

CHAPTER TWO

Murphy and Burke road the train north to Washington, D.C., where Murphy still had his residence just across the border in Virginia. They caught the noon train and would arrive in Washington around nine or ten in the evening.

Burke had a worn leather briefcase. He opened it and removed a stack of reports and gave them to Murphy.

"These are typed," Murphy said.

"My secretary has a new Remington typewriter," Burke said. "It has a new design in the keyboard that allows you to see what you're typing while you type it. She's quite handy with it, I must say."

Murphy scanned the top document. The words *Top Secret W.B.* were stamped in red letters.

"I think I'll walk over to the dining car and get us some coffee," Burke said.

After Burke had left the riding car, Murphy started to read the typed reports. In a span of just three months, fourteen women were murdered on the streets of New York City.

According to reports compiled by the New York City and the Metropolitan police, all the women were known prostitutes. The locations of the murders varied, from the section of Manhattan known as the Five Points, to the Lower and Upper West Side where prostitutes were known to frequent.

Two victims were found on the west side of Central Park near 96th Street.

The city medical examiner's report described the murders as "ghastly" in nature. Each of the victims was, as the medical examiner stated, "gutted like fish." Ovaries, uterus and other vital organs were removed, but not on-site. In the medical examiner's opinion, the women were murdered elsewhere and then dumped.

The combined efforts of the City and Metropolitan police failed to produce a single witness or viable clue as to the identity of the person or persons responsible.

The major newspapers in New York, including the *Times, Post, Sun, World,* and *Tribune,* were demanding action on the part of the police. Women in the city were in a panic and men were demanding the right to carry arms to protect their women and families. The *Times* wrote a piece asking Mayor Franklin Edson to request the use of the National Guard from Governor Grover Cleveland.

Burke returned with two large mugs of black coffee.

"How do you not have one shred of evidence after fourteen murders in a span of a few months?" Murphy asked as he took a mug.

"The more important question is can you put an end to this before the meeting of countries in thirty-four days?" Burke asked.

"Have the mayor and police been notified that I'm being sent as an advisor?" Murphy asked.

"Arthur himself sent a wire to Edson informing him that a member of his Secret Service was coming to assist the police with the investigation," Burke said. "Also, I've booked you a nice room in the Carlton Hotel near Central Park and reserved you a carriage driver. And retained the services of a personal assistant."

About to sip from his mug, Murphy paused. "What was that last part?"

"I've reserved you a personal carriage and driver."

"No, after that," Murphy said.

Burke sighed softly, then sipped from his mug and said, "It was Arthur's idea. The Pinkerton Detective Agency has the best trained personnel in the world. They use the most modern techniques of any police agency in the country. One agent in particular is from Scotland Yard. Squire Melvin Knoop the Third. He came over in 'seventy-three to study American police techniques and was recruited by Pinkerton's in 'seventy-nine. Allan Pinkerton is from Scotland, you know."

"This Knoop is my assistant?" Murphy asked.

"Pinkerton's served as Lincoln's bodyguards during the war before Grant formed the Secret Service," Burke said.

"And look how good that turned out for Lincoln," Murphy said. "Look, Burke, I don't need an assistant, a bodyguard, or a babysitter."

"I'm afraid it's the President's idea and it can't be undone," Burke said. "If someone from Scotland helps end this reign of terror on the streets of New York before the meeting, well, Scotland is part of the UK, and it will sit well with them as our ally."

"Ally? Didn't they burn the White House to the ground in eighteen fourteen?" Murphy said.

"It's done. Knoop is on a train from Chicago as we speak," Burke said. "Now let's talk about your compensation."

"My regular fee and expenses, and I've been thinking that I'd like to go back full time and run the Secret Service," Murphy said.

"I'll speak with the President," Burke said. "I'm sure he'd be delighted to have you head up his protection detail."

Murphy sipped from his mug. "I think I'll go to my room and take a nap," he said. "I'll see you at six for dinner."

In his stateroom, Murphy removed his jacket, tie, and shirt and splashed cold water from the basin on his face. Then he sat on the bed and opened his large satchel that held three bottles of his father's whiskey.

He opened a bottle and poured one ounce into the water glass beside the pitcher on the nightstand. He took a small sip, then stuffed and lit his pipe and sat against the headboard.

The problem with men like Chester Arthur, Edson, and Cleveland was that they were career politicians. Shaking hands and kissing babies was their strong suit, not getting dirty in the real world. And when it came to solving a crisis, immediately wasn't soon enough, and at once was too slow.

But his father was right. His life had been on hold for too long and he needed a sense of purpose again. His grandfather once told him, when as a boy he asked him why he still worked in the fields every day, that "A life without a purpose is called death."

Under President Grant, being a member of his Secret Service squad and personal bodyguard was a joy and a privilege. He had read in a newspaper recently that Grant was living and writing his memoirs in Mount McGregor in New York. He would make time to visit his old commanding officer and dear friend while in New York City.

Murphy finished the whiskey, set the pipe on the nightstand, and took a nap.

"There are some details missing from the police reports," Murphy said as he sliced into a steak.

Burke ordered baked chicken and was cutting into it, then paused briefly. "Such as?" he said.

"Were the victims dressed or undressed when found on the streets?" Murphy said. "Had the prostitutes engaged in recent sexual relations before they were murdered? Were the women drugged with chloroform or ether or opium to render them helpless victims?"

Burke ate a piece of chicken and washed it down with a sip of red wine.

"Were the victims robbed of their possessions?" Murphy continued. "Were there any witnesses to the victims with a potential customer prior to their demise? Even prostitutes have a residence. Did the police locate and search the residences of the victims? Do the victims have relatives in the city, and were they interviewed by the police?"

"I think your questions would be better served if you asked them to the police," Burke said.

Murphy nodded. "These representatives meeting in New York with Arthur are exactly what?" he asked.

"High level cabinet members of their governments authorized to discuss free trade and economics," Burke said. "Each will travel with a party of ten that includes assistants and security. The talks will take place over a period of two weeks in Manhattan, after which a special train will carry them to Washington for a tour of the White House and a state dinner."

"Why not just move the whole shebang to Washington away from the bad publicity of the murders?" Murphy asked.

"The meetings took six months to plan, and New York City was chosen over Washington so as to not intimidate the other representatives by a show of power on Arthur's part."

Murphy ate a slice of his steak and took a sip from his water glass.

"I'll accompany you to New York to introduce you to Mayor Edson," Burke said. "He didn't like Arthur sticking his nose in what he considers a local matter, and it took some smoothing over to calm him down, so I expect you to act accordingly."

"Accordingly?" Murphy said.

"You're a talented regulator and lawman, Murphy, perhaps the best out there, but you're no politician," Burke said.

"God forbid such a state ever befalls me," Murphy said.

Burke lifted his wine glass and said, "I'll second that emotion," and took a sip. "Now we'll stay overnight in Washington and take the early morning train to New York. Only police ride horses in the streets, Murphy, so I suggest you leave that beast you ride in Virginia on your farm. The other thing is only police openly carry a sidearm, so keep that Colt of yours under wraps. The people in New York get upset when they see a man carrying a gun."

"Aren't they a delicate bunch," Murphy said.

"There, that's what I'm talking about," Burke said. "Why are the most accomplished of men oftentimes the most uncouth?"

"Maybe you need to be one to be the other?" Murphy said.

Burke sighed and pulled out his pocket watch. "We'll be in Washington by eight o'clock. Feel like a quick game of chess?"

"If you don't mind losing to someone as uncouth as me," Murphy said.

Murphy walked Boyle from the boxcar to the platform where Burke waited beside a manned carriage.

"We'll meet at ten tomorrow morning and take the ten-thirty train to New York," Burke said. "I'll have breakfast with the President and review our meeting. I made a reservation for you at the Hotel Washington."

"I'll ride to my farm," Burke said as he strapped on his holster.

"In the dark?"

"Boyle knows the way," Murphy said and he mounted the saddle.

"I thought you rented it to a family?"

"I did, but they keep my bedroom available."

Murphy turned Boyle and trotted away from the station and into the night.

Burke climbed aboard the carriage and said, "Let's go, driver."

Lights were on in the large farmhouse when Murphy rode Boyle to the hitching post near the porch and dismounted.

Before he took the first step to the porch, the front door opened and Mal Johnson stepped out with a cocked shotgun in his hands.

Murphy looked at the tall, wiry black man and said, "It's not polite to shoot the landlord."

Mal squinted through the dark at Murphy.

"Mr. Murphy, is that you?" he asked.

"There's a slight chill in the air tonight, Mal," Murphy said. "You wouldn't happen to have a pot of coffee on the stove, would you?"

Mal Johnson was born a slave, as was his wife, Etta. Mal to a large plantation in Georgia, Etta in South Carolina. They met when she was sold to Mal's master for purposes of breeding, as she was of strong stock. The master had a local preacher marry them, and a year later a son was born.

That was in eighteen sixty-one, just before the war started.

The boy died from cholera when he was just a few months old. Life on the plantation continued as normal until, in late 'sixty-three, it was overrun by Grant's troops and the slaves were freed. Many, including Mal, enlisted in the black troops formed in the north. Etta accompanied Mal to Boston, where he became part of the first all-black regiment in American history.

After the war, with nothing to return to the south for, Mal stayed on with the army as a scout, and he and Etta traveled west to the new frontier. After fifteen years of traveling the west with the army, Mal retired and he and Etta returned east. Both were in their forties by then, with two young sons. Mal's meager pension wasn't enough to support them, so he took odd jobs to make ends meet.

Six months ago, when Murphy decided he had enough of Washington, he decided to rent his Virginia property to someone experienced in tobacco farming. Mal and Etta applied.

Mal, like Murphy, was a Grant man and also had years of experience with growing tobacco before the war.

Murphy, more interested in keeping the property value high than being a landlord, rented the farm to Mal and Etta for next to nothing and allowed them to keep the entire value of the crop.

"How was last harvest, Mal?" Murphy asked as Etta filled three cups with fresh coffee.

"Nearly a hundred percent," Mal said. "Maybe two acres lost to pests and such. This one will be even better."

"Good," Murphy said. He sipped from his cup and nodded to Etta. "Fine coffee, ma'am."

"Can I fix you something to eat?" Etta asked.

"I ate on the train," Murphy said.

"I was going to write you, but as long as you're here I might as well ask," Mal said. "Those twenty acres to the south that need clearing, I would like to use some of my profits to buy a team of oxen to clear it. I think in two years I can add twenty acres to the crop."

"How much of an investment will you need?" Murphy asked.

"I priced a team of oxen, equipment, and mule at a thousand dollars," Mal said.

"I'll pay for it," Murphy said. "The team and equipment will become part of the farm, so all you have to do is clear the land. The extra profits are yours to keep."

"I'll do my best to show your faith in me ain't wasted," Mal said.

"You've already shown me that," Murphy said. "How are your boys?"

"Samuel is fifteen now," Etta said. "Moses is about to turn fourteen."

"Both are well?" Murphy asked.

"Yes, sir," Mal said. "They help with the farming when they ain't in the colored school. Samuel is as tall as me almost."

Murphy looked at the cap-and-ball plains rifle that hung on the wall above the front door. "Did you teach them to hunt with that?"

"I did," Mal said.

"Do you know the general store near the border?" Murphy asked.

"Yes, sir," Mal said.

"Tomorrow afternoon, take a ride over there," Murphy said. "There's something there I'd like you to pick up for me."

"Yes, sir," Mal said.

"Etta, how is my room?" Murphy asked.

"Have another cup of coffee while I put fresh linens on the bed," Etta said.

"I'll see to your horse," Mal said.

A man can lie to everyone but himself. As he sat against the headboard with a small nightcap of whiskey and his pipe, Murphy reflected on his own soul. A man needs to do that once in a while to gain perspective on his life.

It was a little more than a year ago that he last saw Sally as he rode off on an assignment commissioned by newly appointed President Chester Arthur. They said their goodbyes and if things had worked out, she would have moved to his home in Tennessee to await his return.

Things didn't work out. A man named Christopher who drove carriages for the White House knew Sally, by coincidence, from her years as a madam and paid her a visit one night and violated her.

Burke told him much later that the reason Sally ran away was not because of the shame of being violated, but because she feared that if he found out, Murphy would commit first degree murder to avenge her honor.

In retrospect, Sally had been correct.

That's exactly what he would have done. In a sense, she saved his life. In doing so, she gave her own. She was pregnant, and Murphy had no way of knowing if the child was his or Christopher's, but it didn't matter anymore. She died giving birth.

The truth was that he couldn't stand the sight of the Virginia property anymore. It was as if Sally's ghost lived in the walls. His father taught him very early on never to sell property if it could be avoided, so he rented it to the Johnson family, a move that benefited all involved.

Drink consumed, pipe extinguished, Murphy blew out the oil lamp on the nightstand and crawled between the very clean, freshly scented sheets.

Murphy took breakfast with Mal, Etta, and their two boys.

"I have a favor to ask of you, Mal," Murphy said as they ate. "I need to go to New York City, and they don't allow horses on the streets. I'd like you to watch Boyle for me for about a month."

"Sure thing, Mr. Murphy," Mal said. "Need me to hitch the wagon and drive you to the railroad?"

"I do," Murphy said. He looked at Samuel and Moses. "Don't get the notion you can put a saddle on him; you can't. Boyle won't allow anyone but me to do that. If you try, you'll wind up with two thousand pounds of angry horse on your hands."

"Boyle be fine, Mr. Murphy," Mal said.

"I know."

At the railroad station, Murphy removed his large satchel and suitcase and then shook Mal's hand.

"Remember to stop at the general store on your way home," Murphy said.

"But we stopped on the way here," Mal said. "And you didn't come out with anything."

"See you in about a month," Murphy said.

Mal nodded, turned the wagon around, and started back along the dirt road.

Murphy stood beside his satchel and suitcase, lit his pipe, and waited for Burke to arrive.

Mal reached the general store that served many of the surrounding farms. The owner, a man called Avery, fought for the North during the war and lost his left leg from the knee down.

You'd never know it, though, as he wore a wooden leg attached at the knee, complete with foot. A slight limp in his step was the only indication the left leg was partially gone.

Mal parked the wagon and entered the store. Avery was behind the large counter and wearing a white apron. A few people were browsing in various aisles.

"Mr. Avery, how are you today?" Mal said. "I'm here to pick up something for Mr. Murphy."

"You're here to pick something up all right, but not for Mr. Murphy," Avery said.

Avery reached under the counter and produced two Winchester Model 75 rifles and two boxes of ammunition and set them on the glass top. "Mr. Murphy said a man can't teach his sons to hunt properly without a proper rifle," he said.

"Must be some mistake," Mal said. "I can't afford no

hardware like this."

"No mistake, Mal," Avery said. "Compliments of Mr. Murphy."

Mal looked at the twin Winchesters.

"Take them home, they're yours," Avery said.

"We should reach the Island of Manhattan by four this afternoon," Burke said. "I wired the driver to pick us up at the station and take us to the hotel. We'll have dinner at Delmonico's on Fifth Avenue and then meet with the mayor for breakfast."

"You wouldn't be trying to make a politician out of me, would you, Burke?" Murphy asked.

"Heaven forbid," Burke said.

CHAPTER THREE

"Careful with those bags," Murphy told the carriage driver. "There are breakables in them."

Seated in the carriage, Burke lit a large cigar and said, "He knows what he's doing, Murphy. Come on and get in."

Reluctantly, Murphy entered the carriage and sat next to Burke.

"How far to this hotel?" Murphy asked the driver.

"About three quarters of a mile," the driver replied.

Murphy looked at Burke. "Three quarters of a mile," he said.

"It's the city, Murphy," Burke said. "Folks are different in the city."

Murphy sighed and pulled out his pipe.

"Let's go, driver," Burke said.

Murphy watched the streets as the carriage rolled along. Dozens, if not hundreds, of horse-drawn carriages lined the wide streets of the city. Every building seemed twenty stories high and the stench of burning coal filled the air.

Every few blocks, a uniformed policeman on horseback was on patrol. Pedestrians clogged the sidewalks, women in the latest fashions, men in fine suits with bowler hats.

Telegraph poles and lines were everywhere, and some even had extra lines for the invention of the telephone.

"Progress, Murphy," Burke said. "It's all about progress. More than a million people live in Manhattan, and do you know what makes that possible?"

"It's an island and they can't get off," Murphy said.

Burke grinned. "I can appreciate your sense of humor," he said. "But the truth is that the science behind making electricity allows people to exist twenty floors in the air. Electricity to provide power to elevator lifts allows people to live up instead of spread out."

A uniformed police officer on horseback suddenly raced by, blowing a whistle as he galloped along.

"How would the Union have fared if our men had been armed with little more than whistles?" Murphy said.

The carriage turned onto Fifth Avenue and Murphy looked at the wall that encompassed the large mass known as Central Park.

"Our hotel is just a few blocks from here," Burke said.

There was a break in the wall where horse-drawn carriages entered and exited the park. A few men rode bicycles.

"Ridiculous-looking things," Murphy said as a man on a bicycle rode past the carriage.

"I imagine they'd feel the same if they saw you riding that massive beast of yours," Burke said. "And their bicycles produce no waste."

The driver steered the carriage to the curb in front of the Carlton Hotel. "I'll get your bags, gents," he said.

Before Murphy could grab his satchel and suitcase, a curbside bellhop took his bags and Burke's suitcase and carried them into the lobby.

The lobby was large, ornate and not for the poor. Women in high fashion and men in expensive suits occupied sofas and chairs and drank tea.

Burke checked them in at the marble front desk and then the bellhop took the bags to one of three elevators.

"We're on the sixteenth floor," Burke said.

When the elevator door opened, it was manned by an operator dressed in a hotel uniform.

Murphy stared at the elevator car, which was primarily a box with mirrored walls.

"Get in," Burke said as he stepped inside the car.

Murphy looked at the operator. "What do you do?"

"I run the elevator, sir," the operator said.

"Is this thing safe?" Murphy asked.

"Perfectly safe, sir," the operator said.

Cautiously, Murphy entered the car, followed by the bellhop.

The operator closed the gate and said, "Floor, please?"

"Sixteen," Burke said.

The operator placed his hand on the lever and slowly the elevator ascended.

Murphy put his right hand on the mirrored wall and after a few flights, his face nearly turned green.

"Surely you've been on an elevator before," Burke said.

"Be quiet, Burke," Murphy said and closed his eyes.

Burke looked at Murphy and grinned. "The Great Regulator."

"Shut up," Murphy snapped.

Murphy didn't open his eyes until the elevator stopped and the operator said, "Sixteen," and opened the gate.

Murphy rushed off the elevator, followed by Burke and the bellhop.

"Rooms 1611 and 1612," Burke told the bellhop.

In front of 1611, Burke gave Murphy the key to 1612. "I'll meet you in the lobby at six-thirty for dinner," he said. "That's in one hour."

Murphy unlocked the door and stepped inside, followed by the bellhop. The bellhop set the bags on the bed and Murphy gave him a dollar bill.

The room was large enough for a family of four. The bed, twice the size it needed to be, was fancy and soft. The entire room furnishings were ornate, as if royalty lived there.

There were two doors in the room. Murphy opened one and it was a large closet. He opened the second and it was an indoor toilet. The name "Thomas Crapper" was inscribed on the bowl. There were also three basins for washing and a wall-mounted shaving mirror.

Murphy went to the window. The view was dizzying, to say the least. At least one hundred and fifty feet high, the room looked down upon the enormous landmass called Central Park.

Most towns in most of the west would fit inside the park with enough room left over for a decent-sized cattle ranch.

Carriages looked small and people like ants.

Murphy turned away from the window and stripped off his clothing. In the toilet closet, he trimmed his beard and washed his face, then combed his hair. He went to the bed and opened his suitcase.

He selected a clean shirt and suit with vest and dressed quickly. From the satchel, he removed a Smith & Wesson .38 caliber revolver and a shoulder harness, and put them on. Then he put on the suit jacket and looked in the mirror. The revolver was undetectable.

Murphy took his key and left the room. He walked to the elevator and looked at the two buttons on the wall. He assumed one was for up, the other down. He pressed down.

It took several minutes, but finally the center car arrived. Cautiously, Murphy entered the car and told the operator he wanted the lobby. As the car descended, Murphy closed his eyes until the car stopped.

When he stepped out, the lobby was abuzz with people. Every chair and sofa was occupied and conversations were anxious and animated.

Murphy went to the desk.

"May I help you, sir?" the clerk behind the desk asked.

"What's got all these people in an uproar?" Murphy asked.

The clerk reached under the counter and produced a copy of the *Times*. "Last night the 'Manhattan Madman' struck again," he said. "That makes fifteen."

"Manhattan Madman?" Murphy said.

"That's what some in the newspapers have started calling him," the clerk said.

"May I have this?" Murphy asked.

"Certainly, sir. I have others."

Murphy took the newspaper to the corner of the lobby and found a vacant chair by a fireplace. A few logs burned and crackled, but the fire gave off very little heat. He scanned the front page and read the story.

At daybreak, a woman was found to be murdered on Centre Street in the Five Points section of lower Manhattan. Details of her death are unclear except that she appears to have been murdered in the same fashion as the previous fourteen victims. Residents of Five Points identified the woman as "Crazy Dora," but have been unable to provide her real name. She appears to be between the age of thirty-five and forty according to the medical examiner.

"Murphy, there you are," Burke said as he walked across the lobby.

Murphy stood, folded the newspaper, and stuck it into his suit jacket pocket.

"Delmonico's is just a few blocks from here so I thought we'd walk," Burke said.

Street lamps placed every twenty feet illuminated the streets so that even though it was now dark, walking was no problem. Carriages out for night rides had two oil lanterns mounted to the front.

"I'm told that by nineteen hundred all the street lamps will be electrified," Burke said. "And that twenty-five percent of all homes will have access to the telephone."

"I can wait," Murphy said.

"Have you even seen the telephone?" Burke asked.

"No, and I can live without it," Murphy said.

"Well, here we are," Burke said. "I had the desk clerk make a reservation for us."

Delmonico's Steak House was advertised as the best steak house in New York and, without a reservation, the wait for a table could take two hours or more.

A maître d' took Burke and Murphy to a window table. There was a buzz in the restaurant among the patrons that wasn't lost on Burke.

"Something is going on," Burke said.

Murphy reached into his pocket and produced the newspaper. Burke looked at the headline, and then scooped up the paper.

"Good Lord," Burke said. "The Manhattan Madman?"

Murphy looked past Burke at the tall man with long hair and partial beard, dressed in a tasseled coat walking to their table.

"Colonel Murphy, is that you?" the man asked in a booming voice.

"Buffalo Bill Cody," Murphy said. "Where on earth did you come from?"

"The West Side at the moment," Cody said.

Burke looked at Cody. "William Cody? Buffalo Bill Cody?"

"One and the same," Cody said.

"What are you doing in New York?" Murphy asked.

"I'm in town with the Wild West," Cody said. "Cowboys, soldiers, Indians, the great Plains War and all that. I've been on the road a year now."

"Sit down and join us," Murphy said.

The waiter brought a third chair to the table and Cody sat.

"How do you know Murphy, Mr. Cody?" Burke asked.

"I was chief of scouts under Murphy during the Plains War

and afterward," Cody said.

"You rode for the Pony Express, didn't you?" Burke asked.

"I did indeed, sir," Cody said.

"Bill once ran for twenty-four straight hours using a dozen horses," Murphy said.

"I was just a kid then and full of juice," Cody said. "These days I'm content to just play make-believe."

The waiter returned and during dinner, Cody told one entertaining story after another. From his experiences with the Pony Express, to his years during the war as a buffalo hunter and army scout, and finally as ringleader of his show about the Wild West.

"My dream is to take the Wild West to Europe and bring the flavor of the American West to the people," Cody said.

"I have no doubt that you will," Murphy said.

"Shall we have coffee and cigars?" Burke asked.

"I'm afraid I left my cigars at the hotel," Cody said.

"They sell them at the counter," Murphy said. "I'll get three."

As soon as Murphy left the table, Burke said, "Mr. Cody, you . . ."

"Call me Bill."

"All right. Bill, you rode with Murphy in the old days. Have you ever heard his Christian name spoken?"

Cody turned to see where Murphy was. "Once," he said. "And it didn't end well for the man who spoke it. Best let that sleeping dog sleep."

Murphy returned with three Cuban cigars.

"I ordered brandy and coffee," he said.

An hour later, Murphy and Burke shook hands with Cody on the street.

"Come see my Wild West and experience the excitement firsthand," Cody said.

"I return to Washington tomorrow sometime," Burke said.

"Murphy?" Cody said.

"I'll come see your show," Murphy said. "I'll let you know when."

"Excellent," Cody said. "I look forward to giving you the tour."

As they walked back to the hotel, Burke said, "The mayor isn't going to be happy in the morning."

"I expect not," Murphy said.

They entered the lobby and the desk clerk immediately flagged them to the desk.

"A gentleman has been waiting for you, Mr. Burke," the clerk said.

"Where?" Burke asked.

"There," the clerk said.

Burke and Murphy turned and looked at the short, plump man dressed in a checkered suit with bowler hat who walked toward them.

"Mr. Burke, Mr. Murphy?" he said.

"I'm Burke, this is Murphy," Burke said.

The man grinned. "I'm Melvin Knoop," he said.

Murphy took a deep breath and sighed as he exhaled.

"I thought we might sit for a while and get acquainted, seeing as how we'll be working together," Knoop said.

"We have a breakfast meeting with the mayor at eight-thirty, so I'm going to turn in early," Burke said. "I'll see you gentlemen at seven-thirty sharp here in the lobby."

"Goodnight, sir," Knoop said.

"Ten minutes," Murphy said and walked to a vacant sofa.

Knoop followed and sat.

"So, Mr. Murphy, I . . ." Knoop said.

Murphy held up his right hand. "First thing, do you have a different suit of clothes?"

"Yes, of course. Why?"

33

"Because you look like a traveling snake-oil salesman," Murphy said.

"I don't . . . what does that even mean?" Knoop asked.

"It means you wear a different suit tomorrow," Murphy said. "Something more professional."

"As you wish," Knoop said.

"Burke tells me you're from Scotland, and that you studied at Scotland Yard before coming to America," Murphy said.

"That's true, but my mother is American," Knoop said. "She was living in Scotland at the time and taught me English as a young child, which is why I have very little accent."

"So you have dual citizenship?"

"I do."

"And you came to America to study American police techniques?"

"I did."

"And how do you find American techniques?"

"To be honest, Mr. Murphy, decades behind the Yard," Knoop said. "Except for Mr. Pinkerton, of course."

"Of course," Murphy said.

"The biography Mr. Burke sent me on you is most impressive," Knoop said. "Civil War hero, one of the first secret agents under President Grant and at the forefront of modern forensic techniques."

"What exactly do you do at Pinkerton's?" Murphy asked.

"Forensic evidence analysis in notorious cases is my expertise," Knoop said.

"Get into the field much?"

"Beg your pardon."

"Do you leave your office in Chicago much and investigate in the field?"

"Actually, this is my first field assignment away from Chicago," Knoop said. "Mr. Pinkerton thought this case was important enough to send me for my expertise."

"We'll see about your expertise in the morning," Murphy said.

"Beg pardon?"

"There was a fifteenth victim this morning," Murphy said. "You'll get to test your expertise right after breakfast. Get some sleep tonight, Mr. Knoop. You'll need to be wide awake in the morning."

About to slip into bed, Burke paused when there was a knock on his hotel door.

He walked to the door and said, "Yes?"

"Burke, open the door," Murphy said.

Burke unlocked the door and opened it. "I'm tired, Murphy and was about . . ."

Murphy walked past Burke and entered the room.

"Please tell me this is some kind of joke," Murphy said.

"If you're referring to Knoop, the President wants his expertise on analysis," Burke said.

"He still has pimples," Murphy said.

"President Arthur and Pinkerton think very highly of his skills in modern forensic science," Burke said. "Arthur wants this mess cleared up before the conference, and he doesn't care how or who gets the job done. Now please let me get some sleep."

Murphy sighed as he reached into his inside jacket pocket and produced a small flask full of his father's whiskey.

"How about a quick nightcap then?" Murphy asked.

Burke took the flask. "If it will make you happy," he said.

CHAPTER FOUR

Murphy met Burke and Knoop in the lobby of the hotel at seven-thirty in the morning. The carriage was curbside with the driver at his station.

Murphy noted that Knoop wore a dark-colored suit with a matching bolo hat.

"Better," he told Knoop as they boarded the carriage.

Burke looked at Murphy, but didn't comment.

After they settled into the carriage, Knoop said, "If I may ask a question, Mr. Murphy? I notice that you're wearing boots with your suit. Wouldn't shoes be more comfortable than boots?"

Burke all but rolled his eyes and looked out the window of the enclosed carriage.

"I wouldn't know," Murphy said.

"I don't understand," Knoop said.

"I wouldn't know because I don't own a pair of shoes," Murphy said.

"I see," Knoop said.

Murphy sighed and watched the New York streets roll by as the carriage headed downtown along the street called Broadway. The streets were clogged with carriages and bicycles and pedestrians, and the air still smelled foul with the stench of burning coal.

"When Mr. Pinkerton told me I was being sent to New York, I did a lot of reading about it," Knoop said. "I thought Chicago was a big city, but New York has it beat by far. Did you know

New York has over one hundred and eighty buildings classified as skyscrapers, more than any city in the world? And that one million two hundred thousand people live in Manhattan? There is a large power plant run by coal and steam on the lower West Side that produces electricity using giant turbines turned by the steam. Also, the Brooklyn Bridge that recently opened connects the town of Brooklyn with Manhattan, so people can commute back and forth every day if they want. And Manhattan is bounded by the East, Hudson, and Harlem rivers. The Lenape Indians were the first settlers long before Columbus or the Dutch. The Dutch called it New Amsterdam. I didn't know that, but they did."

"Mr. Knoop, look at Mr. Murphy please," Burke said.

Burke and Knoop were seated side by side with Murphy opposite them.

"Do you see how his left eye is twitching?" Burke asked.

"Yes," Knoop said.

"Do you know what that means?" Burke asked.

"Perhaps a spot of dust?" Knoop said.

"No, Mr. Knoop," Burke said. "I would wager that Mr. Murphy is seriously thinking of throwing you head first from this carriage."

Knoop stared at Murphy.

"So, if you'd like to remain seated and in one piece until we reach the mayor's office, I suggest you refrain from any additional tour-guide comments," Burke said.

A uniformed police officer escorted Murphy, Burke, and Knoop into City Hall.

Knoop whispered to Burke, "Would Mr. Murphy really have done what you said?"

"Thrown you off the carriage?" Burke said. "If you were lucky, that's all he would have done."

The uniformed police officer led them to a private dining hall where Mayor Franklin Edson and Commissioner of the City Police, George Washington Matsell, were seated at a dining table.

Neither man stood as Murphy, Burke, and Knoop entered the hall.

"I'm William Burke, special assistant to President Arthur," Burke said. "This is Secret Service Agent Murphy, and Pinkerton's forensic specialist Melvin Knoop."

Edson stood. He was a short man, about five-foot-six inches tall, and wore a neatly trimmed beard.

"I must tell you, Mr. Burke, that when President Arthur got in touch and told me that he was sending your men to help with our situation, I was highly insulted and put out that he thought we couldn't deal with the situation ourselves," Edson said.

"We like to keep things in-house, so to speak," Matsell said. "And we don't like interference from outsiders."

"Mayor Edson, let me be perfectly clear," Burke said. "President Arthur isn't concerned with your feelings or your hurt feelings. What he is concerned about is the largest international meeting of world leaders in history taking place in your city while a madman is running around murdering women seemingly at will."

Matsell stood up and glared at Burke. "How dare you outsiders come into our . . ."

"President Arthur has authorized me to tell you that if you fail in any way to give one hundred percent cooperation to Mr. Murphy and Mr. Knoop, he will place the entire city under martial law and have both of you removed until the matter is resolved," Burke said. "Are we clear on this?"

Edson glared at Burke. Finally he nodded and took his chair.

"Mr. Matsell?" Burke said.

"Clear," Matsell said, and he, too, took his chair.

"Good," Burke said.

"Please sit down gentlemen," Edson said. "I'll have breakfast brought in and we can talk while we eat."

A chef from the mayor's staff wheeled in a large trolley and served breakfast.

"I'm going to talk business as we eat," Murphy said. "I hope it won't spoil your appetite."

"Go ahead," Matsell said.

"Yesterday morning the fifteenth victim was found in the area known as Five Points," Murphy said. "The newspaper had no details. Can you provide some?"

"She was killed like all the others," Matsell said. "No real signs of a struggle. Cut open with vital organs removed. Dumped on the street. Like the others, she was a prostitute of low repute."

"What does that mean exactly?" Knoop asked. "Low repute."

"She walked the streets in search of clients," Matsell said. "There are at least a half-dozen brothels a man can visit on the island, so her clients are men of lesser standing, so to speak."

"Isn't prostitution illegal inside the city?" Knoop asked.

Matsell looked at Knoop. "How old are you, boy?"

"Twenty-nine."

"From Chicago?"

"I am."

"Don't they have whores in Chicago?" Matsell asked.

"I'm sure they do," Knoop said.

"And wouldn't it be illegal in Chicago?" Matsell asked.

"Back to my point," Murphy said. "With all the publicity about the murders, wouldn't you think they would refrain from doing business for a while?"

"These women are dirt poor, Mr. Murphy," Matsell said.

"They would rather take their chances on the streets than starve."

"Mr. Matsell, here is what we need," Murphy said. "All evidence in storage, including reports written by the medical examiner, and access to the body of the latest victim. A list of family and friends and the names of those who found the bodies and access to all the police officers directly involved with the investigations."

"Anything else?" Matsell asked.

"A very detailed map of the city," Murphy said.

"Follow me after breakfast to my office," Matsell said.

"Mr. Burke, you will tell President Arthur we are cooperating fully," Edson said.

"Completely," Burke said. "Is there any more coffee?"

In front of City Hall, Burke shook Knoop's hand and then pulled Murphy aside.

"Give the kid a chance to help," Burke said. "He might surprise you."

Murphy looked back at Knoop, who was climbing aboard the carriage.

"And wrap this up quickly," Burke said. "President Arthur is counting on you."

"Expense money and your word you will talk to him about reinstating me as head of the Secret Service," Murphy said.

"I'll leave an envelope in the hotel safe, and you have my word I will talk to Arthur about your desire to come back," Burke said. "Oh, there's my taxi."

Murphy nodded, turned, and walked to the carriage. He glanced back and Burke was entering an enclosed carriage.

Murphy climbed into his carriage and sat opposite Knoop.

Directly ahead of them, Matsell sat in his personal carriage

and when it rolled away from the curb, Murphy's carriage followed.

"Mr. Murphy, do you . . . ?" Knoop said.

"Drop the mister," Murphy said. "Murphy will do."

"All right," Knoop said. "Do you think Mr. Burke would
have done as he said in the meeting?"

"Got Arthur to enact martial law?" Murphy said. "Burke is
the one man I would hesitate to trifle with when it comes to a
test of willpower."

"I see," Knoop said.

The ride ended after just six blocks.

"I guess people don't like to stretch their legs in this town,"
Murphy said.

He and Knoop exited the carriage and met Matsell on the
sidewalk in front of the four-story building that served as police
headquarters.

"We'll meet in my office," Matsell said.

The lobby of the building was a hub of activity. Two
uniformed sergeants manned a long desk and two telegraph
operators worked telegraphs at a separate desk. A long bench
was filled with prisoners in chains. A dozen or more uniformed
officers were engaged in conversations.

"My office is on the second floor," Matsell said and walked
to the staircase.

Murphy and Knoop followed Matsell to the second floor
where, in fact, the only thing on the second floor was his office.

Etched on the glass door were the words *George Washington
Matsell, Commissioner of City Police.*

The office was large with a massive, very cluttered wood
desk, several file cabinets, a separate desk with a Remington
typewriter, a sofa, several chairs, and a conference table.

Matsell removed his uniform jacket and tossed it over a chair.

"Away from all the bullshit and politics, let's talk freely,"

Matsell said.

There was a knock on the door; it opened and a young officer poked his head into the office. "Do you need anything, sir?"

"A pot of coffee and three mugs," Matsell said.

The young officer nodded and closed the door.

Matsell looked at Murphy and Knoop. "Get comfortable."

Murphy removed his jacket, exposing the shouldered .38 revolver.

"You were saying," he said.

"Away from the bullshit, I've never seen or experienced anything like what's happening in this city," Matsell said. "And I've been with the police department since 'fifty-eight."

Murphy and Knoop took chairs at the table in front of a stack of files. Matsell sat opposite them.

"So you missed the war?" Murphy said.

"I did and gratefully so," Matsell said. "My duty as a police officer came first. I understand that you served under Grant as an officer."

"I did. I was a sniper and advance scout," Murphy said. "After the war, I spent several years out west before retiring. When Grant became President, he asked me to head up the newly formed Secret Service."

"I read that in the file Burke sent me," Matsell said. "Do you have much experience on the streets of New York? No offense to your expertise, but New York City is like no other place in the world. Poverty and wealth on the same streets with a million people living in a space meant for a hundred thousand creates unique circumstances."

"My first experience with your streets came in July of eighteen sixty-three," Murphy said. "I was training a squad of men for sniper detail in Tarrytown when the draft riots broke out. Large angry mobs of men took to rioting, looting, and burning the streets. The police were far too few to control the mobs, and Lincoln ordered reserve Union squads to go in and put down the mob. And that is what we did. We shot and killed Americans protesting the draft in order to save your city. I believe we killed one hundred and twenty of your citizens before the mobs were contained. However, they hung a dozen Negros, burned a black school and orphanage, and did damage in the millions before we stopped them."

Knoop looked at Murphy with wide eyes and open mouth.

"It was a terrible time, I agree," Matsell said.

There was another knock on the door; it opened and the young officer entered carrying a tray with a coffee pot and three mugs. He set the tray on the table and left.

"The latest victim, is the body still in the morgue?" Murphy asked.

"It is," Matsell said.

"We'd like to see it as soon as possible," Murphy said.

"I'll have a telegram sent to the medical examiner," Matsell said.

Murphy nodded. "Knoop, let's review these reports. Commissioner, have you that map I asked for?"

"I'll get it."

While Matsell went to his desk, Murphy filled the three mugs with coffee.

"And a red pencil if you have one," Murphy said.

Matsell returned with both map and pencil.

"Knoop, make notes and chart the map," Murphy said.

Murphy and Knoop read each police and medical-examiner report on fourteen victims. The fifteenth hadn't arrived yet, Matsell said. Each location where the victims were found was charted on the map in red pencil and when the last one was recorded, Murphy said, "What do you see?"

Knoop and Matsell looked at the map.

"Random locations scattered throughout Manhattan," Matsell said. "I've placed extra men overnight at these locations for a week now without results."

"That's because they're not as random as you think," Murphy said. "The victims were dumped above 96th Street and below 34th on the East and West Side, with two victims near Central Park. Nothing below 96th or above 34th on the East Side or Central Park West or Central Park East."

"I see that, but I don't know what point you're attempting to make," Matsell said.

"Out west there is a rule of thumb," Murphy said. "You don't build the outhouse too close to your bedroom window."

Matsell and Knoop looked at Murphy.

"South of 96th to north of 34th, east and west, is where all the wealthiest people live," Murphy said. "Whoever is behind this doesn't want to be recognized, so the bodies are dumped far enough away to avoid detection if he's spotted in the act."

Matsell looked closer at the map, then at Murphy. "I see what you're saying, but why hasn't he used Central Park as a dumping ground? It's the size of a small city, and a body could go undetected for days before it's found."

"The park closes at sunset, doesn't it?" Murphy said. "My guess is he transports the bodies by carriage and doesn't want to risk being seen entering the park or leaving by police on horseback after dark."

"By God, I think you're right," Matsell said.

"Knoop, fold up the map and put it in your pocket," Murphy said. He looked at Matsell. "Where is the evidence stored?"

"What there is we have locked in a cage in the evidence warehouse," Matsell said.

"Wire them and let them know we're coming later today," Murphy said. "Right after we see the medical examiner."

"I'll do anything I can and everything in my power," Matsell said.

"We'll get back to you later," Murphy said.

"That little show I put on in Edson's office was for his benefit," Matsell said.

"Sure," Murphy said.

The city morgue was located in lower Manhattan and from the front steps of the building, the island where the Statue of Liberty was under construction could be seen.

"I read in a newspaper they expect to have it finished in two years," Knoop said.

"Taking their sweet time about it," Murphy said. "Let's go."

A uniformed police officer guarded the main entrance to the morgue, but there was a telegram delivered just minutes earlier with Murphy and Knoop's name on it, granting them admission.

New York City's chief medical examiner was a doctor in his mid-fifties named Alfred Winslow. He was short and round and wore Benjamin Franklin spectacles. He was in the processing room when Murphy and Knoop were escorted by a junior member of his staff.

"Matsell's telegram said to expect Murphy and Knoop," Winslow said. "Which one is which?"

"I'm Melvin Knoop of Pinkerton's," Knoop said.

Winslow looked up at Murphy. "Big son of a bitch, ain't you."

"I had nothing to do with it. It sort of just happened on its own," Murphy said. "We want to see the body."

Winslow removed the sheet from the face of the body on a rolling table and said, "Police said all they know her by is 'Crazy Dora,' so that's how I entered the name."

Crazy Dora had black hair speckled with gray. Her face was weathered and worn by a lifetime of poverty and sickness. She could have been thirty, she could have been forty-five; it was anybody's guess.

"Wretched-looking thing," Winslow said. "Check her teeth."

"Her teeth?" Knoop said.

Murphy opened Dora's mouth to expose yellow teeth of which the front upper and lower teeth had been sharpened to a point.

"Somebody did this to her?" Knoop asked.

"She did it to herself," Murphy said.

"I don't . . . why would she do that to her teeth?"

"She filed them to a point so they're weapons," Murphy said. "If a client doesn't pay, she can rob and even kill him with a bite to the neck."

"Good Lord," Knoop said.

"Observations?" Murphy said.

"No facial bruises or bruises to the neck," Knoop said. "None on the shoulders or arms. She went willingly with her murderer, thinking he was a client."

Murphy looked at Winslow. "Any traces of ether or opium?"

"She'd been dead at least twenty-four hours before she was dumped," Winslow said. "Impossible to tell. I did find traces of blood in her teeth and fingernails. Who the blood belongs to is anybody's guess."

"Show us the wound," Murphy said.

Winslow shrugged. "It's not pretty."

"Go ahead," Murphy said.

Winslow lowered the sheet to Dora's knees. Her entire stomach area was nothing but a large open hole.

After a few seconds of silence, Knoop said, "I think . . . I'm . . ."

"Bucket in the corner," Winslow said. "Don't you mess up my floor, youngster."

Knoop turned and ran for a large slop bucket in the corner

of the room and dropped to his knees.

While Knoop vomited, Murphy continued to inspect the body.

"She's been gutted like a fish," he said.

"And expertly so," Winslow said.

"In what way?" Murphy asked.

At the bucket, Knoop made vomiting noises.

"The liver, spleen, kidneys, and appendix weren't just hacked out in some crazed fit of rage," Winslow said. "A fair amount of skill was applied to remove the organs intact. You can see how the organs were carefully cut to remove them without damaging them by the way the remaining organs were sliced."

Murphy looked at Winslow. "Wouldn't that take some medical knowledge and training?" he asked.

"It would," Winslow said.

"The other victims, were they the same?"

"Yes."

"I didn't read that in your reports."

"I put only facts in my reports, not my opinion," Winslow said. "Opinions are for the psychiatrists."

"Her personal belongings?"

"The police took them," Winslow said.

"When the next victim shows up, I don't want you to do an autopsy until I'm present," Murphy said.

"Are you sure there will be a next one?" Winslow asked.

Murphy looked at Winslow. "This one is not going to stop. There will be a next one, count on it."

In the corner, a green-looking Knoop stood up.

Murphy walked to Knoop and said, "Let's go if you're able."

"Where are we going?" Knoop asked.

"The police evidence warehouse is on Eleventh Avenue and Thirty-Fourth Street," Murphy said.

Knoop looked out the carriage window and took several deep breaths.

"We can stop and get something to settle your stomach," Murphy said.

"That didn't bother you one bit, did it?" Knoop said.

"In this one battle in 'sixty-four, the Confederates were charging up a hill," Murphy said. "Always a bad idea, charging a hill. The high ground is always almost impossible to take. Anyway, I watched a cannon ball take the head clean off this Rebel soldier and the funny things is his body didn't drop. It just stayed in place, holding his rifle. No head and holding his rifle."

"God," Knoop said.

"You see enough, you grow a hard bark," Murphy said.

"I could use a cup of tea," Knoop said.

The evidence warehouse was a fortress. Constructed of red brick, the two-story structure had iron bars on all windows and a front door made of reinforced steel.

A uniformed police officer escorted Murphy and Knoop to the cage reserved for the Manhattan Madman murders.

"I have to tell you there isn't much in the way of evidence on this one," the officer said. "Mostly because there just isn't any."

The officer stopped in front of a cage the size of a small prison cell and used a key to unlock the door.

"Would you happen to have any tea?" Murphy asked him.

"Tea? I don't think so."

"Could you get a cup please?" Murphy asked.

"With milk and some honey," Knoop said.

"I'll see what I can do," the officer said.

"Coffee for me if you would," Murphy said.

The officer nodded and walked away.

"Let's see what we got," Murphy said.

Most of the boxes were marked *Unknown Female,* a few with

names and the last one *"Crazy Dora."*

They went through each box and inspected each article of clothing and shoes. There were a few items of jewelry, but no handbags with identification for any of the victims.

Knoop made what notes he could, as they examined each evidence box.

The last box contained the clothing and shoes last worn by "Crazy Dora." White blouse and undergarments, black skirt and black shoes. No jewelry of any kind or money.

The color of the white blouse was stained by a colorless liquid.

Murphy sniffed the collar and gave it to Knoop. He sniffed and looked at Murphy.

"Ether?" Knoop said.

Murphy took out his small tinderbox, removed a wood match, lit it, and touched the stain on the collar. The dried ether immediately burst into flames. Murphy patted out the flame with his hand before the material could burn.

"Would you wager the next victim has ether on her clothing and traces in her throat and lungs?" Murphy asked.

"I would not," Knoop said.

The police officer returned with a mug of coffee and another with tea.

After the officer left, Knoop said, "How do you know about ether?"

"I saw enough doctors use it during the war," Murphy said. "Highly volatile stuff."

Knoop sipped some tea. "It appears our 'Madman' is somewhat intelligent and not without skill. I heard what Winslow said about surgically removing the organs."

"It's possible to be a genius and crazy at the same time," Murphy said. "History has taught us that much."

Knoop sipped more tea.

"Observations on the evidence?" Murphy said.

"The clothing is remarkably blood free," Knoop said. "Not a missing button or torn fabric."

"What does that tell you?" Murphy asked.

"He uses ether to sedate them and then removes their clothing before he . . . cuts them open," Knoop said.

Murphy sipped from his mug and then nodded. "To what purpose?" he asked.

"You mean what does he gain by committing these heinous acts?"

"That's what I mean."

"Maybe . . . maybe he's just crazy, as you said."

"There are all kinds of crazy," Murphy said. "In 'sixty-five, when Lee surrendered to Grant at Appomattox, afterward we visited a few nearby hospitals. I saw many soldiers on both sides suffering from mental breakdowns. Some were talking to themselves, and some were holding conversations as if someone else was talking to them. Just because no one was actually talking back doesn't mean that it wasn't real to the poor bastards. Point is, sane or crazy, who knows what's in someone's mind except that someone?"

"What you're saying is that he could be walking the streets appearing as sane as anyone else and be completely mad at the same time?" Knoop said.

"I've known more than a few," Murphy said. "How's your stomach?"

"Better."

"Good. Let's go."

"Where?"

"This is Centre Street in Five Points," the carriage driver said as he opened the carriage door. "Are you sure this is where you want to go?"

Murphy stepped out of the carriage and stood on the

sidewalk. "Positive," he said.

Knoop stepped down and stood next to Murphy.

The neighborhood called Five Points was still a slum, but there were signs of progress in that several new buildings were under construction and many of the old tenements were gone.

The air was foul, the streets were crowded, and the sidewalks were full of garbage and waste.

"Look at this place," Murphy said. "Who would miss somebody who lived here if they disappeared overnight unless they were dumped in the street for someone to find?"

"At night I would imagine the streets are less crowded," Knoop said.

"The gangs around here have eyes in the back of their head," Murphy said. "Night or day. Let's walk."

"Shall I wait?" the driver asked.

"Yes," Murphy said.

The driver nodded and climbed aboard his seat where he kept a loaded revolver.

Murphy and Knoop walked along the crowded street under the watchful eyes of every person within a block radius.

"On that corner used to be a large old brewery that was converted into apartments for the poor," Murphy said. "I believe it was demolished after the draft riots."

A group of a dozen gang members came away from a tenement building and approached Murphy and Knoop.

"Look at this big dandy taking his little doggie for a walk," the leader of the gang said.

Knoop said, "Is he talking to us?"

"The doggie speaks," the leader said. "Can he do some tricks for us?"

The gang members behind the leader chuckled loudly.

"Let's see what they might have in their pockets," the gang leader said. "Starting with the little doggie."

Murphy took one step forward and smacked the leader across the face with so much force, he spilled backward and knocked three gang members to the ground as he toppled over.

"Speak to me again, and I'll send you to the hospital," Murphy said and started walking.

Stunned, Knoop stayed in place and looked at the fallen gang members.

Murphy paused to turn around. "Are you coming?" he said. "Little doggie."

Knoop caught up to Murphy and they walked a few blocks toward the river.

"That man, that gang, they didn't frighten you in the least," Knoop said.

"Young, stupid idiots wouldn't last five minutes in the likes of Dodge City or Tombstone," Murphy said.

"Where are we going?" Knoop asked.

"Nowhere. Just getting a feel for the neighborhood."

"That story you told about the draft riots, the worst of them happened around here, didn't they?" Knoop said.

"Navy ships in the river bombed the rioters with cannon fire before we took to the streets," Murphy said. "They said we killed one hundred and twenty that partook in the riots, but they didn't count the women and children who were collateral damage."

Near the river was a small park, and Murphy walked to a vacant bench and sat. Knoop sat next to him.

"How do you dump fifteen bodies in various locations around the city without one witness seeing you?" Murphy said as he took out his pipe.

"Under the cover of darkness," Knoop said.

"Yes, but how? And even at night this city is wide awake," Murphy said.

"I imagine that, like Chicago, many people in New York work

at night," Knoop said. "The police, the fire department, hospitals all work at night, as do many others."

"Let's look at that," Murphy said as he lit his pipe. "There are around one thousand police officers in Manhattan, half of whom work at night. Five hundred men to patrol thirty-three square miles where more than one million people reside. Of that five hundred, maybe fifty are on horseback with the ability to get around quickly. That's pretty small odds of spotting one man dumping a body on a dark street."

"One in a two hundred and forty chance of being spotted," Knoop said.

Murphy puffed on his pipe and looked at Knoop. "There is a like number of firemen, and if half work at night, if they aren't out fighting a fire you can bet they are in their bunks sleeping."

"And hospital workers, doctors, and nurses don't leave the hospital grounds until their shift is over, so I'd not consider them a factor," Knoop said.

"That leaves what?"

"In Chicago sanitation workers have night crews," Knoop said.

"A small number I'm sure," Murphy said.

"So the odds of spotting someone dumping a body during the night are pretty slim," Knoop said.

"Let's go back to the hotel," Murphy said. "We need to make notes and hash this about some more."

As they returned to the carriage, Knoop noticed the various gangs on the streets steered clear of them. They glared at Murphy and Knoop as they walked by, but no one made a move to approach them.

Knoop spotted the gang that confronted them earlier in front of a building, but the leader Murphy smacked was visibly absent.

At the carriage, Murphy said, "Driver, take us back to the hotel, please."

★ ★ ★ ★ ★

Murphy and Knoop took dinner in the hotel dining room.

As he cut into a steak, Murphy said, "He needs freedom to move around the city at night undetected."

"How?" Knoop asked.

"In sniper school, you're taught how to blend in with your surroundings," Murphy said. "Not to wear the uniform, to disguise yourself to look like a bush or even a tree branch. Basically to make yourself invisible to the enemy."

Knoop, opting for chicken, sliced off a piece of meat. "He's blending in with his surroundings is what you're saying?" he said. "How?"

"Find that out and we find him," Murphy said.

"I shall give it considerable thought," Knoop said.

The room stuffy, the bed too soft, Murphy awoke around four in the morning, stiff and with a slight headache.

He got out of bed and lit the oil lamp on the nightstand. Then he opened the window to allow fresh air to circulate the room. The bottle of his father's whiskey was on the dresser, and he filled a water glass with two ounces and then stuffed his pipe and lit it.

At the window, Murphy sipped whiskey, smoked his pipe, and looked at the dark streets of the city one hundred fifty feet below. The street lamps gave off a fair amount of light on the sidewalks, but there were a thousand places to hide in shadows.

Across the street Central Park was a huge expanse of pitch black. Dots of light pinpointed the entrance roads from east to west through the park.

A mounted police officer rode slowly down the middle of the street. A few minutes later, a horse-drawn sanitation carriage passed by. One man drove the carriage while two men walked behind it with shovels and brooms and scooped up horse manure.

Murphy sipped whiskey and continued to look out the window. The chilled fresh air cleared the headache, and the whiskey warmed his blood. He was about to close the window and return to bed when he heard the sound of horses on the streets.

He puffed on the pipe and waited to see what horse-drawn carriage or wagon came into view.

It was a large milk wagon pulled by two horses and with two men in the drivers' seats. In the wagon were a dozen or more very large steel milk containers.

Murphy stared at the milk wagon as it passed by and out of sight.

He closed the window.

"It's just that easy," he said aloud.

CHAPTER FIVE

"Milk wagon?" Matsell said.

"Or sanitation wagon," Murphy said. "Or any other service that works overnight that would fit in and not cause someone to take notice."

Burke and Knoop were in Matsell's office at police headquarters, seated at the conference table. Each had a mug of coffee.

"If you're looking for a certain type of individual and that individual makes it so he's part of the normal scenery, it's that much more difficult to spot him," Murphy said.

"The way a trained sniper would," Knoop said.

Murphy looked at Knoop and Knoop shrugged.

"It just could be possible," Matsell said.

"There's more," Murphy said.

Matsell sipped from his mug and then nodded.

"We examined the body of the last victim, and we agree with the medical examiner's findings in that she wasn't just hacked to death in some kind of crazed rage," Murphy said. "A great deal of skill was displayed in removing the internal organs."

Matsell stared at Murphy.

"We found ether on her clothing," Murphy said.

"A doctor?" Matsell said.

"A surgeon," Murphy said. "Or someone with extensive knowledge of surgery."

Matsell sat back in his chair and sighed. "A skilled madman?"

"Wouldn't be the first, won't be the last," Murphy said. "They still talk of Bill the Butcher in the Five Points, and he's been gone since before the war."

"Suggestions?" Matsell said.

"I suggest a night watch, Commissioner," Murphy said. "Triple the amount of mounted police overnight and have them pay close attention to all milk wagons, sanitation wagons, and every other type of wagon regularly seen on the streets. If he's using a wagon to dump the bodies, he's bound to be spotted if we're looking in his direction."

Matsell slowly nodded. "I'm not totally convinced, but I'll agree to what you say. We haven't had any luck so far, so your suggestion might just prove fruitful."

"I'd like two horses from the city stable," Murphy said. "And the use of two police uniforms."

"You wish to work undercover?" Matsell said. "Very well, why not? The police stables are located on Tenth Avenue off Thirty-Fourth Street. I'll send a wire to expect you sometime today. I'll have uniforms sent to your hotel rooms. Mr. Murphy, you may be difficult to fit."

"The hotel has a tailor shop in the lobby," Murphy said.

Matsell stood up. "I have some telegrams to send," he said.

Riding in the carriage to the city police stables, Knoop said, "I have to confess that I don't know anything about horses."

"Don't tell me you've never ridden a horse?" Murphy said.

"Living in Chicago, there is no need to," Knoop said. "Like New Yorkers, I walk or take a carriage everywhere and sometimes a bicycle. It was the same in Scotland."

"Good God, man," Murphy said.

"It's life in a big city," Knoop said.

"We'll think of something." Murphy sighed.

★　★　★　★　★

The city stable for police horses was a large warehouse building and directly next to it was a smaller warehouse where horse-drawn paddy wagons were stored.

"You'll ride in a paddy wagon," Murphy said.

At the stables, a stable manager told them they received the telegram from Matsell about their need for two horses.

"One horse as it turns out," Murphy said. "A large male that isn't afraid to run and doesn't spook at the sound of gunfire."

"Take your pick," the stable manager said. "They're all well trained."

"Now who do we see about a paddy wagon?" Murphy asked.

Murphy checked his appearance in the hotel room mirror. The blue uniform, after some alterations by the hotel tailor, fit him a bit snugly, but wasn't all that uncomfortable. The material was wool, and he knew it would itch so he purchased a bottle of baby powder and doused himself with it before putting on the uniform.

From the satchel, Murphy took out his custom-made Colt revolver and holster. Before strapping it on, he removed the foot-long Bowie knife he always wore on the left side.

In front of the mirror, Murphy strapped on the holster and checked himself again.

"Passable," he said aloud.

Murphy ignored the stares from people in the hotel lobby and took a chair to wait for Knoop.

After ten minutes or so, Knoop came off one of the elevators. His uniform was baggy in the legs and tight around the stomach. The lack of a firearm was obvious, but he wouldn't need one to ride the paddy wagon.

Murphy hid the laugh caught in his throat and stood. "Let's

go," he said.

The carriage was parked outside the hotel and the driver was in his seat and ready. After ten at night, the street traffic was light and they made it to the police stables in less than twenty minutes.

Murphy was partnered with a big German named Gerhard. The man wore a walrus mustache and carried a lead nightstick painted black. A .44 revolver was around his hip and a Winchester rifle hung off the saddle on his horse.

Knoop went with a paddy wagon normally assigned to take drunks off the streets.

Gerhard was a braggart and a ferocious bully to the point his fellow police officers were even afraid of him. On their first night patrolling the streets together, Gerhard simply rode his horse to any drunk they spotted on the streets and clubbed him on the head with his lead nightstick, leaving the drunk bleeding and unconscious.

He had a whiskey flask in his pocket that he sipped from constantly throughout the evening, although the whiskey seemingly had no effect on him.

Murphy put up with Gerhard's bragging, violence, and drinking for three nights. On the fourth night, while patrolling the Chinese neighborhood near the Five Points, they stopped and dismounted in the shadows between two buildings so that Gerhard could relieve himself of the whiskey he'd been drinking.

While Gerhard went to the rear of the alleyway, Murphy stayed with the two horses.

He heard the sounds of a wagon on the streets. It was a milk wagon pulled by two horses and with one driver in the buckboard seat.

Murphy watched it roll by and a feeling came over him that meant something, but he didn't know what.

He watched the wagon reach the end of the block and continue to the next.

Gerhard returned and said, "Reminds me of the time I . . ."

"Quiet," Murphy said. "Look."

"At what?"

"That milk wagon that just passed."

Gerhard looked to his right at the wagon at the end of the block.

"What about it? It's too dark to see properly."

"Every milk wagon I've seen had between ten and twelve canisters of milk on it," Murphy said. "This one had six."

Murphy and Gerhard walked the horses to the street and watched the milk wagon. On the next block, it stopped near the curb.

"There's no delivery site there," Gerhard said.

The driver left the buckboard and went back to the containers. In the dark, Murphy and Gerhard watched the driver dump something onto the sidewalk. Then he returned to the buckboard, and the wagon rolled on at a moderate speed.

Murphy and Gerhard mounted their horses and took off after the wagon.

Gerhard had a brass whistle on a chain and he placed it in his mouth and blew it loudly and repeatedly.

"Shut up, you fool," Murphy said.

Gerhard ignored Murphy and kept blowing the whistle.

Hearing the whistle, the driver of the milk wagon broke the horses into a full run.

The chase went on for ten blocks. Along the way every mounted police officer in earshot of Gerhard's whistle joined the chase. Near Battery Park, the driver brought the wagon to a quick stop, jumped from the buckboard, and took off running.

Murphy turned his horse into the park, which was well illuminated by street lanterns, and, with ten mounted officers behind him, gave chase.

Gerhard stopped his horse just inside the park, drew his Winchester rifle, took careful aim, and fired.

The driver, struck by the bullet, pitched forward to the ground.

Murphy and the others raced to the fallen driver. Murphy dismounted first and knelt beside him. Gerhard's shot had opened up a large hole in his neck. He was still alive, but Murphy knew the driver had just seconds to live.

The driver looked at Murphy.

"He's a great man. A great man," the driver whispered.

"Who?" Murphy asked.

The wounded driver tried to talk more, but the blood gushing from his neck made it impossible.

"Who is a great man? Who?" Murphy said. "Who are you talking about?"

The driver, near death, smiled. "You won't find him. He's gone," he rasped.

"Gone where?" Murphy said.

The driver stopped breathing and his eyes went lifeless.

Murphy sighed and stood up.

Walking his horse, Gerhard said, "That was some bully shot I made, eh."

Murphy walked to Gerhard and punched him in the jaw, and Gerhard fell to the ground.

"You stupid drunken son of a bitch," Murphy said.

Slowly, with blood streaming from his mouth, Gerhard stood up. "No man puts his hands upon me," he said.

The ten mounted police officers stood beside their horses and watched in shock as Murphy beat Gerhard to a bloody pulp. Once Gerhard was unconscious on the ground, Murphy went to his horse and mounted the saddle.

"Five of you men stay here," he said. "The others come with me."

Three paddy wagons were beside the latest victim when Murphy and the five mounted officers arrived at the scene.

Knoop was among the group with the paddy wagons.

"Gutted like the others," Knoop said.

"Put her on a wagon and take her to the morgue," Murphy said. "Another wagon go with these men to pick up the driver."

"Gone? Gone where?" Edson asked.

"He died before he could say," Murphy said. "Thanks to that trigger-happy idiot."

"Gerhard is a twenty-year veteran of the department," Matsell said. "A highly decorated veteran at that."

"He's a drunk and a fool," Murphy said.

"Where is Gerhard now?" Edson asked.

"In the hospital," Matsell said.

"Why?" Edson asked.

"Mr. Murphy beat him to a pulp, something I would have never believed possible," Matsell said.

"Before he died, he said the killer was a great man?" Edson said.

"That's what he called him, a great man," Murphy said. "Then he said we won't find him because he was gone."

"The question remains, gone where?" Edson asked.

"That's when he died," Murphy said.

"Do you believe him?" Edson said. "That he's gone?"

"A dying man's last words, who knows?" Murphy said.

"Earlier you said this requires some surgical skill. We could check doctors who recently left the city," Matsell said.

"I doubt he was practicing medicine," Murphy said. "Your time would be better spent identifying the driver and where the milk wagon came from. That might help locate this great man."

"Yes, very good," Edson said. "What about the victim?"

"We're on our way to the morgue right now," Murphy said. "Feel like taking a ride, Commissioner?"

"Her liver, kidneys, appendix, and gallbladder have been removed," Winslow said. "And ether was found in her nose and mouth and some on her shirt."

Murphy looked at the cavern in her abdomen. "Surgically removed like 'Crazy Dora?' " he said.

"There is little doubt that the man who did this is a skilled surgeon," Winslow said.

"The man, that driver called him a great man," Matsell said. "Could he be talking about his skill with a knife?"

"I couldn't do such detailed work," Winslow said. "So if he was in fact talking about his greatness with a knife, it's possible."

"Have we identified the victim?" Murphy asked.

"Iris Nutley," Matsell said. "I recognized her face immediately. She's a well known prostitute and pickpocket. She works the Five Points and Bowery, but regularly goes uptown to fleece the rich on Fifth Avenue. In her younger days she often worked as a maid and would rob the homes she was hired to clean."

Murphy looked at Matsell. "Let's put men on the streets and see if we can find someone who might have seen her last."

Matsell nodded.

"Where is the driver?" Murphy asked Winslow.

Winslow turned to another table and removed the sheet. "Bullet caught him right in the main artery, poor bastard."

"Clean him up," Murphy said. "We'll have a sketch artist make a drawing of his face, maybe somebody knows him." He turned to Matsell. "What about the milk wagon?"

"I have men checking that as we speak," Matsell said.

"Knoop, if you feel up to it, let's get some breakfast," Murphy said. "Commissioner, you're welcome to join us."

Matsell scooped up some scrambled eggs and washed them down with coffee.

"I have to believe the driver was talking about his skill with a knife when he called him a great man," Matsell said.

"I agree, but how would a driver know that?" Murphy said.

"Right," Matsell said. "I also believe him that this so-called great man has left the city. I think the pressure from the newspapers and police has driven him away."

Murphy ordered pancakes with bacon and sliced into the stack with a fork. "I agree with you that he's gone," he said. "But to where and to what end?"

"Not our concern at the moment," Matsell said. "The objective was to make the city safe again for the President's meeting, and we've accomplished that. For that you have my compliments."

They were in a small restaurant not far from police headquarters.

"May I use the telegraph in your building to wire the President?" Murphy asked.

Knoop looked at Murphy.

Matsell looked at Knoop. "You're not eating, lad."

"My stomach is a bit queasy I'm afraid," Knoop said.

"Understandable," Matsell said.

"We'll walk to police headquarters," Murphy told Knoop. "The fresh air will do you good."

The telegraph room at police headquarters was located behind the front desk and had six stations manned by six uniformed officers.

"Lads, this is Secret Service Agent Murphy," Matsell said.

"He needs to send a telegram to the President."

"Actually, I need you to clear the room," Murphy said.

The six operators looked at Murphy.

"I wasn't asking," Murphy said.

"I'd like to hear your thoughts on the matter, Mr. Knoop," Matsell said from behind his desk.

Seated in a chair opposite the desk, Knoop said, "Naturally I'm glad that we put a stop to his activities here in New York, but . . ."

"But what, lad?" Matsell said.

"If he's gone as that man said, gone where and will he start over again?"

"I see and share your concern, lad, but that doesn't diminish what you've accomplished here," Matsell said.

"I realize that, but I have to wonder what his motivation was in doing what he did," Knoop said.

"Do you know how I became commissioner of police in this, the largest city in the country?" Matsell asked.

Knoop shook his head.

"By enforcing the law and not caring why the criminal commits the crimes that he commits," Matsell said. "The why and where of it is best left to the lawyers, judges, and the head doctors for without me doing my job they don't get to do theirs."

There was a knock on the door; it opened and Murphy entered.

"Mr. Murphy, I trust you had no problem sending your wire?" Matsell said.

"None at all," Murphy said.

"We were just discussing the merits of why criminals commit their crimes," Matsell said.

A desk sergeant walked in behind Murphy.

"We just received a wire, Commissioner," he said. "Our men

have identified the driver of the milk wagon and found his place of residence."

Murphy turned to the desk sergeant. "Can you wire them back?"

"They're standing by."

"Wire them and tell them not to enter the residence until we get there, and keep everybody on the street away," Murphy said.

The desk sergeant looked at Murphy and then at Matsell.

"He wasn't asking, Sergeant," Matsell said.

The sergeant nodded and closed the door.

"I believe I'll go with you lads," Matsell said.

Murphy, Knoop, and Matsell rode in Matsell's police carriage to the Bowery, where the milk-wagon driver had a small apartment on the third floor of a walk-up tenement building.

A dozen uniformed officers stood on the sidewalk outside the building. A small crowd had gathered, and the officers held them at bay.

"Is anybody watching the apartment door?" Matsell asked an officer.

"Two men, Commissioner," an officer said.

"Good. Now keep these people away," Matsell said.

As they entered the tenement building, there was an immediate stench of stale urine.

"The drunks and derelicts who occupy buildings such as this have a habit of pissing on the stairs," Matsell said as they walked up to the third floor. "Some because they're drunk, others because they believe the urine keeps the rats away."

At the apartment door, two officers stood watch.

"Anybody go in?" Matsell asked.

"No, sir."

Matsell opened the door and he, Murphy, and Knoop entered

the dark apartment.

Murphy struck a match and lit several oil lanterns in the apartment while Knoop opened the dark curtains at the windows.

The apartment was a mess. Consisting of a living room, kitchen, and bedroom, every square inch was littered with clutter and filth.

"William Kelly," Murphy said as he read the name on a worn letter he found on the kitchen table.

"Let's have a thorough look around," Matsell said.

In the bedroom, Knoop found a stack of medical books, a cigar box with seven hundred dollars, and an opium pipe with a supply of opium. There were notebooks from Kelly's years as a medical student with notes scribbled in pencil that were faded with age.

In the living room, Murphy found a doctor's bag that contained instruments and various drugs.

"This man went to medical school at Harvard for two years," Knoop said. "What happened to him?"

"Opium, Mr. Knoop," Matsell said. "He developed a taste for opium. I've seen it ruin many a man in my time. The Chinese introduced it to the Five Points back in the 'forties and it's been a problem since."

"Apparently Mr. Kelly's employer, the great man, paid very well," Knoop said. "There's seven hundred dollars in a cigar box in new bills."

"And nothing at all that might identify the great man," Murphy said. "Mr. Kelly might have been an opium addict, but he wasn't stupid. His medical education tells us something about his employer, the great man. Skill recognizes skill."

"Any notes on his recent activities?" Matsell asked.

"None," Knoop said. "Just notes from his college days."

"I'll have everything in the apartment taken into evidence

and searched thoroughly," Matsell said. "If you gentlemen are satisfied for the moment, I suggest we return to headquarters."

"Have your men knock on every apartment door and get statements from all the tenants," Murphy said. "Somebody might know something useful."

At the desk in the lobby, a desk sergeant said, "A report, Commissioner, on the milk wagon," and he handed Matsell a folder.

Matsell scanned the report and said, "Every dairy in the city reports no stolen wagons. It appears the wagon Kelly was driving was homemade."

"Mr. Commissioner, we've been up for thirty-six hours now," Murphy said. "I'm going back to the hotel, have a hot bath, and get some sleep."

Each floor of the hotel had a male and female bathhouse with six tubs and an attendant.

As Murphy lowered himself into a hot tub, Knoop stared at him in wonder.

"I've never seen a man with so many scars," Knoop said as he climbed into the tub next to Murphy.

Murphy had his pipe and lit it with a wood match.

"Where did . . . I mean, how did you acquire so many scars?" Knoop asked.

"The two in my chest near the left shoulder are from musket balls from the war," Murphy said. "The one in my lower right abdomen came from a Winchester rifle a few years back. The one in my left forearm came from a Sioux tomahawk. The two long ones on my back are from a Navajo knife attack. The others I don't even remember much."

Knoop looked at Murphy, who quietly smoked his pipe.

"What are you going to do now?" he asked.

"After my bath, get a steak and then eight hours of sleep,"

Murphy said. "Tomorrow I'll catch a train to Washington and report to Burke."

"Washington is on the way to Chicago," Knoop said.

Murphy looked at Knoop and grinned. "It is," he said.

"After we have supper, why not take in Cody's Wild West Show?" Knoop asked.

"I clean forgot about it."

"It's still early."

Murphy shrugged. "Why not?"

The tent held a thousand or more people. Murphy and Knoop had VIP seats in front near the action. Cody sat atop a tall white horse and served as ringmaster. Screaming savage Indians in war paint attacked soldiers, and they put on quite a show, reenacting the Battle of Bull Run and other famous skirmishes of the West.

The Indians and actors who portrayed the soldiers were highly trained and skilled riders and actors and the crowd ate up every second of the show.

"This is quite a good show," Knoop said.

"Especially if you've never seen the real thing," Murphy said.

CHAPTER SIX

A breakfast invitation from Mayor Edson was waiting for Murphy and Knoop when they checked out of the hotel at seven in the morning.

A driver and carriage waited curbside.

"We have plenty of time to catch the eleven a.m. train," Knoop said to Murphy as the driver loaded their luggage onto the carriage.

Edson and Matsell were waiting in the mayor's dining hall at City Hall.

"Mr. Murphy, Mr. Knoop, the city can't thank you enough for your service in ridding us of this madman," Edson said. "I intend to write a letter to Mr. Pinkerton himself about you, Mr. Knoop, if you wouldn't mind."

"Mr. Mayor, let me be clear on this," Murphy said. "We didn't stop this 'madman,' as you call him, we just relocated him. He'll kill again."

"The purpose of your coming here was to rid the city of him and make the city safe for the President's meeting," Edson said. "You've accomplished that, and that is what matters. Nothing else at this point."

The mayor's chef entered the hall. "Shall I serve breakfast now?" he said.

"Yes," Edson said.

After breakfast, while they took coffee, Murphy said, "How did you men make out with evidence in the apartment and with

70

his neighbors, Commissioner?"

"Nothing of any value from the apartment so far," Matsell said. "And his neighbors all said he was a quiet man who kept to himself, but they always say that. We did learn from his notebooks that at one time he was a brilliant medical student with a bright future before it all went wrong."

"One final thing," Murphy said. "I doubt that Kelly had carpentry skills, or this so-called great man. Have your men check carpenters and wagon makers. Maybe somebody remembers a special request. And he had to get those milk containers from somewhere."

"I shall do that, Mr. Murphy," Matsell said.

Murphy and Knoop, along with hundreds of others, waited on one of a dozen outdoor platforms for various trains.

Murphy lit his pipe and watched trains arrive and depart on the many sets of tracks.

"Do you really believe he will kill again after such a narrow escape?" Knoop asked.

"Count on it," Murphy said. "And soon."

"May I ask why you feel such?"

"He has a purpose in what he's doing," Murphy said. "We may not see or understand it, but like that man talking to himself, he certainly does."

"Do you think he'll continue to target prostitutes?" Knoop asked.

"Yes," Murphy said. "They are readily available and most will never be missed. If he targeted prominent citizens, there would be a public outcry, but who really cares if some prostitutes go missing?"

Knoop nodded.

Murphy looked down the track.

"Our train is coming," he said.

Burke's personal carriage waited for Murphy and Knoop at the Washington station.

"I do believe we've been invited to the White House, Mr. Knoop," Murphy said.

Burke lit a massive Cuban cigar and looked across his desk at Murphy and Knoop.

"More coffee?" Burke asked.

"Why do you ask if I want more coffee when you know full well that if I do, I'll have to get it myself?" Murphy said as he stood and reached for the pot on Burke's desk.

"Now is not the time to be argumentative, Murphy," Burke said. "Arthur is extremely pleased and would like to tell you that personally."

Murphy looked at Knoop.

"What about it, Mr. Knoop, do you want to meet the President?" Murphy asked.

"Yes, of course," Knoop said.

"I'll wait for you here," Murphy said.

Knoop looked his question at Murphy.

"I've already met him," Murphy said. "I wasn't that impressed."

After Burke delivered Knoop to the Oval Office, he returned to his office to find Murphy smoking his pipe at the window.

"Can't you for once just play along?" Burke said.

"I wish they'd do something with the Washington Monument," Murphy said. "It looks ridiculous in two colors."

"It's not colors, it's shades, and . . . oh, never mind," Burke said.

Murphy turned away from the window. "He's not done killing, Burke. Not by a long shot."

"Your mission was to make New York City safe for the President's meeting," Burke said. "You accomplished that. What more do you want?"

"Have your staff send telegrams to every US Marshal and county sheriff's office advising them to respond immediately to your office if prostitutes suddenly go missing," Murphy said.

Burke stared at Murphy.

"You're as crazy as a bedbug, Murphy," Burke said.

"I'll stay here on my farm until I hear from you," Murphy said.

Burke sighed. "You're going to do it anyway, aren't you?" he said.

"I have most of the twenty thousand in expense money you gave me," Murphy said. "I'll just hold onto it for now."

Burke sat behind his desk. "You do that," he said.

About to enter Burke's carriage, Murphy paused to turn around when Knoop called his name.

"Mr. Murphy, where are you going?" Knoop asked when he arrived at the carriage.

"I have a small farm just across the border," Murphy said. "I'll have the driver remove your luggage for you."

"No, wait, I'd like to go with you," Knoop said.

"Why?"

"I believe there is much I can learn from you," Knoop said. "I'd like to go with you when he strikes again. I know that's what you plan to do. Mr. Burke told me so."

"Listen, Knoop, you belong in the city where you can sleep in a soft bed every night," Murphy said. "Where he strikes again might just be far and away from such comforts."

"I don't care," Knoop said. "We started this together; I'd like to finish it that way."

"God help me," Murphy said. He held open the carriage door. "Get in."

As Murphy drove the carriage past acre upon acre of tobacco plants, Knoop said, "This is your farm?"

"It is."

"I didn't know they grow tobacco this far north."

"You can grow tobacco in Vermont if you want to, just not as much," Murphy said. "They grow it in western Massachusetts, although most people aren't aware of that."

"I wasn't," Knoop said as Murphy turned the carriage left onto a dirt road.

After about a quarter mile, Knoop said, "Is that your farm-house?"

"It is," Murphy said.

"Burke called you . . . what did he say?" Knoop said.

"Crazy as a bedbug," Murphy said.

"That's it," Knoop said. "Are you?"

"What do you think?"

"I think Mr. Burke might be the only man in the entire country who could call you that," Knoop said. "And get away with it."

The road turned again and Murphy drove the carriage to the corral where Samuel and Moses were chopping kindling.

On the porch, Etta was shucking beans, and she stood up and looked at Murphy as he stepped out of the carriage.

"Hello Samuel, Moses," he said. "I see your pa is keeping you busy."

"Mr. Murphy, I had a feeling you'd stop back this way," Etta said. "Come on up here and I'll go fetch Mal."

Knoop stepped down and stood next to Murphy.

"They're Negroes," Knoop said.

"You noticed," Murphy said.

"But you're from Tennessee," Knoop said.

"Did you miss the part where I fought for the North?" Murphy said.

Mal came out to the porch with Etta beside him.

"Mr. Murphy, I was just washing up for supper," Mal said. "Etta's making fried chicken. You'll join us?"

"Good. I'm starved," Murphy said.

"You men sit on the porch," Etta said. "I'll bring you coffee." She looked at Samuel and Moses. "Nobody said you could stop working."

"That's your horse?" Knoop said.

Holding a cup of coffee, Murphy stepped up onto a rung and Boyle nuzzled his face.

"This is Boyle," Murphy said. "Nearly two thousand pounds of blood, guts, and raw courage."

"He's . . . big," Knoop said.

"I walked him every day, but he won't let me get near him with a saddle like you said," Mal said.

Murphy rubbed Boyle's neck. "We'll stretch our legs come morning," he said.

"How long you planning to stay, Mr. Murphy?" Mal asked.

"Until I receive a telegram from Washington," Murphy said. "In the meantime, I figure me and Mr. Knoop here can lend a hand clearing stumps."

Mal looked at Knoop with a raised eyebrow.

"What's stumps?" Knoop said.

"You'll find out in the morning," Murphy said.

"The bedroom in the attic is quite comfortable, Mr. Knoop," Etta said.

"Thank you, ma'am," Knoop said. "And this dinner was quite elegant."

"I baked an apple pie with fresh apples," Etta said. "Samuel, go to the kitchen and churn the cream for the pie."

"Yes, Ma," Samuel said and stood up.

"Why don't you men go to the porch," Etta said. "I'll bring the pie and coffee."

"Did you buy what you need to clear the land?" Murphy asked Mal as he stuffed his pipe.

"I did, and Mr. Murphy, those Winchester rifles are . . ." Mal said.

"Nothing more than a simple thank-you for the way you break your back around here," Murphy said.

"The oxen and mule make it much easier, that's for sure," Mal said. "Those stumps can be mighty stubborn."

"What's stumps?" Knoop asked.

"Know what a tree is?" Murphy said.

"Of course," Knoop said.

"Same thing, only shorter," Murphy said.

Etta came out with a tray filled with apple pie and whipped cream.

"Thank you, ma'am," Murphy said.

"I have some chores," Etta said. "I'll leave you men to talk."

After Etta went inside, Mal said, "So how was New York? Exciting?"

"Eventful, but we left unfinished business," Murphy said. "That's the telegram we'll be waiting on."

"Did you see a telephone?" Mal asked.

"I did not," Murphy said. "I meant to, but there wasn't time and I forgot."

"The electrified light bulb?"

"I saw a few in the hotel and at City Hall, but not many," Murphy said. "I did ride in an elevator to the sixteenth floor."

"Sixteen floors. Was it exciting?" Mal asked.

"I'm not entirely sure I trust anything that goes so high powered by electricity on a cable," Murphy said.

"Excellent apple pie," Knoop said. "My compliments to your wife. I'm a bit tired from traveling, and I think I'll turn in."

"Good idea," Murphy said. "We'll be up at four-thirty."

"Four-thirty?" Knoop said.

"My misses will show you to your room," Mal said.

After Knoop went inside, Mal looked at Murphy.

"Squirrely little fellow, ain't he?" Mal said.

Murphy sipped some coffee and said, "He's going to need a horse."

CHAPTER SEVEN

Murphy and Mal swung heavy axes into the wide base of a tree stump for several hours, stopping occasionally to sip water from a bucket on the wagon.

Shirtless, their chests and arms glistened from a layer of sweat in the sunlight.

At the wagon, Knoop wrapped his hands in white gauze. "My hands are bleeding," he said.

"That's because you have the hands of a baby," Murphy said.

Mal went for water while Murphy kept chopping away at the stump. He dipped the ladle into the bucket, took a few sips, and poured the rest over his head.

"It's hard to keep up with the man," Mal said.

Knoop looked at Murphy. "I think he's just plain crazy, if you ask me," he said.

Mal grinned. "Care to tell him that?"

"Not on your life," Knoop said.

"Mal, I think we're ready for the team," Murphy said.

"Can you handle a team of oxen?" Mal asked Knoop.

"Oxen?" Knoop said.

Mal held the reins on the two oxen and waited for Murphy to give him the signal. A thick rope around the massive chest of each ox was tied around the stump.

At the stump, Murphy turned to Knoop.

"Are you ready?" Murphy asked.

"My hands are bleeding," Knoop said.

"Ignore it; it will stop," Murphy said. "Now put your back into it."

Murphy placed his hands on the top of the stump. Knoop sighed and did the same.

"Watch the roots," Murphy said. "Sometimes they snap when the stump breaks ground, and if one hits you in the head it will take it clean off."

"My head?" Knoop said.

"Go ahead, Mal," Murphy yelled.

Mal pulled on the reins and the team of oxen moved forward. Murphy pushed against the stump and looked at Knoop.

"My head," Knoop said.

"Push," Murphy said. "Never mind your head."

Knoop put his hands on the stump and pushed.

As the oxen moved forward, a loud cracking sound came from the stump as thick roots started to break free.

"A few more feet, Mal," Murphy said.

Mal pulled on the reins, and the oxen moved forward and the stump cracked loudly as roots broke and slowly the stump began to upend.

As the stump broke free, Murphy grabbed Knoop by the back of his shirt and yanked him backward.

Mal guided the oxen to the edge of the field where five or six additional stumps were gathered.

"Well, we have time for one more before lunch," Murphy said.

Etta arrived in a small wagon with a picnic basket full of sandwiches and milk. She sat on the buckboard with Knoop while Murphy and Mal worked on the second stump of the day.

"Let me see your hands," Etta said to Knoop.

Knoop held up his hands.

"Best let me tend them," Etta said.

She had a first aid box in the back of the wagon and cleaned Knoop's hands with alcohol, then rubbed salve on them and covered them in a clean white bandage.

"My husband ought to know better than to work a man unused to wielding an ax," Etta said.

"I don't think it was Mal's idea," Knoop said.

Etta looked at Murphy as he swung an ax into the stump. "Probably not," she said.

After a few dozen more chops into the stump, Murphy said, "Get the oxen, Mal. I think she's ready to go."

Knoop and Etta watched as Murphy pushed against the stump. It seemed to Knoop that every large muscle in Murphy's arms and back would burst from the skin as he strained to break the stump free from the earth.

Then, with a loud snap, the oxen yanked the stump free from the ground and dragged it forward.

Murphy stepped back and looked at Etta and Knoop in her wagon.

"Is that sandwiches I smell?" Murphy asked.

"Mr. Murphy, this man can't use those hands in the condition they're in," Etta said.

Eating a cold chicken sandwich, Murphy looked at Mal. "Does Sweetin still sell horses to the army?"

"Sure does," Mal said.

"Mr. Knoop, we're taking the afternoon off," Murphy said.

"Thank God," Knoop said.

The Sweetin ranch was located about twelve miles southeast of Murphy's farm. Murphy borrowed Mal's wagon and drove Knoop to the ranch after lunch.

Sweetin, a tall, powerful man in his sixties, ran the ranch with his two sons. A third generation immigrant from Norway, he spoke with a thick accent and, when angered, was prone to swearing in his native language.

Murphy parked the wagon at a large corral near the main house. Sweetin, on the porch, stepped down and looked at Murphy.

"Congressman Murphy, is that you?" Sweetin asked.

"It is. I've come to buy a horse," Murphy said.

Seated in chairs on the porch, Sweetin served coffee in mugs. Murphy lit and smoked his pipe.

"What happened to that beast you ride?" Sweetin asked.

"Boyle is fine," Murphy said. "The horse is for my friend Mr. Knoop here."

Sweetin looked at Knoop. "What happened to your hands?"

"Blisters from chopping tree stumps," Knoop said.

"Blisters?" Sweetin said.

"Where are your boys?" Murphy asked.

"Left two days ago with one hundred horses for the cavalry," Sweetin said.

"Do you have something small and gentle for my diminutive friend here?" Murphy said.

"Let me get my spectacles, and we'll go take a look," Sweetin said.

After Sweetin went into the house, Knoop said, "I've never ridden a horse in my life, you know."

"It's time you learned, Mr. Knoop," Murphy said.

Inside the corral Sweetin showed a dozen horses he brought from the barn.

"All are broke and gentle," Sweetin said. "Though too small for the army."

Murphy studied the horses.

"Most are bought by men for their womenfolk," Sweetin said. "Never sold one to a man before."

"First time for everything," Murphy said.

"True enough," Sweetin said.

"That little bay there with the white spot on her nose, how old?" Murphy asked.

"Two years and a few months," Sweetin said.

"Let me see her teeth," Murphy said.

Sweetin walked the horse to Murphy.

Murphy opened the horse's mouth and inspected the teeth and gums. "How much?"

"Three hundred, and I'll throw in fresh shoes," Sweetin said.

"Would you have a saddle broken in?" Murphy asked.

"Several. Take your pick. I'll throw it in with the price."

With the bay tethered behind the wagon, Murphy drove the wagon back to the farm.

"Why do I need a horse?" Knoop asked. "I don't know anything about horses."

"We might be going where a carriage ride through the park is unheard of," Murphy said. "Unless you plan to run beside my horse the whole way, you'll need a horse of your own."

Knoop turned around and looked at the bay. "She is kind of pretty," he said.

"Treat her right, and she'll return the favor," Murphy said.

At the corral, Mal said, "She's a fine-looking little bay."

Murphy looked at Samuel and Moses.

"Boys, tomorrow morning while your pa and me are clearing stumps, how would you like to teach Mr. Knoop here how to ride a horse?" he said.

Samuel and Moses raised eyebrows at Knoop.

"But he's a grown man," Samuel said. "How come he don't

know how to ride a horse?"

"I'm from Chicago," Knoop said.

"Don't they have horses in Chicago?" Moses asked.

"Boys, back to your chores," Mal said. "Wood doesn't split itself."

"Think I'll take Boyle out to stretch his legs," Murphy said.

"The saddle goes on like this," Samuel said as he slung the saddle over the bay's back.

"These are for your feet?" Knoop asked.

"Called stirrups," Samuel said.

Standing next to Knoop, Moses laughed. "Don't you know nothing?"

"I know a great deal," Knoop said. "Just not about horses."

"Now watch me," Samuel said after he tied the belt known as a flank billet around the bay's stomach.

Samuel put his left foot in the stirrup, grabbed the saddle horn, and lifted himself into the saddle. "See? Easy," he said.

Samuel dismounted and gave the reins to Knoop. "Now you," he said.

Knoop took the reins. "What's that thing called?" he asked and pointed to the saddle horn.

"That's the saddle horn," Samuel said. "You hold it while you lift yourself up with your foot in the stirrup."

Knoop placed his foot in the stirrup, grabbed the horn, and attempted to mount the saddle. As he hopped on his right foot, he pulled on the reins and the horse walked to her left. Knoop followed and they went in circles.

Moses broke out laughing. "You sure know nothing 'bout horses," he said.

"Go chop some wood or something," Samuel told Moses.

Moses shook his head as he walked away. "He sure don't know nothing about horses," he said.

As Mal drove his wagon to the corral, Murphy said, "Four stumps is a good day's work."

"Sure is," Mal said.

Etta was on the porch shucking ears of corn.

Mal and Murphy stepped down from the wagon and walked to the porch.

"Where's Mr. Knoop?" Murphy asked.

"In the barn soaking in a hot bath," Etta said.

"Did he ride today?" Murphy asked.

"That's why he's soaking in the tub," Etta said. "It appears the only thing he does well on a horse is fall off of it."

At sunup the next morning, Murphy and Knoop went to the corral to saddle their horses. As Knoop tossed the saddle over his bay, she turned and nipped at him.

"She doesn't like me very much," Knoop said.

"You haven't shown her who the boss is," Murphy said. "A horse is a herd animal. They follow the leader in the herd. She needs to know you're the leader. All you've shown her so far is fear. She'll never respect fear."

Murphy mounted Boyle.

"Let's go," he said.

It took several attempts, but Knoop finally managed to mount the saddle. Riding next to Boyle, Murphy stood several feet higher than Knoop.

"Let's see what that little bay can do," Murphy said.

"What does that mean?" Knoop said.

As soon as they reached the road, Murphy gave the reins a yank and Boyle took off running.

The bay, not about to be left behind, opened up, and Knoop

nearly fell from the saddle.

"Murphy . . . stop!" Knoop yelled.

About a mile down the road, Murphy pulled Boyle back and allowed the bay to catch up.

"She has a fine spirit," Murphy said.

"She's as crazy as you are," Knoop said.

"She needs a name," Murphy said.

"A name?"

"Unless you plan to call her horse, she needs a name."

"A name comes to mind, but it wouldn't be fit to say in mixed company," Knoop said.

"Take the lead, Mr. Knoop," Murphy said.

Knoop looked at Murphy. Murphy glared at Knoop.

"I know, I know. You weren't asking," Knoop said.

Knoop tugged on the reins and the bay took the lead. They rode for several miles until Knoop stopped.

"I've thought of a name," he said. "Lexine, after my mother in Scotland. I shall call her Lexi."

"Well, Mr. Knoop, I suggest we ride another mile and then turn around," Murphy said. "Ten miles is a good stretch of the legs for the first day."

"Come on, Lexi, let's go," Knoop said.

It was close to noon by the time Murphy and Knoop returned to the farmhouse. Burke's carriage was at the corral.

Burke and Etta were taking coffee on the porch.

"That's Mr. Burke," Knoop said as he and Murphy dismounted.

Murphy and Knoop put Boyle and Lexi in the corral, removed the saddles, and then went to the house.

"I hate to admit it whenever you're right, Murphy," Burke said and handed Murphy a folded telegram.

Murphy read the telegram and then handed it to Knoop.

"Looks like we're headed to Fort Smith, Arkansas," Murphy said.

Knoop read the telegram. It was addressed to Murphy in care of William Burke. It read *To Murphy Stop Four Prostitutes Have Disappeared Within the Last Week Stop Just Thought You Should Know Stop Judge Parker Fort Smith Arkansas Stop*

"Isn't he the one they call the hanging judge?" Knoop asked.

"Mr. Knoop, I took the liberty of contacting Mr. Pinkerton and advising him that you will be continuing on with Murphy," Burke said. "If you want."

Knoop looked at Burke.

"A man should always finish what he starts," Murphy said.

"I've never been to Arkansas," Knoop said.

"Mr. Burke, will you stay for lunch?" Etta said.

After lunch, Murphy, Knoop, and Burke took coffee on the porch.

"It could be coincidence, Murphy, but Judge Parker felt strongly enough about it to respond to my blanket telegram," Burke said. "It's worth ten hours on a train to find out though."

"We'll leave in the morning," Murphy said.

"I figured you would," Burke said. He removed an envelope from his suit jacket pocket and gave it to Murphy. "Another ten thousand in expense money."

"I'll wire you from Fort Smith," Murphy said.

After supper, Murphy and Knoop went to the corral and took Boyle and Lexi into the barn to brush and groom them.

"Brush with the grain, never against it," Murphy told Knoop. "She'll learn to trust you soon enough and then love you."

"Love?" Knoop said.

"A while back I was after some rustlers," Murphy said. "I was ambushed coming down a mountain, and while I was on the ground bleeding, a highly aggravated grizzly bear had me in his sights. Boyle came to my defense and took that grizzly head on and fought him to a draw and saved my life. A horse wouldn't do that unless it loved you."

Murphy rubbed Boyle's neck and Boyle turned to nuzzle Murphy's hand.

"The number-one rule you remember, Mr. Knoop, is to take care of your horse before you take care of yourself," Murphy said.

Knoop looked at Murphy.

"Never forget that," Murphy said.

CHAPTER EIGHT

On the porch, Murphy shook hands with Mal. Etta and the boys stood by his side.

"Where is Mr. Knoop?" Murphy asked.

"Right here," Knoop said as he stepped onto the porch holding a large satchel.

"I told you to pack light," Murphy said.

"I left half my belongings," Knoop said.

"Mal, take care of your family," Murphy said.

Knoop shook Mal's hand. "I'll send your belongings to the address you left," Mal said.

"Appreciate it," Knoop said.

"It was a pleasure having you," Etta said. "Please come again someday."

As they reached the railroad station, Knoop said, "What do we do with Boyle and Lexi?"

"Take them with us," Murphy said. "In the boxcar."

After purchasing tickets, Murphy sent a telegram, and then he and Knoop waited with the horses at the rear of the station where the boxcar would be once the train arrived. It was fifteen minutes late, but finally rolled to a stop at the platform.

The boxcar could accommodate a dozen horses, but there was just one other in the car besides Boyle and Lexi. After tethering them in stalls, Murphy and Knoop boarded the train and placed their satchels under their seats.

"Get comfortable. We have a ten-hour ride ahead of us," Murphy said.

Knoop purchased a railroad map in the office and studied it. "Except for a thirty-minute stop in Bowling Green in Kentucky, the train runs express," he said.

"Like I said, get comfortable," Murphy said.

Seven hours later, Murphy and Knoop stretched their legs in Bowling Green by walking to the boxcar to check on Boyle and Lexi.

Back on the train, Murphy said, "We should reach Fort Smith around eleven-thirty."

"Where will we stay overnight?" Knoop said. "We'll need a hotel room."

"I sent a telegram. It's taken care of," Murphy said.

As the train rolled to a stop in Fort Smith, Murphy nudged Knoop awake and said, "We're here. Wake up."

Knoop stood and stretched and said, "I don't know if I'm more hungry or tired."

"Let's get the horses, and we'll take care of both," Murphy said.

The dark streets of Forth Smith were somewhat illuminated by street lanterns as Murphy and Knoop walked the horses to a large livery stable near the railroad depot.

A man was on overnight duty in the stable, and Murphy paid in advance for two nights' care for Boyle and Lexi.

"Grab your gear and saddlebags," Murphy said.

As Murphy removed his Winchester from the saddle, Knoop said, "That's a Winchester, isn't it?"

"Not just a Winchester, part of the One in a Thousand series," Murphy said.

"I'm familiar with the term."

"Glad to hear it. Let's go."

"These streets are all mud," Knoop said.

"Must have had some hard rain the past few days," Murphy said. "Walk on the sidewalk."

The sidewalks were constructed of wood planks elevated about six inches off the ground. Footsteps echoed loudly as you walked on them, especially at night. Piano music could be heard from several saloons.

"Where are we going?" Knoop asked. "We need to find a place to sleep."

"Down this street," Murphy said and turned left.

They walked several blocks to the edge of town; Murphy turned right and they walked another block.

A large yellow and gray, two-story home on the fringe of town was lit by a lantern on the porch and several candles in the front windows.

A figure sat in a chair on the porch.

Murphy and Knoop walked to the porch.

"Hello, Kai," Murphy said. "Did you get my telegram?"

Kai slowly stood up. "I got it," she said.

Murphy and Knoop went up to the porch.

"This is Melvin Knoop," Murphy said.

"I have a pot roast keeping warm," Kai said.

"This is wonderful, ma'am," Knoop said.

Kai served the pot roast with potatoes and carrots, bread, and coffee and had an apple pie keeping warm under a towel.

"Thank you," Kai said as she watched Murphy.

Knoop had never seen so handsome a woman as Kai. She was several inches taller than he, with striking high cheekbones and green catlike eyes. He was sure she was part Indian, but of which tribe he hadn't a clue.

"I only had one room available for tonight, but it has two beds," Kai said.

"I'm so tired I could sleep on the floor," Knoop said.

"Not necessary," Kai said, looking at Murphy. "Would you like some pie?"

"I would, and then I'll turn in," Knoop said. "I'm exhausted."

Kai served Knoop and Murphy a slice of pie with fresh coffee.

"The room is the first door on the right on the second floor," Kai told Knoop after he finished his pie.

"Thank you," Knoop said as he stood up.

"I'll join you in a few minutes," Murphy said. "I want to get some air."

"Goodnight, ma'am," Knoop said.

"Goodnight," Kai said.

After Knoop went upstairs, Murphy filled his coffee cup and stood up. "I believe I'll sit on the porch and smoke my pipe," he said.

On the porch, Murphy and Kai sat in the love-seat style swinging chair.

"I thought I would never see you again," Kai said.

"I guess it's been a while," Murphy said as he blew smoke. "Did you ever find the man who killed your husband?"

"No, and I stopped looking," Kai said. "When the marshals bring in the prisoner wagons, I no longer go to the courthouse."

"Why?"

"Instead, I found myself looking for you to ride back into town," Kai said. "It was making me . . . sad, so I stopped."

Murphy looked at Kai. "How is it you have green eyes?"

"Only my mother was Navajo," Kai said. "My father was German and Irish with a touch of Ogunquit."

"I probably should have written you more," Murphy said. "Letter writing isn't my strong suit."

"You owe me nothing, but it would have been nice to receive a few more letters," Kai said.

"I'm not much for . . . I mean writing a woman . . . the words don't seem to come," Murphy said. "I never know what the right thing to say is in a letter."

"You are about the clumsiest man around a woman I have ever met," Kai said. "I think you'd rather be risking your life chasing outlaws than talking to a woman."

Murphy sighed.

"I'll say it for you," Kai said. "I can see in your eyes how nervous I make you, and a man is nervous around a woman only when he has feelings for her. Be an ass and lie to yourself if you like, but I know otherwise. I serve breakfast at six-thirty. Don't be late. I don't save leftovers for stragglers."

Kai stood and entered the house.

Murphy sucked on his pipe.

"Sometimes I think I'm better off with just me and the horse," he said aloud.

CHAPTER NINE

Murphy opted to skip breakfast and take just coffee on the porch with Kai.

They sat in the love-seat swing set. In the morning sunlight, Kai's eyes were emerald green and haunting to look at.

"Will you be gone long?" Kai asked. "I usually don't serve lunch, but since you missed breakfast."

"I didn't miss it. I skipped it," Murphy said.

"That's not an answer," Kai said. "And the result is the same, an empty stomach."

"I don't know," Murphy said. "A few hours, at least."

"Then I will fix you lunch," Kai said.

"You don't have to," Murphy said.

"Don't be a pain in the ass, Murphy," Kai said. "Women have little need for men who are a pain in the ass."

"Lunch will be fine," Murphy said.

Knoop came out and said, "You missed a great breakfast, Mr. Murphy."

Kai stood up. "I have dishes to wash," she said and stood up.

Murphy stood and handed his cup to Kai. "Let's go, Mr. Knoop."

"Where?" Knoop asked.

"To see the judge."

The walk to the courthouse from Kai's house was three quarters of a mile and halfway there, Knoop began sucking wind.

"Wait," Knoop gasped. "I can't keep up with your long legs."

Murphy stopped to allow Knoop to catch his wind.

"It wouldn't do you any harm to skip a breakfast or two," Murphy said.

With his hands on his knees, Knoop said, "I admit I could lose a few pounds, but not all at once."

Murphy gave Knoop another minute, and then said, "Ready?"

"I guess so."

Ten minutes later, they arrived at the steps of the courthouse. It was constructed of brick and stone and was the tallest structure in Fort Smith.

"Wipe the sweat off your face before we go in," Murphy said.

Knoop pulled out a handkerchief and wiped his face.

They went up the steps and entered the lobby. A US Marshal at a desk stood and said, "Firearms are not allowed in court except for law enforcement."

Murphy took out his wallet and showed it to the marshal. He scanned it and said, "Who are you here to see?"

"Judge Parker," Murphy said. "He's expecting us."

The marshal stood. "Follow me," he said.

Murphy and Knoop followed the marshal to the second floor to an office. The words "Judge Isaac C. Parker" were etched into the door.

The marshal knocked and then opened the door. "Judge, Secret Service Agent Murphy is here to see you," he said.

"Send them in and go fetch Sheriff Cooper," Parker said.

The marshal closed the door.

Behind his desk, Parker stood. He was around six feet tall, stout, with white hair worn long, and a white beard that made him appear older than his fifty-seven years. He looked at Knoop.

"Who's this?" Parker asked.

"Judge, this is Melvin Knoop of Pinkerton's," Murphy said.

"Pinkerton's, huh," Parker said. "You don't look like much.

What do you do for Pinkerton's, Mr. Knoop?"

"I analyze data and profile criminal behavior," Knoop said.

"What the hell for?" Parker said.

"Why, to fight against . . ." Knoop said.

"Never mind, never mind. Come on and have a seat," Parker said. "That's a fresh pot of coffee there, Murphy. Why don't you pour us all a cup."

Murphy lifted the pot off Parker's desk and filled three mugs.

"Have a seat," Parker said. "While we wait for Sheriff Cooper."

Murphy and Knoop took chairs opposite the desk while Parker took his chair behind it.

"When I got wind of that telegram sent from the White House, I never expected to respond to it," Parker said.

"That's why we're here," Murphy said. "Tell us about it."

"I'll let Cooper do that," Parker said.

"Tell me, Judge, any sign of Belle Starr and Sam?" Murphy asked.

"Not since you chased them out of here last time you were here," Parker said. "I heard they holed up in Wyoming Territory a while back."

Knoop looked at Murphy. "You chased out Belle and Sam Starr, the famous outlaws?"

"A long story," Murphy said.

"Never mind that right now," Parker said. "Tell me about this . . . hell, I don't even know what to call him."

"Mass murderer, sequential killer, take your pick," Murphy said. "He targets prostitutes and kills them by opening them up as if they were fish. He has skill, though. Surgeon-like in his precision. He killed more than a dozen that we know of in New York City alone."

"Good God," Parker said.

There was a knock on the door. It opened and Sheriff Chris

95

Cooper entered.

"You sent for me, Judge?" Cooper said.

"I did," Parker said.

Cooper was tall and slender, thirty-five years old, and an experienced lawman of ten years.

"This is US Secret Service Agent Murphy and Pinkerton's Detective Knoop," Parker said. "They're here about the missing whores."

"Damndest thing I ever saw," Cooper said.

"What's that?" Murphy asked.

"A big man, almost what I'd call a giant, rode into town in one of those gypsy wagons," Cooper said. "I was across the street from Tool's Saloon, and when he got down from the wagon, he looked to me to be around three hundred or more pounds. He went into Tool's, and then I got called away to break up a fight at the Ace's Saloon."

"And?" Murphy said.

"When I returned, the wagon was gone and so were four whores that work at Tool's," Cooper said.

"When was that?" Murphy asked.

"Five days ago."

"Let's go to Tool's," Murphy said. "Judge, I'll see you later."

Murphy stood up and looked at Knoop.

"Murphy?" Parker said. "Be nice."

Tool's Saloon was a large, two-story structure in the center of town on Elm Street. The first floor held a dozen gaming tables that consisted of cards, roulette, and other games of chance. At capacity, it held three hundred people.

A staircase led to the second floor where the brothel and eight bedrooms were located.

"That's Tool over there dealing blackjack," Cooper said.

"Get him," Murphy said and walked to a vacant spot at the bar.

Cooper looked at Knoop.

Knoop shrugged. "He wasn't asking," he said.

Cooper walked to the blackjack table and whispered to Tool. Tool stood up, waved to another dealer to take his place, and followed Cooper to the bar.

"I'm Sebastian Tool, owner of this establishment. Who are you?" Tool said to Murphy.

Murphy had his wallet out and showed his identification to Tool.

"Maybe we can talk in your office," Murphy said.

Tool sat behind his large desk in the office located behind the bar.

"May I offer you gentlemen a drink?" he said.

"It's nine-thirty in the morning," Murphy said.

"We're open twenty-four hours, except on Sunday," Tool said. "Some stupid temperance laws."

"Tell me what you know," Murphy said.

"Four . . . five days ago, around three in the afternoon I think it was, this big son of a bitch just walks in and immediately the floor goes silent," Tool said. "As tall as you but a good hundred or more pounds heavier and none of it fat. As easy as you please, he walks to the bar and says he wants four whores."

"Who was at the bar?" Murphy asked.

"My regular bartenders," Tool said. "He directed him to me and I escorted him upstairs to the madam. Standing next to him I felt like a child. Arms like anvils, hands like bear claws."

"What about his voice?" Murphy asked.

"Yeah, that's the other thing," Tool said. "He spoke English, but he sounded funny. Foreign-like."

"Is it normal for men to rent out the prostitutes off premises?" Murphy asked.

"I lease the entire second floor to Madam Geraldine," Tool said. "She conducts her business as she sees fit, and I don't interfere."

"Sheriff, let's go have a talk with Madam Geraldine," Murphy said.

Madam Geraldine was around fifty years old, a plump woman with massive breasts that nearly popped out of the top of her too-tight dress every time she took a breath. She met them in a small parlor at the top of the stairs.

"Government man, huh," Geraldine said when she looked at Murphy's identification.

"We're here about your four missing women," Murphy said.

"The government is interested in my four missing girls?" Geraldine said. "Why?"

"The why is my business," Murphy said. "Your business is to tell me what happened."

Geraldine looked at Knoop and Cooper, then back at Murphy. "Aren't you the polite one," she said.

"I don't have time for polite, and my patience is wearing thin," Murphy said.

Geraldine reached down into her bosom and came up with a cigar. She clenched it between her teeth and lit it with a wood match. "Sheriff, pour us a drink," she said.

Cooper went to a table where a decanter of whiskey and glasses rested on a silver tray. He poured a few ounces of whiskey into a glass and gave it to Geraldine. She took a sip and looked at Murphy.

"What do you want to know?" she said.

"From start to finish, what happened?" Murphy said.

"Tool brought this giant into my parlor. I guess it's five days now," Geraldine said. "The giant, he says he wants the use of four of my girls for several days at his camp he has with another fellow. He says he's willing to pay top dollar. Now we rent out local to the boys who live in town or at some of the ranches, but never at a camp, so I put it to the girls. He said he would pay each girl three hundred in advance and the house two hundred per girl."

"That's two thousand dollars," Knoop said.

Geraldine looked at Knoop. "You look like your bean could use a little polishing yourself, sonny boy," she said.

"I don't . . . what . . . I don't know what that means," Knoop said.

"It means wet the pole between your legs with one of my girls," Geraldine said.

Knoop blushed. "No, I couldn't," he said.

"Never mind that," Murphy said. "So what happened?"

"The giant pulled out this roll of bills and counted out the money and put it in my hand," Geraldine said. "The girls drew straws who would go, but the giant wanted two redheads and two blondes."

"Who went?" Murphy asked.

"Stacy, Kim, Janet, and Jane," Geraldine said. "Two redheads and two blondes."

"How did they leave?" Murphy said.

"Back staircase to the alley," Geraldine said. "It's how we normally do it for an outcall."

"Did you see his wagon?" Murphy asked.

"From the top of the stairs. It was one of those gypsy-type wagons. The girls all got in back."

"Tool said he spoke with an accent," Murphy said.

"Like some kind of foreigner," Geraldine said. "I've heard French and German, Mexican and even some Portuguese, but it wasn't any of them."

"How was he dressed?" Murphy asked.

"Like an eastern dude."

"So how do we know these girls are missing and not just at some extended party?" Murphy asked.

"I felt uneasy about it after two days and sent one of my deputies out to where they were supposed to be camped," Cooper said. "There was nothing."

"He told you where they were camped?" Murphy asked.

"Four miles west of town is what the giant said," Geraldine said.

"And no sign of them?" Murphy asked.

"Not due west," Cooper said.

Murphy looked at Geraldine. "Thank you, ma'am," he said.

Geraldine rubbed Knoop's hair. "My girls would love to get their hands on a cuddly little thing like you," she said.

"Who is the best tracker you have, Judge?" Murphy asked.

"That would be Marshal Cal Whitson," Parker said. "And Bass Reeves. Reeves is a Negro and works mostly in the Indian Territory. Both could track a mouse across a frozen lake in the dark."

"Can you spare them for a few days, maybe a week?" Murphy said.

"They're bringing in some prisoners that were holed up in the Indian Territory," Parker said. "They're due back around noon tomorrow. I'll assign them both to track for you, but no more than ten days. I need these men."

"Thanks, Judge," Murphy said.

"What the hell, we're both Grant men," Parker said. "Now get out of here. Court's about to convene."

"I'd surely like to go with you," Cooper said.

"Your place is here in Fort Smith," Murphy said. "Out there is federal business."

"I suppose," Cooper said.

Murphy shook Cooper's hand. "See you later, Sheriff," he said.

Walking back to Kai's home, Knoop said, "What's Indian Territory?"

"Reserved land for the Indian tribes in the mountains," Murphy said.

"Will we see any?" Knoop asked. "Indians, I mean."

"Probably," Murphy said. "But don't let it worry you none. They quit taking scalps years ago."

When they reached Kai's home, a buggy with two horses in the rig was parked out front.

"Maybe she has company?" Knoop said.

Most of the guests were gone for the day and Kai was alone in the kitchen. She was at the table, packing a large picnic basket.

"Mr. Knoop, I have left you something for lunch," Kai said. "It is in the bottom oven keeping warm."

"Thank you, ma'am," Knoop said.

Kai turned to Murphy.

"Grab the picnic basket and let's go," she said.

"Where?"

"Now where else would you take a picnic basket, Murphy?" Kai said.

CHAPTER TEN

Five miles north of Fort Smith, Kai spread a large wool blanket in the shade of a tree that stood beside a mountain stream.

"Bring the basket," she said.

Murphy carried the basket to the blanket and Kai opened the lid. She removed fried chicken, cornbread, fresh fruit, a bottle of wine, and a coffee pot.

"If you'd make a small fire, I'll make a pot," Kai said.

Murphy built a fire and while a pot of coffee cooked, they ate lunch in the shade.

"Did your business in town go well?" Kai asked.

"Yes. I have to go into the Indian Territory though. Probably in the next few days."

"Will you take the little man?"

"Knoop? If he wants to go, I suppose I will."

"He's as helpless as a city woman in the country," Kai said.

"I know."

"There is an extra blanket in the buggy. Could you get it, please?" Kai said.

Murphy stood and went to the buggy for the blanket. When he returned, Kai was at the edge of the creek.

"Kai, what are you doing?" Murphy asked.

In one smooth motion, the dress fell from her body, and naked, Kai stood with her back to Murphy. Her shape was exquisite.

"Oh. Oh, okay, good," Murphy said.

Kai dove into the creek, swam to the center, turned, and stood in neck-deep water.

"Are you coming in, Murphy?" she asked.

"Water looks cold," Murphy said.

"It is."

Murphy stared at Kai.

"Don't tell me the great Murphy is afraid of a little cold water," Kai said. "Or maybe a woman?"

Murphy sighed. He dropped his gun belt and then removed his shirt.

At the sight of his many scars, Kai gasped softly.

Murphy removed his pants and underwear and dove into the water. He burst through the surface and said, "God, that's cold."

Kai swam to Murphy. "So many scars," she said.

"The one in my shoulder is from . . ." Murphy said.

Kai tapped her chest. "I meant in here," she said.

"I don't understand what's happening here," Murphy said.

"I'm courting you, you idiot," Kai said. "Because you are too dumb or shy to court me. Is that so hard to understand?"

"Where I come from a man does . . ." Murphy said.

Kai wrapped her arms around Murphy, stood on her toes, and kissed him. "You talk too much," she said.

Under the second blanket, Kai rested her head against Murphy's chest.

"Usually I have very little use for men," Kai said. "They're stupid, clumsy, and most of the time they smell bad. But you have proven pretty useful, Murphy. Twice today in fact."

Murphy held Kai close and stroked her still-wet hair.

"What is your Christian name, Murphy?" Kai said.

"I'd rather not say."

"If you'd rather sleep in the room with your chubby little friend who probably snores and passes gas all night instead of my bed with me, then . . ."

"Jesus, Kai," Murphy said.

"It's just a name, Murphy. How bad can it be?"

"My parents are from the old country," Murphy said. "They didn't realize when they named me what they were doing."

"Tell me," Kai said.

Murphy sat up. "You don't leave a man much room, Kai."

"None." Kai sat up. "Tell me."

Murphy sighed, and then whispered into her ear.

"Okay? Satisfied?" Murphy said.

Kai looked at Murphy. A smile crossed her lips, and then she started to laugh.

"Ah, I knew it," Murphy said.

"That's . . . that's . . . hilarious," Kai said and toppled over into an uncontrollable fit of laughter.

Murphy looked at her.

"Hilarious," Kai said with tears streaming down her face.

"Dammit," he said.

When Murphy and Kai entered the kitchen they found Knoop seated at the table where he had been writing letters and writing in his notebook all afternoon.

"I see you've been busy," Murphy said.

"Writing reports to send to Mr. Pinkerton," Knoop said.

"You men get out of my kitchen," Kai said. "I need to prepare supper for the guests. Go on the porch and I'll brink you coffee."

Murphy and Knoop went out to the porch where the late afternoon sun cast them in shadow.

Murphy stuffed and lit his pipe. "The trip into the Ozarks won't be easy," he said. "Maybe you'd rather wait here?"

"I'd rather wait in Chicago, but Mr. Pinkerton placed his faith in me to do this job," Knoop said.

"Can you handle any sort of weapon?" Murphy asked.

"Like a gun?"

"What I had in mind."

"No, no, I can't," Knoop said. "I've never had to."

"The mountains are hard country," Murphy said. "It's not a place to go without being healed."

"I don't . . . what's healed?"

"Armed."

"But you and the others will be armed."

"And if we get separated?"

Knoop looked at Murphy.

"Tomorrow, when we go back to town, we'll pick you up some trail clothes," Murphy said.

"Why?"

"Because you'd look ridiculous riding a horse through the mountains looking like a Boston banker," Murphy said.

"I'll get the clothes, but I'm not sure about a gun," Knoop said.

"You weren't sure about riding a horse, either," Murphy said. "We'll figure something out tomorrow."

Kai came out with two mugs of fresh coffee.

"I heard what you said about a gun," she said. "I have an old pepperbox he can have."

"What's a pepperbox?" Knoop asked.

"It's sort of a derringer," Murphy said. "Chambered for the .22 round. Holds six, and they have a tendency to go off all at once. Thanks, Kai, but we'll find something more suitable."

"Since you are the only two here at the moment, I need you to help with some chores," Kai said.

"Chores?" Knoop said.

"I need butter churned and wood chopped," Kai said. "Mr. Knoop, would you care to chop some wood?"

"No, ma'am, I'm more of a butter man myself," Knoop said.

Kai looked at Murphy. "After you finish your coffee, you'll find the ax in the backyard shed and a pile of logs."

"Yes, ma'am," Murphy said.

Kai looked at Knoop. "And the cream and churn are in the kitchen."

"Yes, ma'am," Knoop said.

After Kai went inside, Murphy stood up. "Best get to churning, Mr. Knoop," he said.

Murphy watched Kai brush her long black hair from a chair in front of her bedroom dresser. She wore a simple nightshirt and was barefoot as she stroked her hair with the soft bristle brush.

Murphy remembered as a boy he would watch his mother brush her hair sometimes, and he never understood why she was so adamant about the procedure. He asked his father one time if he understood why Ma brushed her hair every night the way she did. Pa said, "Son, one day when you're grown, you'll come to realize that you haven't a single notion why women do what they do and you never will. It's just a fact of nature."

Kai looked at him in the mirror. "What are you thinking?" she asked.

"I'm thinking that I don't know a damn thing about women," Murphy said.

Kai put her brush down and smiled. "For once we agree on a subject," she said.

She stood and turned down the bed, then removed the nightshirt and got under the covers.

"Are you coming to bed or are you going to stand there with your mouth open?" Kai said.

Murphy removed his shirt and then his pants and got into bed beside Kai.

She blew out the oil lamp on the nightstand.

"Kai, I was thinking," Murphy said.

"Think tomorrow," Kai said and kissed him. "Tonight I need you to be useful one more time."

CHAPTER ELEVEN

Murphy and Knoop sat on the porch with mugs of coffee while they waited for the morning to pass.

"They have a good general store in town where we can pick you up some good trail clothes," Murphy said. "As for a weapon, I have an idea. You can wear the .38 I wore in New York on the shoulder holster."

"I've never fired a gun, .38 or otherwise," Knoop said.

"I know, but we can remedy that later," Murphy said.

Holding a pot and a cup, Kai came out to the porch. She touched up Murphy and Knoop's mug, set the pot on the porch railing, and took the chair next to Murphy.

"I will take you to town in the buggy," Kai said. "I need to shop for supplies, so you might as well ride with me."

"I'll hitch the buggy," Murphy said. "We're ready to leave."

Murphy left the porch and went to the rear of the house where Kai's buggy and horses were kept in a small barn.

Once Murphy was safely out of earshot, Knoop said, "Kai, you seem to know Murphy fairly well. Maybe you can tell me something."

Kai sipped from her cup and looked at Knoop.

"Oh . . . I meant no offense, ma'am," Knoop said. "What I mean is . . . as a person; you seem to get along with Murphy very well. He isn't the easiest person to get along with, you know. He can be quite bossy at times and prone to sudden fits of violence. In New York City, he . . ."

"What is the something you wish to know?" Kai said.

"Oh, well, what I was wondering . . . and this would be just between us," Knoop said. "I would swear I would never tell a living soul. Murphy would probably skin me alive if I . . ."

"Mr. Knoop, before sunset," Kai said.

"Yes, of course," Knoop said. "I was wondering if you know Murphy's first name. His Christian name."

Kai stared at Knoop, and she kept a straight face. Then, out of the corner of her eyes she saw Murphy leading the buggy to the front gate and she smiled and started to giggle.

"What?" Knoop said.

Murphy walked to the porch.

Kai started to laugh uncontrollably.

"What's this about?" Murphy asked.

Kai started to stamp her feet as tears rolled down her cheeks.

"Knoop, did you . . . ?" Murphy said.

Kai fell from the chair to the porch and stamped her feet. "Oh God . . . oh God," she said between fits of laughter.

"Dammit," Murphy said.

Kai rode between Murphy and Knoop in the buggy and grinned the entire time.

At the large general store, Murphy parked the buggy and helped Kai to the sidewalk.

"Don't look so serious," Kai said. "Your secret is safe with me."

"I'm not . . . can you do something for me?" Murphy said.

"Yes."

"Pick up what you need to make a couple of loaves of corn-bread and some corndodgers, maybe a hundred," Murphy said.

Kai nodded. "And Murphy, be nice to him. He's harmless."

Murphy looked at Knoop, who was still in the buggy.

"Are you coming, Mr. Knoop?" he said.

Murphy smoked his pipe as he watched the street from Judge Parker's office window.

A crowd on both sides of the street began to buzz as a large wagon that was basically a cage rolled into town. Five prisoners were locked in the cage. Cal Whitson and Bass Reeves rode in the buckboard. Reeves held the reins, Whitson cradled a shotgun.

"Wagon's here," Murphy said.

Knoop, at the conference table where he was scrawling notes, went to the window.

At his desk, Parker said, "Mr. Knoop, would you step into the hall and tell the marshal on duty I want to see Bass and Whitson."

Judge Parker did most of the talking while Reeves and Whitson sized up Murphy.

"Tomorrow, Judge?" Reeves said. "I was hoping to spend some time with my wife."

"Sorry, Bass, but this is urgent federal business," Parker said. "It can't wait."

Whitson was tall and lean and appeared menacing by the eyepatch worn over his left eye. Reeves, not as tall as Whitson, was more stout. Both men were hard as nails when it came to enforcing the law.

Whitson looked at Murphy. "I believe I heard of you. Who's the little fellow?"

"Melvin Knoop, an agent of Pinkerton's," Murphy said.

Whitson looked at Knoop. "You figure on going?"

"I do," Knoop said.

"This ain't no Sunday school backyard potluck supper we're going on," Whitson said. "It's hard country out there. No pillows and lemonade."

"He knows that," Murphy said. "He goes. We'll leave at eight tomorrow morning. We'll meet in front of the courthouse."

"Any questions about the assignment?" Parker asked.

Whitson shook his head.

"No, Judge," Reeves said.

"Good. Now get out of here and take a bath," Parker said. "You both stink to high heaven."

After Reeves and Whitson left the office, Parker looked at Murphy.

"I hope you know what you're doing," Parker said.

Kai's buggy was gone when Murphy and Knoop walked to the general store.

"My friend here needs two sets of trail clothes and a good set of boots," Murphy told the clerk behind the counter.

"The back of the store," the clerk said.

"I also have a list of goods we'll need in the morning," Murphy said and took a folded piece of paper from his shirt pocket and gave it to the clerk.

The clerk read the list aloud. "Ten pounds flour, ten pounds bacon, one pound of sugar, five pounds jerked beef, six cans condensed milk, ten pounds of beans, five pounds of cornmeal, grease or lard, one large skillet, one small skillet, one coffee pot, four sets of dinnerware, one pouch of pipe tobacco, two one-gallon canteens, one box of .44 long Colt ammunition, one box of .38 ammunition, one sewing kit, two large saddlebags, and four blankets tied into a bedroll."

The clerk looked at Murphy. "This is considerable money," he said.

"I'll pay in advance when we pick out his clothes," Murphy said.

"Excuse me, but would you have fresh oranges?" Knoop said.

"All out," the clerk said.

"Lemons or grapefruit?" Knoop said.

"Got some lemons," the clerk said.

"Add those, please," Knoop said.

As they walked to the clothing section, Murphy said, "Lemons?"

"For rickets and scurvy," Knoop said. "The boat ride from Scotland took one month. They gave us an orange a day to prevent scurvy during the trip."

"I know what . . . we're not taking a . . . never mind," Murphy said. "Pick out your clothes."

"Black or blue seems to be the only choice," Knoop said. "I don't look good in black."

Murphy sighed. "Don't forget a jacket," he said. "The mountains tend to get cold at night."

Knoop picked up a pair of long underwear. "Should I get these?"

"Yes, and a nice Stetson to keep the sun off your face and neck," Murphy said.

"Do you think they have chocolate? Some chocolate for the trip would be nice."

"I don't . . . I'll check."

While Knoop went through the process of selecting and trying on clothes, Murphy returned to the clerk.

"Do you have chocolate?" Murphy asked.

"I do," the clerk said. "Dark chocolate from Switzerland and Germany. I prefer the Swiss myself. Comes in small bars or one pound."

"Add a pound to the order," Murphy said.

The clerk nodded. "Would you like some candy?"

"Candy?" Murphy said. "No, thank you."

Knoop walked to the counter with his arms full of clothes, boots, and hat. "Got everything," he said.

"Wrap the clothes. We'll take them with us," Murphy said. "I'll pay for everything now."

The clerk totaled the bill at two hundred dollars and wrapped the clothes in a sack.

"We'll pick up the order in the morning," Murphy said as he set two hundred dollar bills on the counter.

Carrying his packages, Knoop said, "Mr. Pinkerton is good for all this."

"Never mind that," Murphy said. "Let's get our horses."

Four miles east of town, Murphy dismounted and said, "Here will do."

Knoop clumsily dismounted Lexi and said, "Do for what?"

Murphy removed his jacket to expose the shoulder rig and .38 revolver. He removed it and handed it to Knoop.

"It's heavy," Knoop said. "I didn't realize it was so heavy."

"Put it on," Murphy said.

Knoop went to stick his right arm through a loop.

"Under your jacket, Mr. Knoop," Murphy said.

"Oh," Knoop said and removed his jacket.

He slipped his right arm through a loop and then the left. The .38 Smith & Wesson revolver hung very low on Knoop's left side.

"Turn around," Murphy said.

Knoop turned, and Murphy adjusted the strap so the shoulder rig was tighter on Knoop's chest.

"Better," Murphy said. "Now draw the weapon and get a feel for it in your hand."

Knoop drew the .38 and held it in his right hand.

"Feel the balance of it," Murphy said. "How it fits into your palm."

"It's heavy," Knoop said.

"It needs to be to absorb the force of the loads," Murphy

said. "It will hit what you aim at up to seventy-five feet. That tree there is as wide as a man and about seventy-five feet away."

"What, you want me to shoot at the tree?" Knoop said.

"I hinted at it, didn't I?" Murphy said.

"Well, what do I do?" Knoop said.

"Cock the hammer, point, and squeeze the trigger," Murphy said.

"I don't aim?"

"The bullet will hit what you point the gun at," Murphy said. "Try to hit that tree."

Knoop stared at the tree. Then he cocked the hammer, pointed the .38 at the tree, and pulled the trigger.

The recoil of the .38 round snapped his wrist backward, and Knoop punched himself in the chin and fell backward and sat down.

"That's how not to do it," Murphy said. "Now let's do it correctly."

Knoop slowly stood up.

"Never hold the gun directly in front of your face," Murphy said. "Keep your elbow loose and knees slightly bent to absorb the recoil. Don't close one eye but instead look directly at what you want to shoot and point the gun at it. Hold the grip firmly but not so firm like you want to choke it. That will cause your hand to shake. Once you've committed to taking the shot, hold your breath right before you pull the trigger."

Knoop looked at the tree. Then he cocked the hammer and pointed the .38 with his arm slightly right of his face. He held his breath, bent slightly at the knees, and pulled the trigger.

The recoil was still powerful, but his hand only moved several inches.

"Did I hit it?" he asked.

"Wide to the right by several feet," Murphy said. "Here, I'll give you a target."

Murphy drew his black Colt Peacemaker, cocked, and fired all six rounds into the tree, producing a four-inch-wide grouping.

Knoop stared at the tree.

As Murphy dumped his spent rounds, he said, "I have a box of fifty .38 shells in my saddlebags. We aren't leaving here until you hit that tree."

Knoop hit the tree seven times out of fifty-six rounds.

As they rode back to town, Murphy said, "Slightly better than ten percent accuracy range is no way to win a gunfight, but it will do for a start."

"My wrist hurts," Knoop said.

"Rub some lemon juice on it," Murphy said.

They rode the horses to Kai's house and put them in the corral in her backyard. They found her in the kitchen where she was baking loaves of cornbread.

A tin cookie sheet on the table held rows of corndodgers.

"Will one hundred dodgers and two loaves of cornbread be enough?" Kai asked when they entered the kitchen.

"It will do nicely," Murphy said. "Thank you."

"I shot a gun at a tree," Knoop said.

"Good for you," Kai said as she wiped her hands on a towel. "If you aren't too tired from that, can you churn some butter?"

"I'll have to use my left hand," Knoop said. "My right is sore."

Kai looked at Murphy. "How about you? Are you sore?"

"No," Murphy said.

"There is some wood out back that could use some splitting," Kai said.

Murphy looked at Kai.

"Umm, Murphy, I don't think she was asking," Knoop said.

★ ★ ★ ★ ★

"Will you come back?" Kai asked as she snuggled her face into Murphy's chest.

"As soon as the job is finished," Murphy said. "We'll leave everything we don't need here with you if you can keep the room open. I'll pay for it in advance."

"And then what?"

"I'll let you decide that part," Murphy said. "If I didn't have bad luck with women, I'd have no luck at all."

"You make it sound as if you're playing poker," Kai said.

"That's not what I . . . it's just that every woman I get close to seems to wind up in an early grave," Murphy said.

"Thirty-five years ago, a group of white men wearing masks rode to the little house my father built for us in the middle of the night," Kai said. "They didn't like the fact that my father's tiny little ranch had a squaw and a half-breed living so close to them. That was in Iowa, where white civilized people live. They burned us out in the middle of the night."

Kai sat up in bed and looked at Murphy.

"Soon after that came the 'Gold Rush' and people moved west by the thousands," she said. "So did we, but not for gold but for a place we could live and be accepted. My father thought he found it in Utah. Thousands of Mormons were settling there by Salt Lake. This time it was a tribe of Paiute that came in the night. They killed my father because he was white, and they killed my mother because she married a white man, and they took me as a slave girl because I'm a half-breed. I lived with them until I was ten and they traded me to the Navajo tribe in Nevada for one pony. I'm only half Navajo, so I wasn't worth very much."

Murphy got out of bed and went to his saddlebags on the floor by the door and returned with a bottle of his father's whiskey. He poured an ounce into the two water glasses beside the pitcher of water on the dresser and gave one to Kai.

She took a small sip and coughed. "And you like this stuff?" she said.

"So what happened after that?" Murphy asked.

"I lived with the Navajo until 'sixty-one," Kai said. "Oddly enough, it was the railroad that took me away from the Navajo and returned me to the white man. Even though war broke out between the North and South, there were tens of thousands of soldiers fighting the Indians for land out west for the railroad expansion. I was taken in Wyoming Territory and sent to live in a school for girls in Baltimore. I stayed there until after the war and received a proper white education. I met my husband after he was discharged in 'sixty-six in Baltimore. I was teaching at the school by then when we met. He was from Arkansas and after we married, we moved here. He was killed in 'seventy-seven by outlaws, so don't you talk to me about your bad luck, Murphy. Using bad luck as a reason is an excuse for giving up."

Murphy sipped some whiskey.

"Why did you never . . . ?"

"Have children?"

Murphy nodded.

"Do you know what happens to a young girl's insides when she is forced to service the desires of one too many Navajo men?" Kai said.

Murphy took another sip from his glass.

"I am forty now, Murphy, and I don't have the time to waste while you ride around chasing outlaws trying to decide if you want me or not," Kai said. "If you do, we are still young enough to make something together. If you don't, then go and I will get about my business as usual."

Murphy tossed back the rest of his drink and set the glass on the nightstand.

"Have you ever been to Tennessee?" he asked.

CHAPTER TWELVE

"Wonderful breakfast, ma'am," Knoop said. "Thank you."

"You're welcome," Kai said.

Wearing his new trail clothes and the shoulder holster, Knoop reminded Kai of one of those actors in the Wild West Show that passed through last year. If it weren't for the fact that he was going with Murphy on a dangerous mission, she would find it comical.

"Wait for me outside," Murphy told Knoop. "I won't be but a minute."

Knoop grabbed his jacket and hat and said, "It's been a pleasure staying here, ma'am."

After Knoop left the kitchen, Kai said, "He's a good little man. Make sure nothing happens to him."

"There will be three of us watching out for him," Murphy said.

"And make sure nothing happens to you," Kai said.

She reached up on her toes to kiss Murphy.

"Will I like Tennessee?" she asked.

"She's a real fine lady," Knoop said as he and Murphy rode to the courthouse. "You should think of settling down when we get back."

"As of right now, the only thing you think about is we are embarking on a mission to capture the men responsible for sixteen murdered women and possibly four more, and that's all

118

you think about," Murphy said. "Nothing else matters. A man starts to think about home and gets to missing his loved ones and he gets careless. In our business, careless gets you dead pretty damn quick."

"What do you do, just turn it off?" Knoop asked.

"No choice," Murphy said. "There's no other way to do this kind of work and make it to old age. There's Reeves and Whitson."

Standing beside their horses, Reeves and Whitson mounted up and waited for Murphy and Knoop to arrive.

"We'll head due west and pick up the trail," Whitson said.

Reeves looked at Knoop and Lexi. "Are you up for this?"

"I'll have to be," Knoop said.

"Let's go then," Whitson said.

They rode due west for about an hour and picked up the first sign of wagon tracks. They dismounted to inspect the impressions left in the grass.

"This wagon was heavy," Reeves said. "Like a gypsy wagon loaded down with five or more people."

"How far before the Arkansas River turns south?" Murphy asked.

"Half a day's ride from here," Reeves said. "You think they headed south?"

"No," Murphy said.

They rode until noon and rested the horses for thirty minutes. Murphy shared the corndodgers with the group, which they ate with sips of water.

"They're following the river," Reeves said. "By nightfall it turns south toward Conway and then Little Rock."

"I don't know where they're going, but it isn't to a big town like Little Rock," Murphy said.

"I think he's going to cross the river," Whitson said.

Knoop looked at the high, flowing waters of the Arkansas

River. "How?"

"On a ferry boat," Murphy said. He turned to Whitson and Reeves. "Where is the nearest crossing?"

"Granny's," Reeves said. "About four hours' ride from here."

Murphy opened his saddlebags and removed four sticks of jerked beef. "Let's go," he said as he passed each man a stick.

Around five in the afternoon, they rode into *Granny's River Crossing Ferry/General Store/And Saloon. One Dollar a horse. 50 Cents Extra for Wagons,* or so read the handpainted sign.

Thirty feet from the river stood a log cabin where Granny, her son, and three grandsons lived. Near the cabin was a general store that also served as a saloon. At a long dock was a wide flat raft that served as a ferry boat. The boat was powered by two ropes that anchored it to land and looped through three stations on each side of the raft. Two men on each side of the raft simply pulled the raft across the river to the other side.

Seated in a rocking chair, seventy-two-year-old Granny chewed tobacco and sipped moonshine whiskey from a jelly jar.

"Bass Reeves, Cal Whitson, weren't expecting to see you anytime soon," she said. "Who's your friends?"

"This is Federal Agent Murphy," Whitson said. "We need to cross, Granny."

"On the hour every hour from sunup to sundown," Granny said. "Who's the little fellow?"

"I'm Melvin Knoop of Pinkerton's," Knoop said.

Rocking, Granny spat juice into a can and said, "Pinkerton's. Fine mess you made of the James brothers a while back."

"That wasn't our . . ." Knoop said.

"Never mind that," Murphy said. "We need to cross, Granny."

"On the hour Mr. Federal Agent," Granny said. "On the hour."

Murphy dismounted and walked to the porch. "I need some

information."

"Come up and have a sip with me if you aim to converse," Granny said.

Murphy went up to the porch and Granny handed him the jelly jar.

"Have a seat, Mr. Federal Agent," she said.

Murphy sat, sniffed the moonshine, and took a very small taste. The harsh, colorless liquid burned his throat as if he had swallowed paint thinner.

"Now what information do you seek, Mr. Federal Agent?" Granny asked.

"A wagon crossed here maybe four or five days ago," Murphy said. "Do you remember it?"

"Six or seven wagons crossed here in that span," Granny said.

Murphy handed the jar back to Granny and said, "This wagon was like a gypsy wagon with possibly a really large man driving it."

"Four days ago right around breakfast that wagon showed up and like you said, this really large man was driving it. I didn't see no one with him, and the back of the wagon was closed," Granny said. "He was big all right. Tall as you, but heavier. Spoke kind of funny, too, as I recall."

"Funny how?" Murphy said.

"Like some kind of foreigner," Granny said. "I heard just about every type of foreigner there is come across my ferry, but I can't figure this one."

"Did he mention where he was headed?" Murphy asked.

"Ain't my business, so I never ask," Granny said. "He paid his dollar fifty and rode the ferry like everyone else."

"Did he stop in the store for supplies or a drink?"

"Not as I recall," Granny said. "Best load your horses. It's almost on the hour."

"Thanks for the information," Murphy said.

"Pay a dollar each to my boy on the raft," Granny said. "And I'll see you on the return trip, if you make it."

Murphy, Reeves, Whitson, and Knoop waited at the boarding ramp to the raft for Granny's son and three grandchildren to check the ropes for the crossing.

"They crossed in the morning," Murphy said. "They left town around three in the afternoon so they had to have camped out overnight and crossed in the morning."

"Four days' head start, five come morning, it will be a task to catch them," Reeves said.

Granny's son turned to Murphy. "Board now. That will be one dollar a horse."

After loading the horses, Murphy stood with Knoop at the front of the raft, Reeves and Whitson in the rear.

"I can see why they picked here for the raft crossing," Knoop said. "It's only about three hundred feet across."

"But too deep and current's too strong for our horses to swim," Murphy said.

"You know, if they hooked up a . . ." Knoop said. He turned to Granny's son pulling rope on his right. "If you hooked up a pulley system on each side of the river and let a pair of mules do the pulling, you'd save your back a lot of work. In part, it's how the Egyptians built the pyramids."

Granny's son looked at Knoop. "What's pyramids?"

"They're . . . just a suggestion," Knoop said.

When they reached the other side of the river, Granny's son said, "What was that you said about mules?"

While Murphy, Reeves, and Whitson brought their horses onto land, Knoop stayed back for a few minutes to talk to Granny's son.

"Nice fellow," Knoop said as he walked Lexi off the raft.

"We have about an hour before sundown," Whitson said. "We should use that time to pick up the trail so we can get a quick start in the morning."

The task proved difficult. Hundreds of horses and men and several wagons had crossed the river in the last week and tracks were everywhere. Several times they had to backtrack and change direction before they decided the deep wagon-wheel impressions in the soft earth were made by the gypsy wagon.

At dusk, they found a comfortable spot to make camp.

Murphy built a fire and put on bacon, beans, and coffee to cook.

While the food cooked, they tended to the horses.

As he brushed Boyle, Murphy turned to Knoop. "Check her shoes for pebbles or cracks," he said.

Brushing Lexi, Knoop paused and looked at Murphy.

"Like this," Murphy said and took Boyle's right front leg and bent it backward at the knee. "A small pebble caught in the shoe can cause a horse to go lame. If you find any, pick them out."

After the horses were brushed and fed, Murphy checked the bacon and beans and said, "Let's eat."

He cut into a loaf of cornbread and passed around thick slices.

Whitson looked at Knoop. "I heard what you said back there on the raft about pulleys and ropes. That's good thinking," he said.

"It's just logical," Knoop said.

"What is it you do over at the Pinkerton's?" Reeves asked.

"Forensic science and logical investigation," Knoop said.

Reeves and Whitson stared at Knoop.

"Perhaps a bit more elaboration," Whitson said.

"Oh, well, see . . . for example," Knoop said. "Before I left Chicago, I was working on a system to take to Congress for firearm identification using serial number and ballistics reports."

Reeves looked at Whitson. "He's speaking English, but I have no notion what he's saying."

"See, every handgun and rifle has a serial number etched into the barrel or other places," Knoop said. "Each weapon is test fired at the factory where it's made, and each weapon makes grooves in the bullets that are unique to that weapon. If one bullet is kept and catalogued to the serial number and later that weapon is used in a crime, the gun can be traced to its owner by the store records of who purchased it. Mr. Pinkerton plans to take the proposal to Washington when I return."

Whitson looked at Murphy. "Is something like that true?"

"It is," Murphy said.

"So if I shot this annoying little fellow for being a pain in the ass, you could dig the bullet out and match it to my gun and only my gun?" Whitson said.

"I could," Murphy said.

"Don't even get me started on what we could do with fingerprints," Knoop said.

"We won't," Whitson said.

Reeves grinned at Whitson. "Guess you shouldn't shoot the little fellow then, Cal," he said.

Murphy stood and fetched an unopened bottle of his father's whiskey from a saddlebag. He opened it and added a splash to four coffee cups and then poured coffee. He sat and lit his pipe.

"Marshal Whitson, may I ask you a personal question?" Knoop said.

"During the war I was with a field artillery unit," Whitson said. "I got too close to an exploding shell, and it blinded me in the left eye. I still have the eye, but it's a sight, so I wear the patch."

"Thank you, Marshal, but that wasn't my question," Knoop said.

"Oh? Well, what then?"

"Since it requires two good eyes to have depth perception, I was wondering how you aim and shoot a gun," Knoop said.

"Well I . . . what's depth perception?" Whitson said.

"It requires two eyes to judge distances," Knoop said. "If you close one eye and look at an object, it's difficult to judge how far away it is."

"I just got used to looking at things with one eye is all," Whitson said. "Near or far is all the same to me."

"Pirates with two good eyes often wore an eyepatch to . . ." Knoop said.

"Mr. Knoop," Murphy said.

"Oh, yes, I'm sorry," Knoop said. "I tend to rattle on sometimes."

"Well, I suggest we rattle ourselves to sleep if we're to be up before dawn," Murphy said. "Mr. Knoop, best hobble Lexi."

Knoop stared at Murphy.

Murphy stood. "Come on. I'll show you."

Murphy was up an hour before dawn and built a fire for breakfast. By the time Reeves and Whitson were out of their bedrolls, the coffee was ready. Murphy woke Knoop when the beans and bacon were done.

"It's still dark," Knoop said when he opened his eyes.

"Have some coffee," Murphy said.

"I can still see the morning star," Knoop said as he sat up and took a cup from Murphy.

"The what?" Reeves asked.

"The planet Venus," Murphy said.

Reeves and Whitson looked up.

Knoop sipped his coffee. "My legs and back feel like I've been run over by a fire wagon."

"Eat some breakfast. You'll feel better," Murphy said.

Murphy cut thick slices of cornbread to go with plates of beans and bacon, and they sat around the dwindling campfire to eat.

"We need to pick up the trail and make a good twenty miles today," Whitson said.

"One of us should scout," Reeves said.

"You do it, Bass," Whitson said. "Seeing as I got no . . . what did he call it?"

"Depth perception," Knoop said.

"Yeah, that," Whitson said.

Knoop removed a lemon from his saddlebags and bit off a hunk of the skin.

"What you got there?" Reeves asked.

"A lemon," Knoop said. "They were out of oranges."

"Lemon?" Whitson said. "You planning on making some lemonade?"

"No, but what I am planning on is not getting rickets or scurvy," Knoop said as he sucked juice from the lemon.

"He does have a point about a scout," Murphy said. "Bass, if you take the point, maybe we can take some time to hunt fresh meat."

"We'll split up at noon," Reeves said.

"Northwest along the river," Reeves said. "Makes no sense."

"We'll rest the horses here for thirty minutes," Murphy said.

They dismounted and sat in the shade of some trees. Murphy dug out the sack of corndodgers and gave each man six. They ate with sips of water.

Knoop went through his saddlebags and dug out the pound bar of chocolate. "Mr. Murphy, may I borrow your knife?"

Murphy pulled the Bowie knife from its sheath and gave it to Knoop. Knoop cut off four slices from the bar and gave each man one.

"Thank you kindly," Reeves said. "But I think I'll eat mine in the saddle."

"We'll catch up to you by sundown," Whitson said.

After Reeves rode away, Knoop said, "Those are mountains there in the distance."

"Ozarks," Murphy said.

"He's taking a wagon into the mountains?"

"Look around you," Murphy said. "It ain't exactly Broadway around here."

"You mean he wants the privacy?" Knoop said.

"He's got to know by now to stay away from large cities," Murphy said. "Out west a man can really lose himself."

"Outlaws can stay at large for years in the west," Whitson said. "Many a man with a checkered past in the east went west to lose himself and start over. The west is a big place, and a lot of it got nobody in it."

"Mr. Knoop, if you're done eating chocolate, let's ride to those rocky foothills over there," Murphy said.

They rode about three miles north to a string of foothills belonging to the Ozarks.

As the approached the rocky foothills, Murphy stopped Boyle and rubbed his neck. "Find him for me, boy," he said.

Knoop and Whitson stayed in the saddle while Murphy slowly took Boyle to the foothills.

"What's he doing?" Knoop said.

"Don't know," Whitson said.

Murphy rode Boyle over rocks and the foothills until Boyle had a sudden, nervous reaction.

"Where? Here?" Murphy said.

Boyle snorted and backed up a few steps on the rocks.

Murphy rubbed Boyle's neck and then dismounted. "Stay here, boy," he said.

Knoop and Whitson watched from several hundred feet away

as Murphy drew his Bowie knife and then disappeared from view behind some large rocks.

After about thirty seconds, Knoop said, "Mr. Murphy!" and was about to yank on Lexi's reins when Murphy stood up.

Holding a six-foot-long, headless rattlesnake, Murphy mounted Boyle and rode back to Knoop and Whitson.

"Is that . . . is that a rattlesnake?" Knoop asked.

"No, Mr. Knoop, it's dinner," Murphy said as he wrapped the headless snake around the saddle horn. "Let's pick up Reeves's trail."

Close to nightfall, Murphy spotted a red dot about a mile ahead of them. "Reeves has a fire going," he said.

When they rode into camp, Reeves was drinking coffee with his back against his saddle. "Just made," he said.

Murphy dismounted, holding the snake. "Make a spit, Mr. Reeves, while I skin our main course."

After Murphy cut the snake into slices and they roasted them on a spit, he cooked a pan of beans. When the snake was fully cooked, he tossed the slices into the pan.

"Mr. Knoop, would you fetch a bottle of whiskey from my saddlebags," Murphy said.

Knoop went to Murphy's saddlebags and returned with an open bottle and gave it to Murphy. Murphy added two ounces to the bubbling pan.

"Give it about fifteen minutes," he said.

"How did you know there was a snake in the rocks?" Knoop said.

"Snakes like sun and rocks," Murphy said. "Horses have a natural fear of snakes. It took some doing to get Boyle used to looking for them instead of running from them, but he can find them nine out of ten times."

"I never had snake for supper before," Knoop said. "I've had snails and enjoyed them very much."

"Snails?" Reeves said. "Like in the garden?"

"Escargot, Mr. Reeves," Knoop said. "Giant, tender snails served in melted garlic and butter sauce. It's a delicacy served to kings in Europe."

"My dog digs them up in the garden and eats them," Reeves said. "Ain't got no garlic sauce though."

Knoop, Murphy, and Whitson cracked up laughing and when they quieted down, Murphy dished up plates of food.

"How did you do today, Mr. Reeves?" Murphy asked.

"It's that wagon all right," Reeves said. "Makes deep impressions in the earth. Traveling due east, slightly to the north and in no hurry."

"No way they ride that wagon through high country in Indian Territory," Whitson said.

"No, sir, they have to stick to low ground and ride through the gorges," Reeves said.

"How far ahead of us?" Murphy asked.

"Sixty miles, no more than that," Reeves said.

Knoop looked at Reeves. "We're going into the Indian Territory?"

"Unless they turn around and come to us," Reeves said.

"Will we see any?" Knoop said. "Indians?"

"Probably," Reeves said. "But they all know me and Cal, so they won't bother us none."

"Well, they don't know me," Knoop said. "Will they bother me?"

Reeves grinned and said, "Guess we'll find out when the time comes."

Knoop looked at Murphy.

"Who wants seconds?" Murphy asked.

CHAPTER THIRTEEN

Reeves had little trouble following the trail left behind by the heavy wagon, and by noon, they'd traveled more than ten miles.

They rested the horses for an hour and ate a cold lunch of corndodgers and beef jerky with water.

"I'm not sure, but I think we crossed over into Oklahoma Territory," Reeves said.

"Cherokee Territory," Whitson said.

"This doesn't make much sense," Reeves said. "A foreigner traveling through Cherokee Nation in a wagon with four whores."

Knoop looked at Murphy.

"He's not traveling," Murphy said. "He's looking for the right place to slaughter those women."

Reeves and Whitson looked at Murphy.

There was nothing to stay.

"Let's mount up," Murphy said.

Around three in the afternoon, Knoop rode close to Murphy and said, "Do you see that on our right?"

"They been dogging us for about an hour," Murphy said.

"Cherokee?" Knoop asked.

"I expect so," Murphy said.

"What do we do?"

Reeves and Whitson were twenty feet ahead, and Murphy galloped Boyle to catch up to them.

"Recognize him?" Murphy asked.

"No. He's a scout," Reeves said. "Probably a hunting party. We'll ride another few miles and make camp. They'll want to pay us a visit."

"We passed some turkeys a while back," Murphy said. "Go on and make camp. I'll see if I can catch a few."

"Should I go with you?" Knoop asked.

"Help set up camp," Murphy said and removed his gear bag from the saddle.

As Murphy turned Boyle and rode east, Whitson and Reeves dismounted.

"Mr. Knoop," Whitson said.

Knoop dismounted and looked back at Murphy.

"No need to worry about him," Reeves said. "If they cross paths, worry about the Cherokee."

After hobbling the horses, they gathered wood and built a fire. Reeves constructed two large spits while Whitson broke out the cookware from the gear bag.

"Mr. Knoop, put on a full pot of coffee," Whitson said. "And see how many cups we have."

"Are we expecting company?" Knoop asked.

"Oh, yes," Whitson said.

As the coffee cooked on the fire, two shots rang out in the distance. They echoed slightly and then faded to silence.

"Winchester," Reeves said.

Fifteen minutes later, with two wild turkeys slung over the saddle, Murphy galloped into camp.

"Mr. Reeves, pluck one of these birds. I'll handle the other," he said as he dismounted. "Mr. Knoop, take off my saddle and hobble Boyle."

"Looks like we need more wood," Whitson said.

Thirty minutes later, while the turkeys roasted on the spits and beans cooked in a pan, Murphy lit his pipe and sat against his saddle.

"What . . . what are you doing?" Knoop asked.

"Waiting for our guests," Murphy said. "Mr. Reeves, how many do you figure?"

"Probably sent out a party of twenty after deer," Reeves said. "My guess is they send ten back with the game and keep ten on our tail to see what we're up to."

"Good guess," Murphy said and looked past Reeves.

Whitson, Reeves, and Knoop turned and looked at the ten Cherokee warriors riding to their camp from the north.

One Cherokee warrior rode in front, while the remaining nine rode behind him in a V formation.

"The one out front is Blood Arrow," Reeves said. "He's a holy man and chief. The one to his right is his son, Two Hawks. The others are just soldiers."

Murphy stood and watched as the hunting party approached camp.

Ten feet from camp, they stopped, and Blood Arrow handed the reins from his horse to Two Hawks and then dismounted.

As he walked into camp, Blood Arrow spoke in Cherokee.

Reeves answered him in Cherokee.

Blood Arrow looked at Knoop and spoke in Cherokee.

Reeves shook his head.

"What . . . what did he say?" Knoop said.

"Blood Arrow speaks English just fine," Whitson said. "He does this just to aggravate us."

Knoop looked at Blood Arrow. He was around forty-five years old, of average height but powerfully built. His dark hair was at least two feet long. His eyes were like coal. He wore gray pants with boots and an army scout shirt unbuttoned.

Oddly, a silver chain with a gold crucifix hung around his neck.

Blood Arrow looked at Murphy. "I saw you kill the birds. You are good with a rifle," he said in English.

"I am," Murphy said. "I hunted them for you and your men to eat with us tonight."

"How are you called?" Blood Arrow asked.

"Murphy."

Blood Arrow turned to Knoop. "And you?"

"Melvin Knoop."

"Your men are welcome to share our fire and our food," Murphy said. "Ask them to come and sit."

Blood Arrow turned and spoke in Cherokee, and Two Hawks and the men dismounted.

"Have some coffee while we wait on the birds," Murphy said.

"I like sugar in my coffee," Blood Arrow said.

"I have something better," Murphy said.

Once everyone was seated around the fire, Murphy dug out the last bottle of whiskey from his saddlebags and added an ounce to a cup of coffee and gave it to Blood Arrow.

Blood Arrow took a small sip and nodded his approval to Murphy.

"We hunted deer and brought six back to our people," Blood Arrow said. "What are you hunting, Murphy? It isn't game."

"An evil man," Murphy said. "A killer of women. He is traveling west in a wagon. Have you seen him?"

"We left our village two days ago. We saw wagon tracks traveling west yesterday, but they were three days old," Blood Arrow said.

"At least we're still on the right track," Reeves said.

"He kills women, this man?" Blood Arrow said.

"Yes, many," Murphy said.

"Bad thing, killing women," Blood Arrow said.

"It is," Murphy said.

"Can I . . . I mean, am I allowed to ask a question?" Knoop said.

"To who, Mr. Knoop?" Whitson said.

"Mr. Blood Arrow," Knoop said.

Blood Arrow looked at Knoop. "Ask."

"The crucifix you wear, how is it you wear the symbol of the Christian faith?" Knoop asked.

"The missionary women who have come to live with us," Blood Arrow said. "We have a school for our young, a church, and a hospital is being built. They teach us about the Christian faith and many other things. We also teach them about our way of life. It's a good trade."

"I admit I'm a bit surprised," Knoop said.

"You expected to find us screaming savages covered in war paint like in the Cody Wild West Show?" Blood Arrow said. He turned to Two Hawks. "Say hello to Mr. Knoop."

"Hello, Mr. Knoop," Two Hawks said.

"In French," Blood Arrow said.

Two Hawks spoke in French."

"In Spanish," Blood Hawk said.

Two Hawks spoke in Spanish.

"Now be quiet," Blood Arrow said.

"I confess, I didn't know what to expect," Knoop said. "In Chicago—that's where I'm from—I've seen some Indians, but they went to college and wear suits and ties."

"I expect that one day it will be that way for all of us," Blood Arrow said.

"Well, while we wait for that day, our birds are ready," Murphy said.

"That was a fine meal," Blood Arrow said.

Murphy stuffed his pipe and lit it with a wood match.

"Can you spare some? I didn't bring enough," Blood Arrow said.

Murphy handed Blood Arrow the pouch. "Keep it, I have another pouch."

Blood Arrow nodded. He stuffed his pipe and took a match from Murphy.

"Nice evening," Murphy said.

They were walking away from camp at Blood Arrow's request.

"The little man, he doesn't belong out here," Blood Arrow said. "He can wait at my village until you return."

"Don't sell him short. He's tougher than he looks," Murphy said.

"I don't sell him short, his legs do that," Blood Arrow said.

Murphy grinned. "You have a fine sense of humor," he said.

"There is a good moon for riding tonight," Blood Arrow said. "We will see each other again, Murphy."

Knoop was saddened as he watched Blood Arrow and his group ride away from the fire and into darkness.

"That wild west show is full of crap," Knoop said.

Murphy placed a hand on Knoop's shoulder.

"Don't believe everything you read in a newspaper," he said.

"Yeah," Knoop said.

"I do believe I'll have a piece of your chocolate, Mr. Knoop," Murphy said.

Chapter Fourteen

Murphy was up an hour before sunrise, built a fire, and started a breakfast of beans and bacon and coffee.

Reeves and Whitson awoke next, and they took coffee with Murphy while they waited for breakfast to cook.

"The other day, what he said about the morning star and you said the planet . . . ?" Reeves said.

"Venus," Murphy said.

"Yeah. What was that all about?" Reeves said.

Murphy looked up and then pointed to the bright object in the sky that was Venus.

"See the brightest star in the sky?" he asked.

Whitson and Reeves looked up.

"We see it," Reeves said.

"They call it the morning star and sometimes the night star, but it isn't a star at all," Murphy said. "It's one of the eight known planets in our solar system. It's about the size of Earth and is seen only one hour before sunrise and one hour after sunset. Look for it tonight about an hour after sundown."

Whitson looked at Reeves.

"You ever get the feeling our education is sorely lacking?" Whitson asked.

"I can't even spell 'sorely,' " Reeves said.

They heard Knoop yawn and looked at him.

"Have some breakfast, Mr. Knoop," Murphy said. "I expect

we'll make twenty miles in the saddle today, so you best eat."

Murphy was packing away the last of the gear when he glanced to his right and saw Blood Arrow and Two Hawks riding toward them.

"Bass, Whitson, company," Murphy said.

"It's Blood Arrow and his son," Reeves said.

Knoop, behind Lexi, stepped out. "They're alone."

"We figured we didn't want such an evil man in our territory," Blood Arrow said when they reached Murphy. "We'll ride with you."

"Sure enough," Murphy said.

Blood Arrow and Reeves rode the point. Ten feet behind them, Murphy and Whitson rode side by side, and ten feet behind them rode Knoop and Two Hawks.

"How did you come to be named Two Hawks?" Knoop asked.

"On the morning of my birth, my father saw two hawks fighting each other in the sky," Two Hawks said. "My father took it to be a sign of good fortune. What about your name?"

"I'm from Scotland, which is part of the United Kingdom," Knoop said. "Our Christian names don't mean a thing."

"The missionary women tell us many names for whites come from your bible," Two Hawks said.

"That is true," Knoop said. "But that doesn't mean they mean anything."

Two Hawks nodded.

"I notice that you carry a rifle and bow and arrow, a tomahawk and a knife, but no sidearm," Knoop said.

"I have no use for a sidearm," Two Hawks said. "The rifle is to defend myself from attackers. The bow is for hunting game. The knife is for skinning game. And the tomahawk is to defend myself against an enemy up close. A sidearm is just weight around my middle I don't need."

Knoop rubbed his stomach with his left hand. "I have some of that myself," he said.

Two Hawks grinned.

"Hey, we're stopping," Knoop said.

"The horses need rest," Two Hawks said.

"So does my back," Knoop said.

"How are these called?" Blood Arrow asked.

"Corndodgers," Murphy said. "Up north I believe they call them fritters."

"Tasty," Blood Arrow said. "Did your woman make these?"

Murphy paused before answering and then said, "Yes."

"Good woman," Blood Arrow said. "Hold on to her."

"Fifteen miles so far today," Reeves said. "I think we can make another ten before sundown. I think we gained considerable time on him."

"A day and a half to two days ahead of us at most," Blood Arrow said. "If it was summer and the days were longer, we could catch them in one day."

"Do you figure he knows he's being followed?" Whitson asked.

Murphy shook his head. "I've seen no sign he's speeded up his pace."

"Something I've been wondering about," Knoop said. "We know he took four women in Fort Smith in his wagon. We know he's killed at least sixteen women. If he . . . I mean . . . why . . . ?"

"Why haven't we seen signs of the women if they've been murdered?" Murphy said. "I've been wondering that myself."

"Maybe when we catch him they will still be alive?" Whitson said.

"What will happen to this man when we catch him?" Blood Arrow asked.

"If he lets us take him alive, we'll bring him to New York to stand trial on federal charges," Murphy said.

"I'd just as soon hang the bastard on the spot," Whitson said.

"I tend to agree," Reeves said.

"We can argue the merits of the law later," Murphy said. "First we have to catch him, and we won't do that sitting around talking about it."

Late in the afternoon, Two Hawks split from the group to hunt some small game.

With an hour of sunlight left, Murphy picked a flat piece of terrain to make camp. He built a fire and put on a pot of coffee and a pan of beans.

Just before sunset, Two Hawks rode into camp with two large hares draped over his saddle.

"I'll help you skin them, son," Murphy said. "Mr. Knoop, we'll need two spits."

An hour later, as they ate a supper of hare, beans, and corn-bread, Blood Arrow set his plate down and stood up. He looked west and walked away from camp about twenty feet.

"Murphy," Blood Arrow said.

Murphy put his plate down and walked to Blood Arrow.

"Did you hear something?" Murphy asked.

"I smell something," Blood Arrow said.

"What?"

"Faint, but there on the breeze," Blood Arrow said. "Smoke."

Reeves, Whitson, Knoop, and Two Hawks joined Murphy and Blood Arrow.

"What is it?" Whitson asked.

"Smell the breeze," Blood Arrow said.

"Smoke," Two Hawks said.

"Very faint, but I smell it too," Murphy said.

"What do you suppose it is?" Reeves asked.

"I don't know, but it isn't good," Murphy said.

"Supper's getting cold," Whitson said.

Murphy nodded. "Yeah."

Murphy added a few more pieces of wood to the fire before getting into his bedroll.

Beside him, Blood Arrow said, "I can still smell it, the smoke."

"I can, too," Murphy said.

In his bedroll, Knoop closed his eyes and waited for sleep.

"I have killed many men in my time," Blood Arrow said. "I imagine so have you?"

"Yes," Murphy said. "Many men. In war and enforcing the law."

"I have never murdered anyone though," Blood Arrow said.

Knoop opened his eyes.

"I never have, either," Murphy said. "Although I have to admit that the end result is the same."

"For the dead," Blood Arrow said. "For what you Christians call my soul, that part of me is clear."

"I like to think mine is, too," Murphy said.

"What is in a man's heart that drives him to murder women that have done him no harm?" Blood Arrow asked.

"Evil," Murphy said. "Sometimes that's all there is to it."

In his bedroll, Knoop nodded and then closed his eyes.

"The smell of smoke is strong," Blood Arrow said. "It's not far from here."

After riding since dawn, they had traveled around twelve miles and the wagon tracks were visible even from a distance.

"Let's give the horses a half hour to rest," Murphy said.

Even though they'd had only a light breakfast of cornbread, corndodgers, and water, no one was hungry and all they took was sips of water.

"I can scout ahead," Reeves said.

"We'll stick together," Murphy said.

When the horses were rested, they rode for about an hour and on point. Murphy suddenly stopped and removed his binoculars from his saddlebags. He looked at something in the distance, replaced the binoculars, and then opened Boyle up into a full run.

The others tried to keep up, but fell many seconds behind Murphy.

The wagon was still smoldering when Murphy and the others arrived. The steel frame was intact but covered in soot. What remained of the wood was very little.

Murphy slid from the saddle and walked to the wagon.

The remains of four skeletons were mixed in with the charred wood and ashes.

Still in the saddle, Knoop made the sign of the cross.

"Is that the four women?" Blood Arrow asked.

"What's left of them," Murphy said.

Blood Arrow dismounted and inspected the tracks made by the two horses that had pulled the wagon.

"The second horse wasn't in tow," he said. "Both had riders."

"Two men," Reeves said. "There were two men."

"If you brought a shovel, get it out and we'll give the remains a proper burial," Murphy said.

They had three folding shovels. Reeves and Whitson took turns digging, as did Blood Arrow, Two Hawks, and Knoop. Murphy kept his shovel and didn't break except to take sips of water.

By late afternoon, two graves were dug and the skeletons of the four women were divided into the two sites.

"We should say a prayer over them or something," Whitson said.

"You go right ahead," Murphy said and mounted Boyle. "At the moment, I have little use for the man upstairs."

"Where are you going?" Knoop said.

Murphy didn't answer and yanked Boyle into a run.

Two Hawks walked to his horse.

"No, leave him be," Blood Arrow said. "Make camp upwind of the smoke."

As Whitson cut hunks of turkey meat off the bone, he looked at Murphy.

"We didn't hear a shot," he said. "How did you catch it?"

"Turkey is not a smart animal," Murphy said. "I rode into a flock of thirty and roped one of them like a cow."

"Damn," Whitson said.

Blood Arrow bit into a thick leg, chewed and swallowed, and said, "What now?"

"I go on," Murphy said.

"Bass and me have to turn around," Whitson said. "Judge Parker will be mad as a wet hen if we don't return."

"I know," Murphy said. "Blood Arrow, in the morning you and Two Hawks return to your village. Take Mr. Knoop with you. He can wait with the missionaries for me or return to Chicago."

"Like hell I will," Knoop said.

"The game has changed, Melvin," Murphy said. "The rules have gone from gray to black. I can't afford to worry about you and go where I have to go."

"Then don't worry about me then," Knoop said.

"Melvin, I swear . . ." Murphy said.

"I'm a Pinkerton's agent on assignment," Knoop said. "And you have no official jurisdiction over me in that capacity."

Murphy stood and grabbed Knoop by the shirt, yanked him to his feet, and lifted him off the ground so they were eye level.

"You might be the scariest son of a bitch I've ever met, but unless you kill me right now, I'm going," Knoop said.

Murphy nodded and lowered Knoop to the ground.

"Well, that was fun and unexpected," Whitson said.

"I still have some chocolate. Who wants a piece?" Knoop asked.

"Murphy, are you awake?" Blood Arrow asked.

Murphy turned in his bedroll and looked at Blood Arrow. "Yes," Murphy said.

"Do you think those women we buried were dead before he burned the wagon?"

"They were dead," Murphy said. "He likes to cut them up and gut them like fish. They were dead, all right, and if it could be said of such a thing, that was a blessing."

"I think maybe I'll ride with you a ways more," Blood Arrow said.

After breakfast, Murphy shook hands with Whitson and Reeves.

"Tell Judge Parker I owe him one," Murphy said.

Reeves and Whitson shook hands with Knoop. "I'll keep an eye out for the morning star," Reeves said.

"Let's go if we're going," Murphy said.

"The horse on the right is ridden by a big man, bigger than you," Blood Arrow said. "The impressions are deep."

"And they have a bigger lead on us now," Murphy said.

"They do," said Blood Arrow. "Tell me, Murphy, what kind of lawman are you that you wear no badge?"

"Secret Service," Murphy said. "It's a federal agency, like a marshal. We protect and serve at the President's wishes."

"In a way, you're no different than my people," Blood Arrow said. "We serve at your President's wishes."

Murphy looked at Blood Arrow. "In a way, you are right," he said.

At noon they rested the horses. Murphy took the time to make coffee and when it was ready, they sat around the fire with cups.

Murphy dug out his maps and studied the territory.

"We're in Oklahoma, we know that," Murphy said. "The tracks lead northwest."

He traced the route with his finger.

"We're on a direct path to Muskogee," Murphy said.

"What's there?" Blood Arrow asked.

"A local railroad stop," Murphy said. "Where you can catch a short ride to a dozen major railways."

"To anywhere?" Knoop said.

"We best get moving," Murphy said.

"There's just enough bacon, beans, and cornbread for breakfast," Murphy said when they made camp at dusk.

"A day's ride to the town of Muskogee," Blood Arrow said. "In the morning, my son and I turn back."

"I understand," Murphy said.

"If you travel back our way, come and visit," Blood Arrow said. He looked at Knoop. "And you, too."

In the morning, after breakfast, Murphy and Knoop shook hands with Blood Arrow and Two Hawks and watched them ride east.

"The map shows Muskogee about twenty miles from here," Murphy said. "We can reach it by nightfall if we push hard."

Shortly before dusk, Murphy and Knoop rode down Main Street in the town of Muskogee. It was a small, bustling town of four thousand residents, most of whom depended upon the fur trading business and railroad for their livelihood.

"My back feels like it's about to shatter," Knoop said. "And my legs are numb."

"There's a hotel at the end of this block," Murphy said. "I'm sure you'll be able to get a hot bath there."

They rode to the hotel and dismounted.

"Register us and wait for me in the lobby," Murphy said.

"Where are you going?" Knoop asked.

"To find the sheriff."

Murphy walked several blocks to the sheriff's office, a squat, red brick building that housed three cells.

A deputy sat at a small desk against the wall. A second, larger desk against the window was vacant.

"Are you the sheriff?" Murphy asked when he entered the office.

"I'm Deputy Maitland."

"Well, Deputy Maitland, who and where is the sheriff?"

"Tom Ward is town sheriff, and right about now he's having supper at the Muskogee Café up the street," Maitland said.

"Obliged," Murphy said.

"Wait. Who are you?" Maitland asked.

Murphy turned and left the office. Maitland got up and followed.

At the end of the street, Murphy turned and entered the Muskogee Café. Sheriff Ward was alone at a window table. He was eating a steak and reading a newspaper.

Murphy had his wallet open to his identification.

"Sheriff Ward, my name is Murphy," he said and placed the wallet on the table.

Ward set the newspaper aside and read the identification.

"Secret Service? Is the President coming through for a visit?" Ward said.

Maitland came up behind Murphy and Ward said, "It's all

right, Deputy."

"You sure?" Maitland said.

"Yes. Return to the office. I won't be long."

Maitland turned and left the restaurant. By now, about thirty patrons at various tables had eyes on Murphy.

"Now what can I do for you, Murphy?" Ward asked.

"Two things I need right now," Murphy said. "Information. Use of your telegraph office. And a cup of hot coffee."

"That's three things," Ward said.

"So it is," Murphy said.

"Have a seat," Ward said. "Let's start with the hot coffee."

On the way to the sheriff's office, Murphy stopped at the hotel to pick up Knoop.

"No, Sheriff, I didn't see anybody like he just described in the past few days," Maitland said.

"We didn't see the second man," Murphy said. "He might have been the one to buy the tickets."

"If he even stopped here," Maitland said. "They might have just kept riding."

"They rode here deliberately for the railroad," Murphy said. "It's where they went from here that concerns me."

"The station is a tenth of a mile outside of town to the north," Ward said. "The town council didn't want smoke so close to town."

"Is the station open?" Murphy asked.

"Only when trains are scheduled," Ward said.

"Where does the station manager live?"

"He lives in a room behind the station," Ward said. "But right about now, you can find him in the Fifty Cent Saloon drinking his supper."

Murphy looked at Maitland. "Go get him and bring him here," Murphy said.

Maitland looked at Murphy.

"I wasn't asking," Murphy said.

Maitland looked at Ward, then walked to the door and went outside.

"Sheriff, I need to send a telegram," Murphy said.

"Office is closed."

"Open it," Murphy said. "Knoop, wait here for the deputy."

Ward had to find the telegraph operator, a man of about fifty named Skylar. He was about to sit down for supper with his wife in the small home they lived in on the west side of town. He wasn't happy about being disturbed.

"We don't need you to open the office," Murphy told him. "Give the keys to the sheriff, and I'll send the telegram myself."

"Make sure nothing is disturbed," Skylar told Ward.

The telegraph office was located across the street from Ward's office. Once Ward unlocked the door, Murphy lit an oil lantern and took a seat at the desk.

The first telegram was to Burke. After tapping in the special code to the White House, Murphy wrote: *To William Burke the White House Stop Have pursued the suspect from Fort Smith to Muskogee Stop Will send more information as it becomes available Stop Murphy*

The second telegram was to Kai. *In Muskogee. Will write or wire with more information soon Stop Tennessee weather is very nice this time of year Stop Murphy*

"I'm done," Murphy told Ward when he stepped out of the telegraph office and met the sheriff on the sidewalk.

"When you said he'd be drunk, I didn't think you meant passed out blind drunk," Murphy said.

Slumped over Maitland's desk was forty-five-year-old Lars Swenson, station manager at the railroad station. He was thin to the point of skinny and wore a walrus-type mustache that made his face appear even thinner.

"Six, seven months ago his wife ran off with a traveling salesman of women's undergarments," Ward said. "He took it hard I'm afraid. Oh, he still functions during the day and manages the schedule all right, but at night, he drowns his sorrows. Her name was Mabel and she must have weighed two hundred and fifty pounds, but he adored her."

Murphy grabbed Swenson by the hair and lifted his head.

"Hey, wake up," Murphy said. "Swenson, wake up."

"He can't hear you," Ward said. "He's blind drunk."

Suddenly, Swenson urinated in his pants.

"Dammit," Murphy said. He released Swenson's hair and Swenson flopped over to the desk.

"Is that coffee pot full?" Murphy said of the pot resting on the flat woodstove.

"I just made it," Maitland said.

"Go over to the café and get a pound of salt," Murphy said.

A few minutes later, Murphy filled a cup with coffee and added a large amount of salt to it.

"Deputy, hold his head back," Murphy said. "Knoop, you hold his nose."

Maitland took hold of Swenson, tilted his head back, and Knoop pinched his nose. After a few seconds, Swenson opened his mouth to breathe and Murphy poured salted coffee down his throat.

Swenson gagged and coughed.

"More," Murphy said and poured salted coffee down Swenson's throat.

Again, Swenson gagged and coughed.

"All of it," Murphy said.

When the cup was empty, Murphy refilled it with coffee and salt.

"Deputy Maitland, do you have a bucket handy?" Murphy asked.

"Under the desk," Maitland said.

"After we get this second cup in him, get it out," Murphy said.

After the second cup of salted coffee was gone, Swenson opened his eyes, bent over, and vomited into the waste bucket.

He vomited for nearly five minutes.

When he finished, he sat back in the chair and slurred, "Mabel, my beautiful Mabel."

"Lars, it's Tom," Ward said.

"Tom?" Swenson mumbled. "Have you seen my beautiful Mabel?"

"No, Lars, not since she run off," Ward said. "Now listen to me, Lars."

"Mabel, my beautiful Mabel," Swenson sobbed.

"Another cup," Murphy said. "Then we'll let him sleep for a few hours."

After boarding Boyle and Lexi at a livery stable, Murphy and Knoop had a steak dinner at the hotel restaurant, and then took hot baths in the bathhouse on the second floor of the hotel.

They returned to the sheriff's office at nine-thirty in the evening. Ward was at his desk and Swenson was sitting up on a cot in an open jail cell.

"He's awake and almost sober," Ward said.

"Good. Bring him out," Murphy said.

Ward brought Swenson from the cell and sat him at Maitland's desk.

"What am I doing here, Tom?" Swenson asked. "I need a drink, Tom. I need a drink bad."

"Mister, one sip of whiskey, and you'll be vomiting for the next week," Murphy said.

Swenson squinted at Murphy. "Who are you?"

"Federal agent, and I need some information," Murphy said.

"Get me a drink," Swenson said. "I need me a drink."

Murphy looked at Ward. "Got a bottle?"

Ward produced a bottle of whiskey from his desk and handed it to Murphy. It was three quarters empty. Murphy pulled the cork and gave it to Swenson.

Swenson immediately took a long swallow. Ten seconds passed and he set the bottle on the desk, leaned into the bucket, and vomited.

"Now answer my questions or I will hold you upside down by your feet and slap you like a piñata," Murphy said.

With drool on his chin, Swenson looked at Murphy.

"What?" Swenson asked.

Knoop wet a towel at the water basin in the back room and gave it to Swenson. Swenson wiped his face.

"I'm after two men," Murphy said. "They rode into town one or two days ago and I'm sure they purchased tickets for the railroad. Are you with me so far?"

Swenson nodded. "My stomach. What did you all give me made me so sick?"

"Salted coffee," Murphy said. "Now pay attention. One of the men I have no description of, but the second man is very tall and very large. Probably around three hundred pounds or more."

Swenson blinked at Murphy.

"Come a think of it, I did see this giant fellow waiting outside the window while this other fellow bought a pair of tickets," he said.

"Tickets to where?" Murphy said.

"I need me a drink, mister," Swenson said.

"You'll only throw it up again," Murphy said. "Tickets to where?"

"Lemme think," Swenson said. "Course, I think better with a taste."

"Go ahead. You'll just puke again," Murphy said. "Now in about ten seconds I'm going to get angry and . . ."

Knoop stepped in front of Murphy.

"For God's sake man, where did he buy tickets for?" Knoop said.

"Topeka," Swenson said.

"You're sure?" Knoop asked.

"I'm sure, but that wasn't where they were going," Swenson said. "I saw him looking at the map and his finger traced the route to Dodge City."

"Did they pay extra for their horses?"

"Not as I remember, no."

Murphy looked at Ward. "Sheriff, best keep him overnight in your jail. If he gets to drinking tonight, it just might kill him."

"Where are we going?" Knoop asked as he did his best to keep up with Murphy.

"Livery stable."

"Why?"

"If they didn't take their horses, maybe they sold them."

"Do you have to walk so fast?" Knoop puffed.

"It's just another block," Murphy said.

They turned off Main Street and walked to the edge of town where the livery stable was located.

A different man was on duty in the office than earlier.

"Where's the other man?" Murphy asked.

"Home asleep, I figure."

"Can you read?" Murphy asked.

"Some."

Murphy pulled out his wallet and showed his identification to the man. "Do you know what this means?"

The man nodded.

"I'm after two men," Murphy said. "They rode into town and took the railroad, but not their horses. I'm wondering if they sold them."

"Nobody sold any horses in a while," the man said. "But two days ago we found two horses, saddles and all, hitched outside the railroad station house."

"What did you do with them?" Murphy asked.

"Follow me," the man said.

Murphy and Knoop followed the man into the stables to the last two stalls on the left. "That's them," the man said.

"Quarter horses," Murphy said. "They could have pulled that wagon clear to California. What about the saddles?"

"Those two hanging on the back wall."

Murphy inspected the saddles. They were well-worn and not marked with a brand or name.

"What about the brands on the horses?" Murphy asked the man.

"What about them?"

"Do you recognize the brands?"

"I do not."

"What now?" Knoop asked.

He and Murphy were having a drink in the hotel lobby.

"We take the next train to Topeka and then to Dodge City," Murphy said.

"What's in Dodge City?" Knoop asked.

"A great deal of cattle, a lot of cowboys, and gambling houses," Murphy said. "And a whole lot of prostitutes."

CHAPTER FIFTEEN

After breakfast in the hotel restaurant, Murphy and Knoop walked to the railroad station where Swenson was on duty behind a caged counter. Swenson wore a railroad uniform and hat, needed a shave, and had bloodshot eyes, but otherwise was alert and coherent.

"You again," Swenson said when he saw Murphy. "What in the hell did you do to my stomach?"

"Have some soft boiled eggs and a glass of milk for breakfast and you'll be fine," Murphy said. "We need two tickets to Topeka and boxcars for our horses."

"That will be eleven dollars," Swenson said. "Train is scheduled to arrive at ten and depart at ten thirty. Be on the platform at ten fifteen to board your horses."

"What time does it arrive in Topeka?" Knoop asked.

"If the train doesn't get robbed or breaks down or gets hit by lightning, and if this lunatic doesn't kill anybody in route, around ten p.m. tonight," Swenson said.

"Do you think they went to Dodge City for the prostitutes?" Knoop asked.

"He didn't go there for the gambling or to sell beef," Murphy said.

Knoop nodded. "I've been asking myself a question. Do they have a certain destination in mind, or are they picking places at random?"

"It appears well thought out," Murphy said. "The gypsy wagon, abandoning it close to Muskogee where the railroad stops. Even leaving the horses behind. They have a method and plan of some kind and apparently the means to carry it out."

"That's what I can't figure out," Knoop said. "What are they after? All this can't be just to kill prostitutes. That makes no sense at all. There has to be something more at work here."

"Melvin, let the lawyers and head doctors worry about the why," Murphy said. "My job . . . our job is to find them and bring them in alive or dead."

"Alive is better," Knoop said. "They can't be analyzed and studied if they're dead."

Murphy stuffed and lit his pipe. After a few puffs, he said, "Melvin, sometimes the choice of alive or dead isn't up to the law. Sometimes, the men we chase prefer dead. If it comes to that, you have to be ready for it, or you can wind up on the wrong side of that coin."

Knoop stared at Murphy.

"Dining car is open," Murphy said. "Let's get some lunch."

Murphy and Knoop walked Boyle and Lexi from the boxcar to the street in Topeka just before eleven at night.

As they walked from the railroad platform into town, Knoop was surprised at the size and sophistication of the western town. Situated along the Kansas River, Topeka, the capital of Kansas, boasted a population of fifteen thousand residents, thanks in part to the railroad industry that made the town a hub. At least ten percent of the population consisted of freed slaves from the war, and they lived and worked in town like everybody else, although segregated to living in one isolated neighborhood.

A dozen saloons were open and bustling, and piano music could be heard for blocks.

"Since our train to Dodge doesn't leave until morning, we

need to find a hotel for the night," Murphy said.

The first three hotels they tried had no vacancy. The fourth, several blocks away from Main Street, had several available rooms and a small livery for guests.

"Is there a place open for a late supper?" Murphy asked the clerk at the desk.

"Several on Main Street," the clerk said.

After bringing his rifle and saddlebags to his room, Murphy and Knoop walked to Main Street and found a restaurant that was open. It was nearly full and loud with conversation and music from a scroll piano.

A Negro waitress took their order once they were seated.

"I've been thinking a lot of what you said on the train about being on the wrong side of the coin," Knoop said. "I don't think I could ever kill a man."

"Melvin, that kind of thinking may be a luxury back in Chicago from behind a desk," Murphy said. "But when you stand between an outlaw and his freedom, that kind of thinking will put you into a very early grave."

"Maybe so, but . . ."

"There are no buts when it comes to life," Murphy said. "If you're in the position where an outlaw knows his only choice is kill or be killed, he'll choose kill every time."

The waitress returned with two cups of coffee. "Your steaks will be ready in a few minutes," she said.

"Thank you," Murphy said.

After the waitress left, Knoop said, "Do you think they know they're being pursued?"

"I think they have a plan and they're sticking to it, no matter what," Murphy said.

"One more thing I want to say, and then I'll be quiet on the subject," Knoop said. "You're not just an officer of the law, Murphy. You're like me in a lot of ways. We're both men of forensic science and we want to know things. Things that can't be found out by killing."

"That's quite a riddle," Murphy said.

"What?"

"Which is the more valuable, knowledge or life?" Murphy said.

The ride to Dodge City from Topeka took eight hours. At four in the afternoon, Murphy and Knoop led their horses through the dusty streets of the booming cattle town. Although it had a population of only two thousand residents, the population swelled during cattle drive season as Dodge was the destination stop along the Chisholm Trail. Cattle auction houses lined the back-row streets where dozens of cattle pens were located.

"We'll try the Hotel Dodge for a room," Murphy said. "I've stayed there before, and it's a decent place."

"There're a lot of cowboys walking around, but none of them are armed," Knoop said.

"There's an ordinance against openly carrying weapons in Dodge to keep the cowboys from shooting each other when drunk," Murphy said. "Keep that .38 hidden under your coat jacket."

The Hotel Dodge had two vacant rooms on the top floor. After registering, Murphy and Knoop took their saddlebags to their rooms. Murphy also took his Winchester.

The hotel also had a livery out back and after they put Boyle and Lexi in stalls, Murphy led Knoop toward the center of town.

They passed an office that used to belong to Mary Kate Ritchie, a powerful cattle broker who teamed up with Belle Starr and went bad. The office was now vacant and boarded up.

"Where are we going?" Knoop asked.

"See the marshal," Murphy said. "He's an old friend of mine."

After reading Murphy's identification, a deputy marshal said, "Marshal Poule transferred to Wyoming about three months ago."

Murphy looked at the deputy behind his desk. "Who's marshal now?"

"He's at the Golden Nugget Saloon," the deputy said. "You won't have no trouble recognizing him."

Murphy and Knoop walked three blocks from the marshal's office to the Golden Nugget Saloon. It was a large building with swinging doors, extremely well lit by dozens of oil lanterns and several chandeliers that held a dozen candles.

The bar was forty feet long with a mirror almost as long behind it. There were six card tables, four roulette wheels and two blackjack tables, two tables for dice, and a dozen tables just for drinking. Around two hundred patrons were crammed into the large room. A piano player played soft music in the background.

Seated at a table for six, three men drank shots of whiskey with mugs of beer. Two of the men smoked long cigars. The third man had a rolled cigarette between his lips.

Murphy walked to their table with Knoop by their side.

"I thought this town had some class," Murphy said.

The three men looked at Murphy.

"Melvin Knoop, I'd like you to meet Wyatt Earp, Bat Masterson, and Doc Holliday," Murphy said.

Knoop had seen their pictures in newspapers and in dime-store novels, but seeing such famous men in person left him speechless.

Earp toyed with his walrus mustache as he looked at Knoop. "Look here, Doc, Bat, it appears old Murphy got himself a pet dog and is taking him for a walk."

"Don't be impolite, Wyatt," Murphy said as Holliday laughed.

"Have a seat and a drink with us," Masterson said.

Murphy and Knoop took chairs.

"I see you got that mess in Tombstone cleared up," Murphy said.

"Not guilty on all counts at the trial," Earp said.

"Which is not the same thing as being innocent," Murphy said.

"Goodness, who in their right mind thinks we're innocent?" Holliday asked.

"It's good to see you, Murphy," Masterson said. "I thought your ass was polishing a desk in Washington?"

A saloon girl came to the table.

"Drinks all the way around," Earp said.

She nodded and went to the bar.

"What are you doing in Dodge?" Murphy asked.

"Fall cattle drives," Masterson said. "Twenty, maybe thirty thousand head coming through since September. I've been hired as marshal to replace Poule to keep the cowboys in line. I needed a good deputy and sent for Wyatt. He agreed to stay until the drive is over, for a fee, of course. He brought along Doc."

Murphy looked at Holliday. "You're wearing a badge?"

Holliday coughed several times before he said, "I'm just along for the ride."

"Tell me, Doc, did you really kill Johnny Ringo by that big oak like they say you did in the newspapers?" Murphy said.

Holliday grinned. "What do you think?"

The saloon girl returned with a tray of drinks and set a shot glass in front of each man. Holliday set a ten dollar gold piece on the tray. She winked at him and walked away.

"What about you, Murphy? Why are you in Dodge?" Earp said. "And does he talk?" he said and looked at Knoop. "Or does he just bark?"

"He talks when he has something to say," Murphy said.

"How about it, little doggie, do you have something to say?" Holliday asked.

"Was Johnny Ringo as fast as they say in the dime novels?" Knoop asked.

"It speaks," Earp said.

"Now, little doggie, if John Ringo was as fast as they say, he would be sitting here and I wouldn't," Holliday said.

Murphy lifted his shot glass and took a small sip. "Melvin Knoop is a Pinkerton's agent and he's helping me with . . ."

Murphy paused when he heard a booming voice from a table halfway across the room.

"Where did you learn to deal blackjack, back east?" the voice echoed.

Murphy looked across the room at the table. The man had his back to Murphy as he continued to ridicule the dealer.

Murphy stood, walked across the room, and quietly stood behind the man.

"A man who violates a woman is no man at all," Murphy said.

The man stiffened. Immediately everyone at the table froze.

"I recognize that voice," Christopher said.

"Stand up and turn around, rapist," Murphy said.

Slowly, Christopher stood. "I ain't armed," he said. "On account of the town ordinance."

"Turn around," Murphy said.

As he turned, Christopher reached inside his jacket for a .32 revolver hidden in a belly holster.

Murphy chopped down on Christopher's wrist and the revolver fell to the floor.

"Not armed, huh," Murphy said.

"There's law in this town, Murphy," Christopher said.

"You're right," Murphy said. "And right now I'm it."

Christopher grinned and then reached for the knife hidden inside his jacket.

Murphy cracked Christopher across the face with a massive right fist, and Christopher hit the table with so much force the table shattered.

The room fell silent, including the piano.

"Get up," Murphy said.

Christopher didn't move. Murphy reached down and grabbed Christopher by the hair and yanked him to his feet. Christopher stabbed at Murphy with the knife, and Murphy slapped it from his hand.

As the knife hit the floor, Murphy grabbed Christopher's throat in his right hand.

"She died giving birth to the child conceived when you raped her," Murphy said.

Murphy's grip around his throat was like that of a coiled snake. Christopher slapped punches at Murphy's shoulders, which he just ignored. Christopher began to choke as Murphy bent him backward.

"He's going to kill him," Knoop said.

"Appears so," Earp said.

"Aren't you going to stop him?" Knoop asked.

"Never get between a big dog and his bone," Holliday said. "You'll live longer."

Christopher slumped to his knees and desperately yanked on Murphy's arm.

"You miserable wretch," Murphy said.

Knoop jumped up and ran to the bar.

"A bucket of cold water," he told the bartender.

"A what?" the bartender said.

"Water. A bucket of water."

The bartended reached under the bar and produced a wood

bucket. Knoop grabbed it, ran to Murphy, and threw the cold water in Murphy's face.

Murphy released Christopher, and he flopped over to the floor and gasped for air.

"Well, that was certainly unusual," Masterson said.

Murphy looked at Knoop.

Knoop dropped the bucket.

"The least you could do is get me a towel," Murphy said.

Murphy sat on the corner of Masterson's desk and sipped coffee from a metal cup. Masterson sat in the chair behind the desk. Earp and Holliday stood against the wall. Knoop sat behind the deputy's desk.

"He was a carriage driver for White House staff," Murphy said. "While I was sent on assignment, he broke into my home and raped the woman I was to marry. She became pregnant. She told my friend William Burke she had to leave because she feared if I found out what happened, I would murder him in cold blood. She was right, I would have. I looked for her everywhere, but when I finally found her she was dead from complications in childbirth. The last place I expected to see him was here."

Holliday struck a match and lit a rolled cigarette.

Masterson sighed.

Earp toyed with his mustache.

Knoop looked away and wiped at his eyes.

The door that lead to the cells opened and the town doctor walked out.

"Well, he'll live, but he won't say much for a while," the doctor said.

"Thanks, Doctor," Masterson said.

The doctor nodded and left the office.

"There is a federal warrant for his arrest, so I'd appreciate it if you'd arrange to have him taken to Washington," Murphy said.

"Save the bother," Holliday said. "I'll shoot the miserable wretch right now."

"Doc," Earp said.

"Hung or shot, the result is the same," Holliday said.

"I'm tired," Murphy said. "I'm going to the hotel and sleep."

Murphy stood, set the cup on the desk, and walked out of the office.

Masterson looked at Knoop.

"Why is he here?" Masterson asked.

"It's a long story," Knoop said.

"We got time," Earp said.

CHAPTER SIXTEEN

When Murphy walked down the stairs to the hotel lobby and entered the dining room, he was surprised to see Masterson, Earp, and Holliday at a table where they were drinking coffee.

"We are in need of your assistance, sir," Masterson said.

Murphy took a chair at the table.

"I'm here on special assignment," Murphy said. "In fact, I was about to ask for your—"

"Your little friend told us all about it," Masterson said. "The problem is, Dodge has at least one hundred sporting women on hand and sometimes twice that number during drive season to accommodate the necessity of the cowboys."

"We have visited every house and brothel in town last night and this morning and asked every madam to take inventory of their girls," Earp said. "That number won't be available for at least a few days."

"From what the little fellow tells us, you need to know if any of the ladies has gone missing in order to act," Masterson said. "In the meantime, instead of waiting around town doing nothing, we thought you'd enjoy helping us with a slight problem."

"Christopher?" Murphy asked.

"On his way to Washington with two deputies as we speak," Earp said.

"Where he will presumably be hung," Holliday said.

"What slight problem?" Murphy asked.

"North of town some local cattle ranchers are upset with a

163

group of ranchers that started raising sheep for the wool," Masterson said. "It's started a blood feud, and we have to stop it before any more are killed."

"I don't fancy waiting around for a head count, so I might as well be useful," Murphy said.

"Good," Earp said.

"And please, sir, refrain from choking anyone lest we bring a bucket of water with us," Holliday said.

Masterson grinned.

"Good morning, all," Knoop said as he approached the table.

"Ah, we can order breakfast now," Holliday said.

"So, what are we doing today?" Knoop asked.

"Apparently, stopping a cattle war," Murphy said.

"That's a fine horse you have there, sir," Holliday said to Knoop. "A mite small, but I expect she makes up for it in spirit."

Masterson, Earp, Holliday, and Knoop were mounted outside the post office while they waited for Murphy.

After a few minutes, Murphy emerged and mounted Boyle.

"Where to?" Murphy asked.

"The man leading the cause is a rancher named Bill Coffey," Masterson said. "We'll visit him first."

"Is he up for this, your little friend?" Holliday asked Murphy as they rode out of town.

"Are you?" Murphy asked Holliday.

"I have tuberculosis, sir," Holliday said. "But I ain't short."

The Coffey ranch was small but profitable with about six hundred head of cattle. In his fifties, Coffey was a hardened rancher who prided himself on hard work and he instilled this same trait in his two sons.

From behind his desk in the study of his ranch house, Coffey glared at Masterson and said, "If I were a tobacco farmer and my crops were infested with the tobacco worm, I would do everything in my power to rid my crops of the nuisance before it destroyed them all. The sheep is no different."

"I would hardly compare a worm to a sheep," Masterson said.

"I know who you are and what you've done," Coffey said. "Except for the big fellow and the little one. You don't scare me none. I worked this ranch since 'fifty-nine, and what's mine is mine and that's all there is to the matter."

"No one is saying what belongs to you is anything but," Earp said. "On the other hand, the open range where your cattle feed doesn't belong to you. It's free range owned by the government."

"Do you know what sheep do to the land?" Coffey said. "Cattle graze to a certain point and move on. Sheep eat the grass down to the root and it never grows back. Cattle can't eat dirt. Me and others figure we got the right to protect our livelihood."

"Don't lecture me, Coffey," Earp said. "I was born on a ranch. Just because you were here first doesn't give you the right to kill sheep on land that isn't yours. We have reports that forty sheep were killed by your men. If one more is killed, we will return with warrants to arrest you and your sons. Is that understood?"

"Sheep ain't men," Coffey said. "If they continue to graze, it won't be animal blood that's spilt."

Murphy stepped forward.

Coffey looked up at him. "You don't frighten me," he said.

"He should," Masterson said.

"Mr. Coffey, I'm from Washington," Murphy said. "The land your men killed sheep on is federal property. Unless you agree to back off and do nothing until we resolve this matter, here is what's going to happen. First, I will arrest both of your sons, as we have witnesses that they did most of the killing. I expect each will get five years. Then I will send for a hundred government laborers, and they will completely fence in all land that belongs to the government. Your cattle will have sparse grazing land and even less water. If one of those government men is so much as harmed, you will rot in Yuma alongside your sons. Am I being clear, Mr. Coffey?"

Coffey looked at Masterson. "Can he do such?"

"Oh, yes," Masterson said.

"Mr. Coffey, be in town at ten tomorrow morning," Murphy said.

Coffey stared at Murphy.

"Mr. Coffey, I wasn't asking," Murphy said.

"I do love it so when he says that," Holliday said.

"Think he'll comply?" Masterson asked Murphy as they rode northeast.

"He'll comply," Murphy said. "Because he's scared for his sons."

"Where are we going?" Knoop asked.

"See a man named Tom Luck," Earp said. "He's the biggest sheep rancher in the territory."

Tom Luck lived with his wife, Elizabeth, and twin boys who were five years old. From Ohio, Luck took advantage of the Homestead Act of 'sixty-two, moved west, and settled on two hundred acres of land. After several years of struggling, he sold his one hundred head of cattle and purchased sheep. His flock of forty had grown to more than two hundred.

Luck's cabin was large enough, but modest. Most of the furniture was handmade by him and his wife during the winter months. Two large barns and a pen sat behind the house where the sheep spent those same winter months.

The kitchen table held eight, enough room for everybody to

sit while Elizabeth poured coffee.

"Bill Coffey doesn't own the open range," Luck said. "And he's well aware of the laws on free grazing."

"We know that," Masterson said.

"Then you also know he has no legal right to kill my sheep on open range," Luck said. "Forty, to be exact, and more from the other sheep ranchers."

"We have your complaint. We're aware of the numbers," Masterson said.

"Well, what are you going to do about it?" Luck asked.

"That's what we're going to talk about," Earp said.

"Look, I know sheep graze a range bare, but they have the same right to the grass as cattle," Luck said. "I took to ranching sheep because I don't have to lead them to slaughter; I can shear them once a year for a tidy profit while at the same time I farm a hundred and sixty acres of my land. That Coffey doesn't have no problem wearing clothes and sleeping on blankets made from wool, now does he?"

"Mr. Luck, be in town at ten tomorrow morning," Murphy said. "We'll resolve this issue then."

"I'll be there," Luck said. "But no promises."

"Murphy, this is Madam Lisa," Masterson said.

They were in one of a dozen brothels located above saloons scattered all over Dodge.

"You're a big one," Lisa said as she looked up at Murphy.

"Did you do as I asked?" Masterson said.

"My girls are all present, accounted for, and occupied at the moment," Lisa said. "If you'd care to wait for a few to free up?"

"Any girls missing from your stable?" Earp asked.

"Nope," Madam Pearl said as she looked at Knoop. "Ten for ten on hand and smelling like baby powder."

"You're sure?" Earp asked.

"Of course I'm sure," Pearl said. "I ought to know how many girls I got."

"Not a one missing, Bat," Madam June said. "Sorry."

"How many ladies do you employ?" Murphy asked.

"Nine, and all are here," June said.

"Thank you," Masterson said.

"Why, Josephine, I didn't know you were in town," Holliday said. "How are you these days?"

"That Cheyenne doctor cured me of the pox," Josephine said. "Now all I do is madam, but I wouldn't mind giving you a turn on the mattress, Doc."

"Duty calls," Holliday said. "About your girls?"

"All accounted for." Josephine looked at Knoop. "What about you, little fellow?"

"Like he said, duty calls," Knoop said.

"How many establishments are left?" Murphy asked as he sliced into a steak.

"Four," Masterson said.

They were in the Dodge House Restaurant having a late supper.

"We'll hit them right after we eat," Earp said.

"Maybe from here he just caught the railroad to somewhere else?" Earp said.

"Possible," Murphy said. "But I don't think they can pass up such a steady supply of available ladies without taking a taste."

The waitress stopped by the table to fill the coffee cups. "Anything else I can get you, just ask," she said.

"Do you have any pie?" Knoop asked.

"Apple and cherry."

"Would you also happen to have ice cream?" Knoop asked.

"Just vanilla. We had chocolate and strawberry, but we ran out."

"I will have apple pie warmed with ice cream on top," Knoop said.

"Anybody else?" the waitress asked.

"You know, we'll take pie and the ice cream all the way around," Earp said.

The waitress nodded and walked away.

Holliday looked at Earp.

"What?" Earp said.

"Sorry, boys, all my girls are occupied with cowboys at the moment," Madam Kate said.

To check the last four brothels, they decided to stick together, as all four were within a two-block walk.

"But are any missing?" Earp asked.

"No, none are missing."

The next to last brothel was a fairly ornate establishment on the second floor above a Chinese laundry. It was the only brothel in town not associated with a saloon.

The greet-and-wait room was furnished with expensive furniture and had a full bar. Red drapes covered the windows. Oil lanterns with red globes added to the mystique.

Madam Jasmine owned the building, including the laundry below. Her prices were the highest in town, but as she was fond of saying, "Quality costs."

"Why hello, Bat," Jasmine said. "I figured you might be coming around tonight. You were right; two of my girls have gone missing."

"Which two and since when?" Earp asked.

"Joanne and Agnes, and as far as I can figure it's been two or three days."

"Three days?" Murphy said. "How is that possible without you knowing?"

"I have eight rooms and twelve girls," Jasmine said. "I make sure each of my girls gets two days and nights off a week. They had two days off and were due back today. Joanne and Agnes didn't show."

"Where do they live?" Murphy asked.

"A mile south of town. They have a cabin. They're sisters."

"Do they have a wagon or carriage?" Murphy asked.

"Wagon," Jasmine said. "They ride in together and ride home together. Everybody in town knows that."

"A mile south of town?" Murphy said.

"Take Elm Street south and keep going," Jasmine said.

"Thank you," Murphy said.

"Before you go, boys, show me your beans," Jasmine said. "Biggest and smallest bean gets a free one. That's my policy."

"That's a kind offer, Jasmine, but duty calls," Holliday said.

"There's a good moon tonight," Murphy said. "We probably won't need to light torches, but keep them handy."

Riding parallel with Masterson slightly in the lead, they rode south on Elm Street to the edge of town and then onto the dark plains. After about a hundred yards, Murphy said, "Hold up a moment," and dismounted.

The deep impressions in the grass made by wagon wheels were clearly visible in the moonlight.

"They travel the same route every day and night. They made their own road over time," Murphy said. He got back in the saddle and said, "We'll just follow their road."

A hundred yards from the cabin, it became visible against the moonlit backdrop of soft clouds.

"No lights in the windows and no smoke from the chimney,"

Murphy said.

"It's after eleven," Earp said. "They probably are asleep."

"On a cold night like tonight, would you go to bed without making a fire?" Murphy asked.

"No sir, I would not," Earp said.

They reached the small corral in front of the house. It was empty. Connected to the corral was a barn large enough for a few horses and a wagon.

They dismounted at the corral and Murphy lit his torch with a wood match. He entered the barn and reemerged a few seconds later.

"No horses, no carriage," Murphy said. "Light your torches."

The front door was unlocked and Murphy entered the cabin first, followed by the others. The combined light from five torches brightly illuminated the living room. The furniture consisted of a love-seat, two comfortable chairs, a small desk, a bookcase lined with books, a spinning wheel and chair, and a large woodstove.

"Nothing out of place," Murphy said. "Melvin, check the stove."

Knoop felt the stove and then opened the door. The stove was filled with ashes. Next to the stove was a large basket filled with firewood.

"Stone cold and full of ashes," Knoop said.

"Check the rest of the cabin," Murphy said.

Each sister had a bedroom. Both bedrooms were neat as a pin with beds made, closets full, dresser drawers full, and nothing seemingly out of place.

The kitchen and pantry were stocked and well organized. The woodstove, like the one in the living room, was cold and full of ashes.

"Melvin, check the desk," Murphy said as he poked around the kitchen.

"I hate to admit this looks rather suspicious," Masterson said.

"Yeah," Earp said.

"Suspicious?" Holliday said. "The only thing missing is a corpse on the floor."

"Found something," Knoop said from the living room.

Murphy, Masterson, Earp, and Holliday went to the desk where Knoop held an open strongbox full of cash.

"Best take that to town," Murphy said.

Knoop handed the box to Masterson.

"It's all we can do tonight," Murphy said. "Melvin, we'll return in the morning and see if we can pick up their trail. Right now I want another word with Madam Jasmine."

"Changed your minds about dipping your beans, huh," Jasmine said. "I'll have a few vacant rooms in about . . ."

"Your girls are missing," Masterson said. "We went to their cabin. Everything is there except their wagon and horses."

"Maybe they took a trip or something?" Jasmine said.

"And left a box full of cash behind?" Earp said.

Jasmine slowly sat in a chair. "Oh, dear," she said. "And they were planning on retiring in another year."

Murphy stepped forward. "Have any strangers been in to see the girls?"

"They're cowboys off a drive," Jasmine said. "They're all strangers."

"I mean foreigners," Murphy said. "A man with a strange accent or mannerisms."

"Come to think on it, there was such a fellow," Jasmine said.

"Describe him," Murphy said.

"Well, he was tall," Jasmine said. "Not as tall as you, but tall. He had dark hair, was clean-shaven, and dressed real nice. He spoke English just fine, but . . . well, he sounded kind of funny."

"What do you mean, funny?" Masterson asked.

"Like some kind of foreign accent," Jasmine said. "But don't ask me what."

"Was Joanne or Agnes one of the girls he selected?" Murphy asked.

Jasmine shrugged. "That I can't tell you."

Seated at a table in the Golden Nugget Saloon, Murphy ordered a shot of whiskey and a beer for each of them.

Murphy smoked his pipe.

Earp and Masterson had cigars, and Holliday smoked a rolled cigarette.

"Do you intend to track their wagon, providing you can pick up the trail?" Earp asked.

"Seems we have no choice," Murphy said. "We've come too far at this point to give up and wait for the next victims to come to light."

"By the way, I counted two thousand dollars in that box," Masterson said. "I'll put out a wire to see if they have any folks. If no one claims the money, I'll give it to the church."

"Pity," Holliday said. "I always heard that charity begins at home."

"Forget it, Doc," Earp said. "Your charity begins and ends at a card table."

"True, but a pity nonetheless," Holliday said.

CHAPTER SEVENTEEN

Luck and Coffey glared at each other as they sat in chairs opposite Masterson's desk.

Behind his desk, Masterson looked at Murphy, who was standing.

"I understand the differences between cattle and sheep grazing, but for the sake of peace, here is how it's going to be," Murphy said. "You will share the range and water, cattle and sheep. Mr. Luck, before the sheep eat down to the roots, you will move them on to a new pasture. Mr. Coffey, as long as Mr. Luck follows that directive, you and the other ranchers will treat his sheep as if they were cattle. Mr. Luck, if you fail to do as directed, Mr. Masterson will arrest you, and I've authorized him to close the open range and everybody loses. Am I understood?"

Coffey and Luck nodded.

"Good. Now get the hell out of here and quit wasting everybody's time," Murphy said.

While Murphy was in the general store, Knoop stood on the wood sidewalk with Masterson, Earp, and Holliday.

"Let me ask you fellows a question," Knoop said. "Would any of you happen to know Murphy's first name?"

"My new little friend, that is one road you don't want to travel on," Earp said.

"How bad can it be?" Knoop said.

Murphy emerged from the store with four large sacks tied with rope. "How bad can what be?" he asked as he tied the sacks to Boyle's saddle.

"The weather this time of year in Kansas," Masterson said.

"Twisters and lightning storms come right out of the blue," Earp said.

"Very dangerous weather," Masterson said.

"I'll keep an eye out for that," Murphy said. "Ready, Melvin?"

"Did you get the oranges?" Knoop asked.

"Yes."

"We'll be out to check the cabin and lock it up later today," Masterson said.

After handshakes all the way around, Murphy and Knoop mounted their horses and road south.

"You didn't tell him about the telegram," Earp said.

"You saw him the other day," Masterson said. "He'd go completely crazy."

"What telegram?" Holliday asked.

"Came this morning," Masterson said. "It seems that Christopher had a shaving razor hidden in the lining of his coat. He used it to escape at a water stop in route to Washington."

"Damn," Holliday said.

Masterson sighed.

"Let's go fight some crime," he said.

"As long as we can do it at Madam Jasmine's," Holliday said.

"Doc," Earp said.

Murphy and Knoop dismounted at the corral and tied the horses on a gate.

The sunlight gave a new perspective to the cabin and grounds. Footprints were visible in the soft earth in front of the corral.

"No horse tracks to the cabin not hooked to a wagon," Knoop

said as he knelt to inspect the footprints. "They walked."

"Or hitched a ride with the sisters," Murphy said.

Knoop measured one set of prints against his own boot.

"I'm an eight," he said. "This print is about a nine. What size boot are you?"

"Fourteen," Murphy said.

"Check out the bigger print," Knoop said.

Murphy placed his right boot in the footprint of the bigger man.

"It has to be at least a sixteen," Knoop said.

"Check the cabin again," Murphy said. "I want another look in the barn."

"Right."

Murphy entered the small barn. If it weren't for the fact that the wagon and two horses were missing, it appeared perfectly normal. Nothing was out of place. There was hay in the stalls, oats in a grain barrel, tools hanging on the walls.

In the rear of the barn were two wood platforms designed for storing saddles. They were vacant.

Murphy left the barn and went to the house. Knoop was at the desk reading some documents.

"These documents are from a bank in Nevada," Knoop said. "They were fixing to buy a small piece of property in a little town called Reno. Ever hear of it?"

"Can't say as I have," Murphy said. "It looks like they took the saddles from the barn along with the wagon."

"There's a book from the Dodge Bank and Loan," Knoop said. "They had four thousand dollars in a savings account."

"Let's check the house again and see if we missed anything last night," Murphy said.

At the end of the hallway between the two bedrooms was an unlocked door. While Knoop was in one of the bedrooms, Murphy opened the door and looked out to a small yard. There was a patch of land where the sisters grew vegetables during the summer months and the outhouse.

He took the three steps to the ground and walked to the outhouse. It was a two-seater with two separate doors. He opened the door on the right and the stall was empty. He opened the door on the left and on the floor of the stall was a white handkerchief.

Murphy picked up the handkerchief and sniffed it. Holding the handkerchief, he returned to the cabin where Knoop was in a bedroom.

"Nothing out of place," Knoop said.

"Look at this," Murphy said. "It was in the outhouse."

Knoop took the handkerchief and sniffed. "Ether," he said.

"We know what happened here," Murphy said. "Let's pick up the wagon tracks."

The wagon tracks weren't difficult to spot in the soft dirt around the cabin. They traveled south and slightly west.

Once they reached open range country, the tracks became more difficult to follow, and several times Murphy had to dismount and check the grass.

"Grass is very resilient," he said. "It will spring back and continue to grow even after one day. After a week, it's like a wagon never traveled over it."

"How far ahead of us are they?" Knoop asked.

"At least four days."

"What's south of us?"

"The little panhandle of Arkansas and then Texas."

"I don't think they want to return to Arkansas," Knoop said.

"No, but they need to pass through the panhandle to get to Texas," Murphy said. "Let's go. We need to make ten miles before lunch."

★ ★ ★ ★ ★

Murphy filled two cups with coffee and passed one to Knoop.

Lunch consisted of hunks of fresh cornbread, an orange, and a chocolate bar. At Knoop's insistence, Murphy bought the chocolate bars and oranges at the general store in Dodge.

"Six hours of daylight left," Murphy said. "We'll track for another five and make camp for the night."

Knoop nodded. "Some things I've been thinking about," he said. "From all accounts these men appear to be foreigners, yet they seem to know the country very well. They travel where they want and seem to never be lost for direction."

"They could have been here for quite some time and traveled extensively," Murphy said.

"It certainly seems like it," Knoop said. "The other thing is they appear to be quite well off. They left two thousand dollars sitting there in the desk as if it were an old newspaper."

"Money does appear to be no problem for these two," Murphy said. "They probably never even checked the cabin once they got what they came for."

Knoop ate some cornbread and took sips of coffee. He looked in the distance as if lost in thought.

"Something else on your mind?" Murphy asked.

"Have you ever read about the ancient Mayans?" Knoop asked.

"I have," Murphy said. "And the ancient Egyptians, Romans, Persians, and Greeks. What are you alluding to, Melvin?"

"The Mayans practiced human sacrifice," Knoop said. "As did many other ancient people. The way they go about killing their victims reminds me of human sacrifice or perhaps some sort of satanic ritual."

"The sacrifices were made to please their gods," Murphy said. "To ensure a good harvest or fertility or to keep the sun shining or the moon from falling to earth or some such nonsense. We've seen no evidence of any such rituals."

"No, we haven't," Knoop said. "Still, I can think of no other reason for their behavior, can you?"

Murphy shook his head. "No."

By late afternoon, they came upon the empty wagon and they dismounted to search the area.

"They left the wagon and took the horses," Murphy said.

"I don't understand," Knoop said. "All four of them?"

"There's blood in the wagon," Murphy said. "And a lot of it."

Knoop touched the dried blood with a finger. "At least two or three days old," he said.

Murphy looked to his left. About a hundred yards away were two freshly dug graves. He jumped back into the saddle and raced Boyle to the graves and dismounted.

Knoop was just seconds behind and dismounted Lexi.

"Ah, Jesus," Knoop said.

"Come on," Murphy said. "We have a good hour of daylight left, and I don't want to lose their trail."

Murphy removed the waxed paper from two well-salted steaks and placed them into a fry pan coated with melted butter.

"The butter will last a week or more in this glass jar because it's salted," Murphy said.

"I will remember that," Knoop said.

Murphy checked the other pan, where beans were boiling.

"Depending upon the trail we might have to hunt for fresh meat," Murphy said.

"When will we reach Texas?" Knoop asked.

"Sometime tomorrow afternoon," Murphy said. "If that's where the trail takes us."

"Murphy, have you . . . have you considered that we might

need reinforcements for this job?" Knoop asked.

"No," Murphy said. "This is a job for a small army or one or two men. We already are the latter."

"Mr. Pinkerton is not going to be happy with me if we fail," Knoop said.

"I don't give a damn what Pinkerton is or isn't happy with," Murphy said. "Do you?"

"Odd, but not anymore," Knoop said.

"Steaks are done," Murphy said.

"They made camp here," Murphy said after they rode most of the following morning.

"Where is here?" Knoop said.

"Texas."

"Looks just like Arkansas."

"It's after noon. We might as well rest the horses here and have a bite ourselves," Murphy said.

"I could use some coffee."

"I'll make a pot," Murphy said. "The Canadian River isn't far, so we have plenty of fresh water."

While a pot of coffee cooked on a small fire, Murphy stuffed and lit his pipe.

"I've been thinking about what you said about Pinkerton not being happy with you, Melvin," Murphy said.

"What of it?"

"I would not like to see you lose your employment because you stayed away from Chicago too long."

"To be honest, what I've learned the past month would fill volumes," Knoop said. "Sitting behind a desk in Chicago just doesn't seem all that appealing anymore."

"Are you saying you don't want to return to Pinkerton's?"

"I'm wondering if there might be a place where I might be more useful," Knoop said.

"Like Washington or New York?"

"I haven't seen my family in many years," Knoop said. "I was thinking of returning home and maybe get a position with Scotland Yard."

"That's a fine idea worth pursuing," Murphy said.

The coffee was ready and Murphy filled two cups and cut hunks of cornbread.

"But first I would like to conclude our business here," Knoop said.

"The way this is going that could take weeks, even months."

"I didn't say I was in a hurry," Knoop said. "Besides, when we do catch them, think of what we can learn about the mental condition of the criminal. The knowledge gained in criminology would set law enforcement on its ear."

Murphy sipped some coffee and looked at Knoop. "That .38 I gave you, it's not just for show. There may and probably will come the time when you have to use it."

"As strange as this may sound, they are worth far more to us alive than dead," Knoop said.

"Melvin, most of the time the choice of alive or dead belongs to the criminal," Murphy said. "We talked about that."

Knoop sighed deeply. "I know, but . . ."

"When the outlaw goes to take your life, there are no buts," Murphy said. "Even sitting behind a desk in Chicago."

An hour before sunset, they reached the northern banks of the Canadian River. It was a long, winding river that stretched across northern Texas into New Mexico on the west and Arkansas to the east.

"They stopped for water and made camp not two days ago," Murphy said as he inspected the ashes from a campfire.

"We gained on them," Knoop said. "They're in no hurry. They don't suspect they're being followed."

"They do not, or they simply don't care," Murphy said as he removed his holster and slung it over the saddle. He rubbed Boyle's neck and said, "I'll tend you in a few minutes."

Boyle turned his neck and nuzzled Murphy.

"Yes, I brought you sugar," Murphy said.

He sat and removed his boots, then stood and stripped until he was naked.

"What are you doing?" Knoop asked, marveling at the many scars on Murphy's chest and legs.

Murphy opened his saddlebags and reached in for a bar of soap. "Before we lose the sun, I'm taking a bath."

He walked to the bank of the river and quickly waded in, then dunked under. When he emerged, he said, "Damn, that's some cold water. I should have made a fire before jumping in."

"How cold?" Knoop asked.

"Do you plan to take a bath?"

"It would be nice."

"Make a fire first," Murphy said as he scrubbed his hair with the soap.

Before getting into his bedroll, Murphy tossed as much wood as he could find onto the fire.

"I didn't think it got this cold in Texas," Knoop said from inside his bedroll.

"This is northern Texas," Murphy said. "We're just a few days' ride to the Colorado border. It warms up as we move south."

"Where do you think they're headed, Murphy?"

"Can't say," Murphy said. "I once chased a killer west clear across the Rockies, only to catch him east in Bryce Canyon."

"I suspect they aren't satisfied just yet," Knoop said. "I think they'll go where there's a ready supply of prostitutes."

"I agree."

"They're using prostitutes for their rituals because they're readily available and they won't be missed," Knoop said. "Somebody has to speak for them. It might as well be us."

"Melvin, you can't allow your emotions to guide you when hunting an outlaw," Murphy said. "Why and because are things you best forget until after the job is done. Then you have the luxury of reflecting on the inhumanity of what's been done. And only then."

"You're right," Knoop said. "I know you're right."

"Get some sleep," Murphy said. "We'll be up early."

Knoop rolled over and closed his eyes.

Murphy looked up at the stars. It was a clear night and the bright moon obscured many of them, but even so, millions were visible. He watched the stars and waited for sleep, but somehow and against all his very own rules, Kai crept into his mind. With her catlike green eyes, silky black hair, and tall slender frame, she was a sight to behold.

But even more than that.

For nearly twenty years he carried around the burden of guilt over the deaths of his wife and child. Eighteen months ago along came Sally Orr, and she started to fill in the large hole in his chest where emotions used to be. When she died so suddenly, it was as if he was just returning home from the war to face the loss of his family all over again.

In a short span of time, just days really, Kai closed the hole to a fraction of what it was and . . . Murphy almost laughed out loud and would have, if Knoop wasn't six feet away.

You should listen to your own advice more often, he thought and closed his eyes.

After washing and drying the dishes and pots and pans from dinner for her eight guests, Kai set the table and readied the kitchen for the next morning's breakfast. In-between she had to fight off the advances from the balding and bespectacled little banker in town on business from Boston. He said she was a handsome, noble savage and actually offered her wampum for a roll in the hay.

She put a pot of water on the stove to boil and then carried it to her room and mixed the hot water with cold in a basin and gave herself a sponge bath before putting on her nightgown.

Then she sat in front of the mirror at the dresser and brushed her hair one hundred strokes. She set the brush on the dresser and was about to turn down the covers when she remembered the mail.

Earlier she had gone to town for supplies, stopped by the post office for the mail, and completely forgotten about it. She grabbed the pile and brought the oil lantern to the nightstand and flipped through the stack.

She stopped when she saw the letter addressed to her from Murphy. The mark said he mailed it in Dodge City.

She tore it open and read the one-page letter written in pen.

Dear Kai,

I'm in Dodge City with Mr. Knoop and we are about to depart after the outlaws we are in pursuit of. I have no notion of when I will return to Fort Smith and to you, but rest assured I will return. If you want me to. Sometimes when time and distance are involved people change their minds about the way they feel about other people. Rest assured that is not the case on my part. I find myself thinking about you often and missing you a great deal, something I shouldn't be doing while on a job, but I can't seem to help myself. I meant what I said about visiting Tennessee with me when I finally do return. I am from the south and a bit old-fashioned in that I believe a man should

bring a woman home to meet his mother before asking for her
hand. I want to say more, but there isn't time.

Much love,
Murphy

"He wants to say more, this idiot," Kai said aloud. "I'm half
Navajo and was raised by the Sioux, and I have better social
etiquette than this bumbling fool."

Nonetheless, Kai tucked the letter under her pillow and went
to sleep feeling like the sixteen-year-old girl asked to her first
cotillion.

CHAPTER EIGHTEEN

"Ever get sick of beans, bacon, and cornbread?" Knoop asked as he sat against his saddle and ate breakfast.

"Out here you eat to stay alive and not as a social gathering," Murphy said.

Facing southwest, Knoop noticed a cloud of dust on the horizon. "Do you see that? What is that, some kind of storm?" he asked.

"Horses," Murphy said. "Eight I would say, and moving fast."

"Right at us," Knoop said.

"Appears so."

"What do we do?"

"Wait."

Finished with breakfast, Murphy and Knoop took the cookware to the riverbank and rinsed them clean. They returned to the campfire and Murphy said, "Melvin, take the pot and fill it. Our guests might like a cup of coffee."

By the time the second pot of coffee was boiling in the fire, eight riders were just a hundred yards away.

Murphy and Knoop watched as they rode hard into camp. The men were Texas Rangers, and from the looks of them had been in the saddle for days.

They brought their horses to a slow trot the last fifty feet with one man in the lead. He dismounted first.

"I'm Captain Junius Peak of the Texas Rangers," he said. "Who am I addressing, sir?"

"Federal Agent Murphy. This here is Melvin Knoop of Pinkerton's. Coffee is fresh made. Why not have a cup and give your mounts a rest?" Murphy said.

Peak turned to his men. "We'll rest the horses thirty minutes. Those that want coffee, break out your cups."

Murphy stuffed his pipe while Peak's men filled their cups.

"Federal agent you say," Peak said to Murphy.

Murphy pulled out his wallet and showed the identification to Peak.

"I see," Peak said. "And what are you doing out here?"

"Tracking two killers," Murphy said. "They're a couple of bad ones."

"Can you sidestep for a few days?"

"How so?"

"We're chasing Blue Duck and his band of about a dozen."

"Blue Duck? I thought he was mixed up with Belle Starr and her bunch."

"You know Blue Duck?"

"We've tangled," Murphy said. "I should have killed him, but he was unconscious at the time and I'm not the sort to kill in cold blood, even the likes of Blue Duck."

"Excuse me, but what is a Blue Duck?" Knoop said.

"A murderous outlaw of the Cherokee Nation," Peak said. "Him and his band have been raiding small farms and ranches all across northern Texas and Arkansas. He's stolen cattle and horses, and kills women and children and anything else in his way. That is what a Blue Duck is."

"Where are you headed?" Murphy asked.

"We got a spy in his band that gave us information as to his hideout," Peak said. "There's a little box canyon in the Davis Mountains where he supposedly holes up after he's rustled cattle and horses."

"That's a day's ride northwest of here," Murphy said.

"It is," Peak said. "And if your business isn't too pressing, I'm inviting you to join us on the hunt."

"Captain, we're after some pretty dangerous men ourselves," Murphy said.

"If Blue Duck eludes us, more men, women, and children will be killed on his rampage, and I need not explain what happens to the women before they are killed," Peak said.

Murphy glanced at Knoop.

Knoop sighed and nodded.

"All right, Captain, we'll join you, but just to the Davis," Murphy said. "If he isn't there, my partner and I need to tend to our own business."

"He'll be there," Peak said. "My spy is a reliable source."

Murphy and Peak rode the point northwest toward the Davis Mountains. The seven rangers and Knoop followed closely in a column of two.

"Coming on noon," Murphy said. "We best break and rest the horses a bit."

"That mount you're straddling looks like he could ride through the night," Peak said.

"He can. I wasn't talking about my horse," Murphy said.

"You're probably right," Peak said. "We'll break for thirty minutes."

Peak's men made a large fire, and two pots of coffee were put on to boil.

"You're welcome to some cornbread and jerky," Murphy said.

"We have possibles of our own to share," Peak said.

He was a tall man, thin and hard, around Murphy's age. He had short hair and a neatly trimmed mustache. He was promoted to captain after he was instrumental in the capture of the notorious Bass gang that was robbing the Texas Pacific Railroad.

Knoop approached Peak. "Would you like a bar of chocolate?"

"Chocolate, eh," Peak said. "I would, thank you."

"Captain, we can make the Davis by nightfall," Murphy said. "Do you have the exact location of this box canyon?"

Peak turned and shouted to one of his men. "Sergeant, get the maps from my saddlebags."

The sergeant brought the maps and Peak squatted and opened them. "My man, my spy in Blue Duck's camp, sent this map just a week ago."

Murphy squatted beside Peak.

"We should reach this spot here by sunset," Peak said and put his finger on a red x on the map. "We head west into the box canyon to the place marked here. It's a trail that leads directly to the murderous bastard's hideout."

"Can we go in after dark?" Murphy asked.

"If the sky is clear, we have a three-quarter moon tonight," Peak said. "We can go in no problem."

"It's another twenty miles to that box canyon and looks another five after that," Murphy said. "Your horses look pretty well spent."

"They'll hold," Peak said.

Murphy nodded. "Let's go if we're going then."

"Captain, we best walk your horses through the canyon," Murphy said. "They're spent, and another mile or so will end them for days."

Peak held up his right hand and his rangers came to a stop behind him.

"Dismount," Peak said. "We walk from here."

Once everyone was on foot, Peak said, "Fifteen minutes rest. We have several miles ahead of us."

Murphy took some water and then stuffed and lit his pipe. "Captain, best have your men eat something. There's a long haul ahead of us, mostly uphill."

Peak sighed. "I push them too hard, I know," he said. "But innocent lives may be at stake."

"Do you believe they have hostages?" Murphy asked.

"Not hostages, prisoners," Peak said. "And womenfolk, most likely."

"Are your men prepared to kill?"

"They're Texas Rangers," Peak said. "They will do what is required."

Peak and Murphy took the point while Knoop and the seven rangers walked single file behind them.

After an hour on foot, Peak held up his right hand and made a circle with his fist. The rangers and Knoop gathered around him.

"There's a slight aroma of a campfire in the air," Peak said. "I guess about a mile ahead of us, maybe a bit more."

"Captain, I suggest we hobble the horses here and take the high ground so we can observe them undetected," Murphy said.

"Agreed," Peak said. "Men, hobble the horses, take your Winchesters, and make sure you have ample ammunition."

Once the horses were hobbled and every ranger and Murphy had a Winchester, Murphy led the way up a hundred-and-fifty-foot-high ridge to flat ground.

"Single file, and put your men on hand signal only," Murphy said.

They walked for about twenty minutes and with each passing minute, the aroma of a campfire grew stronger.

Murphy stopped when he heard voices below, a gibberish of English and Cherokee.

"Captain, come with me," Murphy said.

They walked to the edge and got down on their bellies. A large campfire with food cooking gave off enough light for them to see five men lazing about on blankets with bottles of whiskey and plates of food.

An additional four men were forcing themselves on four women on blankets around the fire. The women were gagged to prevent them from screaming.

"Captain, bring the men over," Murphy whispered.

Peak gave the hand signal and the rangers and Knoop came to the edge and got down on their stomachs.

They watched as the men took turns with the women and Murphy signaled Peak to fall back.

They walked about a hundred feet from the edge.

"Captain, who is your best man with a handgun?" Murphy asked.

"Best how? Fastest or most accurate?"

"Accurate."

"That would be young Norris here."

Twenty-one-years-old, Norris had a baby face on a stout body.

"You ever kill, son?" Murphy asked.

"No, sir."

"He'll do his duty," Peak said. "Rest assured."

"Captain, wait for me and Norris to show in their camp, then open fire with the Winchesters," Murphy said. "Norris, if you can take three, I'll handle the other six."

Norris looked at Murphy. "Just do as I do, son," he said. "Captain, let me borrow your Colt. Norris best borrow one as well. We won't have time to reload."

Armed with two handguns, Murphy and Norris walked fifty feet away and started to descend the hill.

Peak, the rangers, and Knoop returned to the edge.

It was a cool night, but Knoop found he was drenched in sweat from a combination of excitement and fear.

It seemed like an hour, although he knew it was just a matter of minutes before he spotted Murphy and Norris below. Each held two Colt revolvers. Calmly, Murphy led the way toward the outlaws' campsite as if taking an evening stroll.

When they were within ten feet of the campsite, Peak gave the signal to open fire and a hail of Winchester bullets rained down on the outlaws.

Seven outlaws were on blankets with bottles of whiskey. Two were in the act of violating women. The other two women were hog-tied on the ground. At the crack of the first shot, all nine froze in place for a moment, then drew their guns and looked up at the dark hillside.

Knoop watched, astounded, as Murphy simply walked into camp and started shooting. Completely off guard, the outlaws were sitting ducks. Murphy shot them one by one and Norris joined in.

The outlaws tried to return fire, but Murphy was so deadly accurate, they were confused and helpless.

The skirmish was over in just seconds. Murphy killed six Apache outlaws. Norris killed two. One was still alive and crawling away on his belly.

Knoop watched in horror as Murphy followed the outlaw for several feet and then shot him dead with a bullet to the head.

Murphy looked up at the hill. "Captain, there's women need tending to," he shouted.

They put the four women on the outlaws' horses and walked them back to where they'd hobbled their own and made camp for the night.

The women were in shock, and if they responded to words at all, it was to cry or scream in terror. The men did their best to comfort the women and kept them warm under blankets.

"We'll post a guard all night to make sure they don't try to run away during the night," Peak said.

"What about . . . what about the dead?" Knoop asked.

"What about them?" Peak said.

"Shouldn't we bury them?"

"By what them savages believe, without a proper Apache burial they won't get into the promised spirit world," Peak said. "Let 'em rot where they lay."

Knoop stared at Peak.

"Was he there? Blue Duck," Knoop said.

"No."

Peak walked away and sat in front of the fire and reached for a coffee pot.

Knoop spotted Murphy seated against a tree with a cup of coffee and his pipe. He walked over and sat down next to him.

"He's really angry," Knoop said. "I didn't mean to upset him."

"He's angry, but not at you," Murphy said. "Blue Duck left those women as a diversion, knowing the Rangers wouldn't try to follow him with women in their care. Captain Peak is angry because Blue Duck outsmarted him this time."

"I see," Knoop said.

"He'll get his some day," Murphy said. "No outlaw's luck holds forever."

"What you did back there, I will never forget it," Knoop said.

"Those are exactly the kinds of things you best forget if you expect to stay sane," Murphy said.

Knoop nodded. "What's going to happen to these women?"

"They'll need a lot of care," Murphy said. "Their families have probably all been murdered I expect. Blue Duck tends not to leave witnesses to his crimes."

"If he had been there, would you have killed him?"

"I would have tried not to," Murphy said. "Captain Peak and the Rangers would have preferred to bring him back to be hung."

"I think I'm going to try to get some sleep," Knoop said.

"That's a good idea."

Knoop went to his bedroll near the fire and got under a blanket.

Norris approached Murphy and said, "Mind if I sit?"

"Go ahead."

Norris sat next to Murphy. He appeared ashen and nervous. "I never kilt a man before," he said.

"You did your job as a Texas Ranger," Murphy said.

"I know that," Norris said. "It don't make feeling sick inside any easier."

"If you didn't feel sick inside after killing a man, you wouldn't be human," Murphy said. "You'd be just as dead inside as the man you killed."

"But I watched you shoot seven men like they was ducks at a shooting gallery," Norris said. "You mean you feel sick as I do?"

"Every time," Murphy said. "When you stop feeling sick is when you become just like the outlaw you're chasing. Remember that."

"I will," Norris said.

"Good. Now I think I'll try to get some sleep," Murphy said.

CHAPTER NINETEEN

"I'm in your debt," Peak said. "I know I cost you time away from your own business, but you prevented a lot of unnecessary bloodshed."

"Where will you take the women?" Murphy asked.

"They're not fit for a long ride," Peak said. "Oneida in the Llano is the nearest town with an army outpost and a doctor."

"Melvin and I will ride with you to Oneida to resupply," Murphy said.

To prevent the women from falling off their horses, their hands were tied to the saddle horns and their legs secured to the stirrups with rope. They made frequent stops to ensure the women weren't harmed by their bonds. At noon, they rested the women and horses for one hour and tried to get the women to eat, but they did little besides take sips of water.

It was after eight in the evening when they finally arrived in the small town of Oneida. It was a dry, dusty town of about five hundred residents, many of whom worked on the railroad construction site that would later, when renamed Amarillo, turn the town into a major cattle town for transport.

A quarter mile outside of town was a small army outpost with a contingent of thirty soldiers. They bypassed the town and rode directly to the outpost.

Two soldiers on guard duty manned the locked gates from a watchtower sixteen feet high.

"Captain Peak of the Texas Rangers," Peak said to the two soldiers on guard duty. "We have sick women in need of a doctor. Who is your commanding officer?"

A sergeant escorted Peak and Murphy to the office of Major Thomas Fuller, where a full report was made by Peak.

"Sergeant, have the cook open the mess hall and prepare a hot meal for Captain Peak's men," Fuller said. "Bring the women to the infirmary and then have a rider go to town and bring the doctor to assist Captain Brown in case he needs it."

"Yes, sir," the sergeant said.

"And have the guest barracks prepared for Captain Peak and his men."

After the sergeant left, Fuller said, "You men look as if you could use a drink."

Fuller opened a desk drawer and produced a bottle of whiskey and three shot glasses. He filled each glass and gave one to Peak and Murphy.

"That son of a bitch Blue Duck is a menace to every civilized human being in the State of Texas," Fuller said. "It bothers me a great deal I don't have the men to properly track him down, even if I do have the best Navajo scout in the territory."

"Who would that be, Major?" Murphy asked.

"In English his name means Silver Fox," Fuller said. "He likes to be called Sam for some reason."

Murphy tossed back his shot of whiskey and gently set the glass on Fuller's desk. "Major, I wonder if I may borrow Sam for a few days."

Murphy and Peak joined the rangers and Knoop in the mess hall where the cook prepared a steak with all the fixings for each of them.

Major Fuller sat with them, although he took only coffee.

By the time dessert and coffee were served, Silver Fox walked into the mess hall.

"You sent for me, Major?" he asked.

Around fifty years old, Silver Fox was of average height, but stout and muscular. He wore a combination of army uniform and Navajo dress, attire common for Indian scouts.

"An hour ago," Fuller said.

"I was in town, Major."

"At that whorehouse, no doubt."

"Playing cards with some of the railroad men," Silver Fox said. "My two favorite whores have gone missing."

Murphy and Knoop exchanged glances.

"Sam, I wonder if I could speak with you in private," Murphy said.

Silver Fox studied the maps on Fuller's desk.

"My guess is you wouldn't have been able to track them much farther," Silver Fox said. "Tracking through the Llano requires not just a keen eye, but the experience of knowing the country."

"That's why I asked for you," Murphy said.

Silver Fox nodded. He put a finger on the map. "This is where you met up with the rangers. A day's ride southwest would take you to Oneida. If you were able to track them to here, they still have several days' ride on you. By now at least five or more."

"Can you track these men?" Fuller asked.

Silver Fox nodded. "But it won't be easy."

"How late does the bordello stay open?" Murphy asked.

"It doesn't close," Silver Fox said.

"Feel like taking a ride?" Murphy asked.

Silver Fox looked at Fuller.

"Go on," Fuller said.

"This here is Madam Claudine," Silver Fox said. "She's French."

Claudine looked at Murphy. "And you are?"

Murphy took out his wallet and showed her his identification.

"Oh, my," Claudine said. "How exciting."

"He's interested in your two missing girls," Silver Fox said.

"How odd," Claudine said. "Most men are more interested in the girls who are here instead of the ones who aren't."

"The two that are missing, what are their names and how long have they been gone?" Murphy asked.

"Jenny and Maude, and who said they're missing?" Claudine said. "Both girls are real buffalo heifers, if you know what I mean, but for some reason the men love them. The railroad camp about twenty miles west of here requested a few girls for the company and asked for them by name. I employ a man for protection, and he took them there by wagon. He has yet to return."

"Since?" Murphy asked.

"Four days ago."

"Did you report this?" Murphy asked.

"To who and for what reason?" Claudine asked. "My man is probably off drunk somewhere, and my girls are probably happily bringing some entertainment to otherwise miserable railroad workers."

Riding back to the outpost, Murphy said, "We'll leave at first light."

"Morning chow is at five-thirty," Silver Fox said. "We have a first-rate cook. You won't want to miss it."

CHAPTER TWENTY

After breakfast, as dawn slowly broke, Murphy shook hands with Captain Peak at the gates of the outpost.

"You'd make one hell of a Ranger, Murphy," Peak said.

"Captain, it's been a pleasure riding with you," Murphy said. "And thanks for the supplies, we needed them," he said to Major Fuller.

Peak nodded to Knoop. "And take care of him," he said.

Murphy looked at Knoop. "Mount up. Sam, lead the way."

It took most of the morning and into early afternoon for Silver Fox to positively identify the tracks made by Claudine's wagon.

They stopped to rest the horses and eat a quick, cold lunch.

"It's about twelve miles west to the railroad camp," Silver Fox said. "We can make it before nightfall. Then we will know for sure if they are there or not."

Sipping water after eating a hunk of cornbread, Knoop said, "How long have you been scouting for the army?"

"Since I realized we can't beat them," Silver Fox said. "If you can't beat somebody, it's best to coexist with them."

"Where did you learn such a vocabulary?" Knoop asked.

"When I was a boy, I learned French and English from the missionaries who traveled with the French fur traders," Silver Fox said. "They taught me about your Jesus Christ. Much later, I was recruited to scout for the Union Army during the war. I scouted for General Meade at Gettysburg, and General Buford.

And some for Reynolds. Afterward, I stayed on and I've been scouting ever since. Meade was a stickler for education, and I had some of the best tutors from Boston and New York. He figured an educated man was less likely to make mistakes in the field. I attended Meade's funeral at Laurel Hill in 'seventy-two."

"You speak three languages?" Knoop said.

"French, English, Navajo, Sioux, and Crow, and a bit of Latin," Silver Fox said. "Latin is a dead language you know."

Knoop stared at Silver Fox.

"So much for the noble savage theory," Silver Fox said.

"I'm learning," Knoop said.

"You said that like you're from across the pond," Silver Fox said. "Not England, maybe Scotland or Wales."

"Scotland," Knoop said.

"Are you familiar with William Wallace?" Silver Fox asked.

"Yes."

"We shall discuss the merits of his death when we have more time," Silver Fox said. "Right now we best push on."

They mounted up and rode another mile or so in silence before Murphy said, "When Claudine called them buffalo heifers, she meant they are big girls, correct?"

"Each of them outweighs me by fifty pounds," Silver Fox said.

"Why are they in such demand?" Murphy asked.

"Two sweeter, nicer women you'll never meet," Silver Fox said. "Hearts of gold in the both of them. They'll make you chicken soup when you're sick and donate to the church when the *padre* is in need. And it doesn't hurt that a man can lose himself on their giant bosoms as if he's being whisked away on feather pillows."

Murphy grinned. "No, I guess it doesn't hurt."

Silver Fox suddenly stopped his horse.

"What?" Murphy asked.

Silver Fox dismounted. "Don't know," he said.

He stood perfectly still as his eyes scanned ahead. "Let's walk a bit."

Murphy and Knoop dismounted and followed Silver Fox as he walked and continued to scan the area.

"Wait here," Silver Fox said.

He mounted his horse and galloped west for a quarter of a mile, stopped and turned east, then raced back.

"Two riders came from the west," Silver Fox said.

Murphy and Knoop mounted their horses and followed Silver Fox as he rode northwest toward the Llano.

"Wait," Silver Fox said and stopped his horse.

Murphy and Knoop stopped their horses alongside Silver Fox. For several minutes Silver Fox appeared not to move a muscle as his eyes scanned the terrain.

Knoop watched Silver Fox carefully, completely fascinated by the man's personality and demeanor.

"Can you smell it?" Silver Fox said barely above a whisper.

"What?" Knoop asked.

"Death," Silver Fox said.

Knoop looked at Murphy, but Murphy was gazing in the distance.

Silver Fox removed a pair of army binoculars from his saddlebags and scanned the area in the distance.

Calmly he lowered the binoculars and put them away. Then he yanked on the reins and raced forward, leaving Murphy and Knoop behind.

By the time Murphy and Knoop got their horses running, Silver Fox was a hundred feet ahead of them.

Murphy pushed Boyle and slowly he gained on Silver Fox. When they were side by side, Murphy saw in the distance. Tiny black dots circling in the sky.

Buzzards.

Murphy and Silver Fox thundered closer, and when they were within a hundred feet of the dead body on the ground, Murphy pulled his Colt and fired six shots at the buzzards picking flesh off the corpse.

They reached the body and dismounted. Murphy looked back at Knoop, who was hundreds of feet behind.

"Stop," Murphy yelled. "You don't want to see this."

The buzzards had picked the meat off his face, beginning with his eyes, then neck and hands, before they tore away at his clothes. Then they ate away at the flesh of his chest and belly until they reached the internal organs.

"Charlie MacLean, Claudine's man," Silver Fox said.

"His neck's been broken," Murphy said. "Twisted one hundred and eighty degrees."

"Two riders," Silver Fox said. "They took the wagon with their horses in tow."

"I'll bury him," Murphy said. "See if you can get a bead on where they're going."

Silver Fox nodded. "He was a good man, old Charlie. Say a few Christian words over him."

Silver Fox mounted his horse and followed the wagon tracks.

Murphy removed the folding shovel from the saddle and patted Boyle on the rump. "Go find some grass," he said. "I'll be a while."

"I can help," Knoop said.

"You want to help, find some wood to make a proper cross," Murphy said. "With room to carve his name."

Two hours later, Murphy stuck the wood cross with Charlie's name carved in it in the gravesite.

"That's all we can do for this soul," Murphy said.

"Silver Fox is returning," Knoop said.

"They turned east onto the Llano," Silver Fox said when he

arrived and dismounted.

"What is the Llano exactly?" Knoop said.

"A plateau of baked earth and desert a hundred square miles," Silver Fox said.

"Why go there?" Knoop asked.

"Because who is stupid enough to follow?" Silver Fox said. "That is a fine cross. Did you say words?"

"Not yet," Knoop said.

Silver Fox removed his cavalry hat and said a short prayer in Navajo.

"That will do," Murphy said. "Let's find a place to make camp."

They rode about a hundred yards, and then Murphy stopped and turned Boyle around. At least a dozen buzzards were on the ground, picking at the earth for scraps. He withdrew his Winchester, cocked the lever and then fired, cocked the lever twice more, and fired two more shots. Three buzzards fell dead. The others flew and hopped away, squawking.

Murphy replaced the Winchester, turned Boyle, and looked at Knoop and Silver Fox. "When there is nothing else to eat, those filthy creatures will eat each other," Murphy said.

As they rode on, Knoop glanced back and the buzzards were picking at the three that Murphy had shot.

Silver Fox had six steaks covered in salt and wrapped in brown paper given to him by the army post's cook. He also had five pounds of potatoes. They made camp and cooked three steaks with baked potatoes and beans and a pot of coffee.

After eating, Murphy opened his last bottle of whiskey and added some to three cups of coffee.

"There is a small stream coming off the Canadian," Silver Fox said. "We will fill up on water before we reach the Llano."

Murphy stuffed his pipe and lit it. He looked at Silver Fox.

"How far are you willing to go?" he asked.

"As long as it takes," Silver Fox said.

"As far as we know, Charlie is the first man that they killed," Murphy said. "That means they are willing to do whatever it takes to obtain more victims."

Knoop nodded.

"That means we have to be willing to do whatever it takes to catch them," Murphy said.

"I understand," Knoop said.

"These two are bad medicine," Silver Fox said. "The worst kind."

Murphy puffed on his pipe and watched the stars.

Silver Fox looked at Knoop.

"What do you know about William Wallace?" Silver Fox asked.

"Every Scot knows the Guardian of Scotland," Knoop said.

"What fascinated me the most was not that Wallace fought against the King of England for the freedom of his people and became their hero, but that he was betrayed by those same people and died at the hands of the king as a traitor," Silver Fox said. "In many ways, his story reminds me of my own people."

"I can see the parallel between the two people," Knoop said.

Silver Fox nodded. "People do evil things," he said. "Here and across the pond."

"Yes, they do," Knoop said.

"I expect to ride hard tomorrow," Murphy said. "Best get some sleep."

CHAPTER TWENTY-ONE

Silver Fox had a pouch of twelve hard-boiled eggs. He gave two each to Murphy and Knoop to go along with a pan of bacon, cornbread, and oranges.

They were in the saddle a few minutes after sunrise. Silver Fox took the point and road about a hundred feet ahead of Murphy and Knoop. By noon they had covered ten miles and were traveling on the bone-dry plateau known as the Llano.

Silver Fox pulled up and Murphy and Knoop stopped their horses at his side.

"We'll rest the horses thirty minutes," Silver Fox said.

They ate cornbread with sips of water while the horses rested.

"The trail turns northeast from here," Silver Fox said.

"There's nothing here but baked ground," Knoop said.

"Llano Estacado, the Staked Plain," Silver Fox said. "Once called the Great American Desert. Once past the Canadian River, you can ride for two weeks without finding water."

Murphy pulled out his folded map of Texas and studied it for several minutes.

"We're about here," he said and touched the map with his finger. "If we continue on this path it will bring us here around nightfall."

Silver Fox glanced at the map. "Correct."

"What's there?" Knoop asked.

"Adobe Walls," Silver Fox said.

"What is Adobe Walls?" Knoop asked.

Just before sundown they rode into the remains of what was once the city of Adobe Walls. Established in eighteen forty-three as a trading post for buffalo hunters, the town, trading post, saloon, and fort were demolished by two battles fought at the site first in eighteen sixty-four and then a decade later.

All that remained were the walls of the buildings and a few crumbling rooftops.

They dismounted at the crumbling walls of what was once a fort.

"They stopped here," Silver Fox said. "And rode away on two horses and took the other two in tow."

Murphy looked into the fort and saw two blankets on the ground. He, Silver Fox, and Knoop walked to the blankets. They were army green and stained with dried blood.

"Oh, Jesus," Knoop said.

"Where's the gravesite?" Murphy asked.

He looked at the end of the fort and through the crumbled wall. He walked across the overgrown ground and looked over the wall at the freshly dug grave a few yards away.

Silver Fox and Knoop came and stood beside him.

"Those women never harmed a soul," Silver Fox said.

"We best make camp," Murphy said. "Sam, see if you can find where they took the wagon."

They returned to the horses and Silver Fox was about to mount his, when a shot rang out and a bullet struck a wall to their right.

Murphy pulled his Colt and ducked behind the wall, as did Silver Fox, leaving Knoop standing alone.

"Melvin, get down," Murphy shouted.

Knoop turned and ran behind the wall and squatted beside Murphy.

"Did you see where the shot came from?" Murphy asked.

"No," Silver Fox said. "But the door frames all face east so it came from the west."

"All the doors face east?" Knoop said. "Why?"

"Melvin, now is not the . . ." Murphy said just as another shot rang out.

The bullet struck the wall opposite them and bounced to the ground a few feet away. Murphy reached for the flattened bullet and picked it up.

"A .50 caliber plains rifle," he said.

"What's that?" Knoop said.

"Black powder," Murphy said. "I haven't seen a slug like this in more than ten years."

"It's my wagon," a man's voice called out. "Get yourin. This one's mine."

"The wagon," Murphy said.

Another shot fired and bounced off the wall.

"What the hell?" Murphy said.

"No thief in the night steals what's rightfully mine," the man shouted. "Get yourin wagon, you blasted wagon thieves."

"Wait here," Murphy said.

He walked to the rear of the crumbling building, stepped over the wall, turned left, and slowly walked from building to building, checking inside each one. At the ninth building, inside the crumbling walls was the wagon.

An old man sat on the ground beside an open door frame with a plains rifle in his hands.

"Hear me, thieves," the old man shouted. "It ain't yourin, it's mine."

He fired the rifle and then proceeded to reload, a process that took about thirty seconds.

Murphy stepped over the wall and cocked the Colt.

"Old man, that's enough," he said.

The old man turned and looked at Murphy.

"Put down the rifle," Murphy said. "No one wants to steal your wagon."

The old man sighed heavily and set the rifle on the ground.

"You got any coffee?" he asked. "I ain't had me no coffee in quite a spell."

"Name is George Went. I thank you kindly for the coffee."

"How old are you, George?" Murphy asked.

"What year is it?" George asked.

"Eighteen eighty-three," Murphy said.

"I was born in nineteen aught five," George said.

"Seventy-eight?" Knoop said. "You're seventy-eight-years-old."

"If you say so."

"George, what are you doing here?" Murphy asked.

"I live here."

"How long have you lived here?" Murphy asked.

"Moved here in 'fifty-one to trap and trade buffalo skins," George said. "Course all that changed after the war in 'sixty-four came along."

"The Civil War?" Knoop asked.

"The Indian war against Kit Carson," George said. "Then came the second war against the Indians, and there weren't much left after that. Just what you see now."

They were in a building at the rear of the Walls. It was mostly intact and the roof had been repaired considerably.

"What do you live on?" Knoop asked.

"Look around you, boy," George said. "What do you see?"

Knoop looked around the interior of the building. There was a mattress stuffed with straw. A pillowcase also filled with straw. Some cookware, knives and forks, and cups. Two large canteens, a pile of furs, and a well-used fireplace in the west wall.

"Bent's Creek ain't but a mile west of here," George said. "Before the second war we buried several barrels of black powder and thousands of rounds of ammunition. I fish off the creek, hunt hare and the occasional snake, and sometimes small mule deer. I get by on my wits mostly."

George looked at Silver Fox. "Apache?"

"Navajo."

"Never had no trouble with Navajo."

"George, tell me about the wagon," Murphy said.

"You ain't taking it from me, is you?"

"No, it's yours," Murphy said.

"I plan to make it my bed," George said.

"It will make a fine bed, George," Murphy said. "All I want to know is how you came by it."

"Three, maybe four nights now, these two fellows showed up in the wagon," George said. "Say, you wouldn't happen to have something to sweeten this here coffee?"

Murphy nodded to Knoop.

Knoop stood and went outside to the horses.

"About the two fellows?" Murphy said.

"Odd they had two horses in tow," George said. "In back of the wagon they had two women. Big women, and I figure they was asleep. One fellow was a giant, or seemed like it. But the other, much smaller man was the boss. He ordered the big man around and he obeyed."

Knoop returned with Murphy's bottle of whiskey and poured some into George's cup. "Thank you kindly," George said.

"Go on, George," Murphy said.

"They didn't bother to look around none. They must have figured no one was about. The giant, he carried the women into the building you was at. That used to be the fort, you know."

George sipped some coffee. "What is that?"

"Bourbon," Murphy said. "Go on, George, tell more."

"I hid until dark," George said. "I could smell they made a fire and had some grub cooking. I crawled on my belly along the back walls and got a peek into the old fort."

George paused to drink some coffee. "Could use a mite more sweetening."

Knoop added whiskey to George's cup. He sipped and nodded.

"Go on," Murphy said.

"I could hear them talking," George said. "Gibberish if you ask me."

"What do you mean?" Murphy asked.

"Couldn't understand a word what they was saying," George said. "Gibberish. Thing is, they spoke English just fine some of the time."

"When they spoke English, what did they say?" Murphy asked.

George took another sip from his cup. "Something about taking scalps and to be careful," he said.

"Taking scalps?" Silver Fox said.

"Are you sure?" Murphy asked.

"No I ain't," George said. "Like I said, most of the time it sounded like gibberish."

"What did you see?" Murphy asked.

"Say, what do you got in the way of grub?" George asked. "I was fixing to roast a lizard with some cactus stew."

"Cactus stew?" Knoop asked.

"We have steak, beans, cornbread, bacon, some hard-boiled eggs, what would you like?" Murphy said.

"Beefsteak?"

"Texas beef," Silver Fox said.

"Ain't had beefsteak since . . . since I don't know when," George said.

"I'll make a fire and get things going," Silver Fox said.

"Use my chimney there," George said.

"Okay, George, what did you see?" Murphy asked.

"Something I'd just as soon forget," George said.

"We need to know," Murphy said. "Tell us. Please."

George sipped from his cup, and then said, "Got anything to smoke? I ran out of tobacco back in 'seventy-five."

"Melvin, I have a spare pipe in my saddlebags," Murphy said. "Bring it and a pouch."

While Silver Fox made a fire, Knoop went for the pipe and tobacco.

"Here you go, George," Knoop said when he returned.

"Thank you kindly," George said.

Murphy waited for George to stuff the pipe and then Murphy lit a wood match.

"Ain't seen a match since the last war," George said.

"How do you make a fire?" Knoop asked.

"Easy," George said. He stood and went to the fireplace where Silver Fox was adding wood from a pile stacked against the wall. He slipped the powder horn from around his neck, removed the top, and sprinkled a bit onto the wood. Then he picked up two stones and smacked them together to create a spark. After several tries, the sparks ignited the powder and created a small flame.

"See, easy," George said.

"We'll get chow going in a minute, George," Murphy said. "Now tell us what you saw."

George sat beside Murphy.

"They kilt them women," George said. "As sure as I'm sitting here, they kilt them women."

"How, George?" Murphy asked.

"They carved them up like they was hogs," George said. He looked at Murphy, and Murphy could see the horror of the memory in the old man's eyes.

"Go on, George," Murphy said.

"The big fellow, he went to sleep after they was done, but the little one, he stayed there all night just watching them two women," George said. "I felt the evil in them like it was Satan hisself come to earth. And the really strange thing is them women never made a sound while they was being slaughtered like sheep."

"Are you sure they were still alive when he cut them up?" Knoop asked.

George nodded. "I seen this doctor once put a man to sleep right before he sawed off his leg," he said. "He put this cloth over the man's face and then put drops from a little bottle on the cloth and the man went right to sleep."

"That's what they did to the two women?" Murphy asked.

"Yes, sir," George said.

Knoop looked at Murphy. "Ether."

Murphy nodded.

"The fire is ready," Silver Fox said. "I'll get supper going."

"What happened after that, George?" Murphy asked.

"I gathered up what I needed and went to the creek," George said. "Stayed two nights. Came back yesterday morning and they was gone, but they left the wagon."

"Okay, George," Murphy said. "We'll talk more about it later."

"I cut the steaks into four and put on the beans," Silver Fox said.

"Melvin, fix George another cup of coffee," Murphy said.

While Knoop stayed with George, Murphy and Silver Fox left the building and took a short walk.

"Tomorrow morning, see if you can pick up their trail," Murphy said. "We may have to hitch up the wagon and take George with us if the trail is on the way to a town."

"Closest is Oneida," Silver Fox said.

"I know that, Sam, but if they're not going to Oneida?" Murphy said.

"The closest major town from here would be Wichita Falls where they're building the Fort Worth and Denver Railroad. They built the town near the Wichita River, but there has never been a falls."

"How far?"

"Four days."

"Pick up their trail in the morning and we'll make plans from there."

They returned to the building where Knoop was busy with the food and George was sitting against the wall, smoking Murphy's pipe.

Murphy looked at the old man. He was gnarled and grizzled, with white hair past his shoulders and a peppered beard reminiscent of Saint Nick.

"Murphy," Knoop said. "A moment."

Knoop and Murphy walked to the rear of the building.

"I've been giving it some thought, what George said," Knoop said. "Obviously they were speaking their native language mixed with English. I think George mistook the word scalpel for scalp. A scalpel is even sharper than a straight razor, isn't it?"

"Yes, of course," Murphy said.

"What does all this mean?" Knoop asked.

"I wish I knew, Melvin," Murphy said.

"Supper is ready," Silver Fox said.

They ate around the fireplace for light and warmth.

"That beefsteak was everything I remembered it was," George said.

"Want some fresh coffee?" Knoop asked.

"Believe I will, if you can sweeten it a bit," George said.

Knoop filled four cups with coffee and splashed whiskey into each cup.

"I have some chocolate, George. Would you like a piece?" Knoop said.

"Chocolate? The last time I had me a piece of chocolate was the Fourth of July party in 'seventy-three."

Knoop dug a chocolate bar out of his saddlebags and gave it to George. The old man removed the wrapper and took a bite. "Tasty," he said.

"George, we're going to sleep in here with you tonight, is that okay with you?" Murphy said.

"If you don't mind an old man snoring," George said.

"Where's he off to?" George asked shortly after sunrise.

"See if he can pick up their trail," Murphy said. "We're lawmen, and those two are wanted for murder."

"Murder, you say," George said. "I expect after what they did, murder is the right word."

"More coffee, George?" Knoop asked.

"Believe I will," George said. "After you fellows pull out, I'll probably go to my grave without another cup."

"Have you ever thought about leaving, George?" Murphy asked.

"Hell, I never even intended to stay," George said. "I left here the first time after the first war and moved my wife to San Antone. She died of the consumption in 'sixty-eight. I didn't see no reason to stay, so I moved back to hunt buffalo. After the second war, when the place was in ruins and everybody pulled out, I figured I'd stay and hunt buffalo until I had enough hides to sell and retire in my old age. Then tragedy struck and placed me here forever."

"What happened?" Knoop asked.

"I had a hundred pelts and figured that was enough," George

said. "I went down to the creek to wash my clothes and to wash me. I was gone maybe four hours. When I returned, my horse, mule, and pelts were gone. Apaches took 'em. They left me an arrow with their mark on the band."

"So you just stayed?" Knoop asked.

"Would you like to walk eighty miles across the Llano with one canteen of water and no possibles?" George said.

"No, I wouldn't," Knoop said.

"I figured I already lived beyond my years and this ain't a bad place to die," George said. "Only I didn't die, and time just sort of went by on its own accord. I see some Apaches in the distance once in a while, but they think I'm just some crazy old man, so they leave me alone."

"That's an amazing story, George," Knoop said.

"I sort of have a feeling for rattlesnake for supper," George said. "Want to help me trap a few? If you got more beans, I can fix us a tasty stew."

"You go, Melvin," Murphy said. "I have to wait for Sam."

"How do you hunt rattlesnake?" Knoop asked.

"It ain't that difficult once you get the knack," George said.

"What the hell," Knoop said. "I've done every other damned thing on this trip."

After Knoop and George left, Murphy sat against his saddle and wrote a letter to Kai in pencil. Words came hard, and it took a while to fill just one page. When he finally finished, he carefully folded the paper and tucked it into his saddlebags.

George had a long stick with a V notched on one end. He had sharpened the tip of the V to a sharp point. Knoop carried the stick, George carried a machete. "First thing is to find a den," George said as he guided them to rocky hills to the north. "Snake is a cold-blooded bastard that needs direct sunlight to keep warm. They tend to make their dens where they can sun themselves on rocks as the rocks heat up."

Knoop remembered the way Murphy killed a snake in the mountains.

"Course it took me a while to prefect my technique," George said. "I always felt shooting a snake turns the meat bad, you see."

"How do we find a den?" Knoop asked.

"We climb the rocks and look for places they like to hide in," George said.

They walked about a half mile to the rocky hills where George began to search for snake dens.

It took about fifteen minutes for George to locate a shallow den between several large rocks.

"When I snatch him out, you put that stick over his head so he can't move," George said.

Knoop looked at George.

"Get ready," George said.

"Are we sure about this?" Knoop said.

George squatted in front of the hole. Then he reached in with his right hand, grabbed the snake by its rattle, and yanked it from the hole. The angry snake immediately turned and hissed at George.

Laughing, George said, "Get ready, boy," and lowered the snake by the tail to the ground. It tried to slither back into the hole, but George pulled on the rattle and yelled, "Now."

Knoop slammed the V notch over the snake just behind the head, trapping it. Holding the machete in his left hand, George slammed the machete down and cut the snake's head off with the one slice.

George held the snake at arm's length. "It's a nice one. We get one more like it, and we got a decent supper."

"Wait," Knoop said. "I have to start my heart first."

Murphy was brushing Boyle when he spotted Silver Fox riding in from the east. He was about twenty minutes away, so he continued with the grooming.

When he arrived, Silver Fox was covered with trail dust. He dismounted and used his hat to brush off.

"Fresh coffee is on the fire," Murphy said.

"I could use some. Where's the old man and Knoop?"

"Out hunting snake. Come on."

Murphy put the brush away in his saddlebags, and he and Silver Fox entered George's adobe building.

After filling two cups, Murphy said, "What did you find out?"

"Trail leads to Wichita Falls no doubt," Silver Fox said. "Two riders, two horses in tow. One rider is a big man, a very big man."

Murphy sighed. "We'll have to take the old man with us," he said.

"That's no way to make time," Silver Fox said.

"They already have a five-day head start and, I'm not worried about picking up their trail," Murphy said. "They leave the corpses of women in their wake."

Silver Fox nodded. "You tell him," he said. "They're here."

Murphy turned as George and Knoop entered the adobe building. George had two decapitated snakes slung over his right shoulder.

"Will make a right nice stew for tonight," George said.

"George, do you have any other clothes?" Murphy asked.

"I do," George said. "Course, being just me all this time, I have no reason to put them on."

"George, tomorrow morning we're leaving for Wichita Falls, and we want to take you with us," Murphy said.

"What fer?" George asked.

"So you can enjoy your last remaining years in comfort," Murphy said.

"Who said I ain't comfortable here?" George asked.

"George, since you've been here there's been unbelievable progress made in the world," Knoop said. "The electric light bulb, the telephone, the phonograph record, and I've read that within ten years there will be such a thing as a horseless carriage."

"I got no notion of what you're saying, but what's that got to do with my comfort?" George said.

"You can sleep in a soft bed every night, eat good food every day, and drink as much coffee and whiskey as you want," Knoop said.

"I can?" George said.

"Of course," Knoop said.

"George, where are your other clothes?" Murphy asked.

George walked to the rear of the building. With his foot, he brushed away some dirt to expose a short rope.

"In here," he said.

Murphy, Knoop, and Silver Fox walked to George.

George grabbed the rope and lifted the wood door covered with dirt to expose a large hole beneath the floor. In the hole were a chest of clothing, two barrels of black powder, two black powder revolvers, and a metal money chest.

"What's in the cashbox?" Murphy asked.

"Two thousand gold eagles," George said. "Belonged to the soldiers before the second war. After they were all kilt and the others left, I buried it with my other possibles."

"That's forty thousand dollars," Knoop said. "George, you're a rich man, a very rich man."

"We'll take your clothes and cashbox in the wagon," Murphy said. "With this kind of money, you'll live out your days in comfort and style."

"Now hold on there," George said. "I ain't said I'm going nowhere yet."

"You're going," Murphy said. "If I have to tie you up in the back of the wagon, you're going."

George looked at Murphy.

"Sam, grab George's chest of clothes," Murphy said. "He's going to have a haircut and a bath."

"A bath?" George said. "What fer?"

"You stink," Murphy said. "Let's go to the creek and have us a bath right now."

George stared at Murphy.

"George," Knoop said. "He wasn't asking."

"Untie me, you sons a bitches," George yelled.

He was tied across Boyle's saddle. Murphy, Knoop, and Silver Fox walked alongside the horse until Murphy stopped him near the creek.

"Now come on, George, a bath won't kill you," Murphy said as he gently pulled the old man from the saddle.

"I'll put a curse on you," George said as Murphy removed the rope from George's wrists. "A devil's curse. An old Apache woman taught me."

"Apaches don't believe in the devil," Silver Fox said.

George turned and attempted to run, but Murphy grabbed him by the collar of his filthy shirt.

"Melvin, break out the soap and clean clothes," Murphy said.

"All right, damn you," George said. "I'll go in but I can't swim. One of you go in with me or I'll drown."

"I could use a bath," Knoop said.

Silver Fox nodded. "Soap and water won't hurt me none, I guess."

Murphy sighed. "Okay, George, we'll all take a bath."

Murphy removed his holster and placed in over the saddle,

then started to remove his clothing. Knoop and Silver Fox sat on the ground to remove their boots.

Surprisingly quick for his advanced years, George snatched the Colt revolver from the holster draped over Boyle's saddle and aimed it at Murphy.

"Now all o' you get in the creek and leave me the hell alone," George said.

Murphy sighed, then whistled twice, and Boyle stepped forward and nudged George in the back.

"Quit that, ya stupid horse," George said.

Murphy whistled again.

Boyle nudged George a second time.

"I said . . ." George said.

Boyle nudged George harder and as he fell into the creek, Murphy snatched the Colt from George's hand.

Murphy replaced his Colt in the holster and said, "We'll be right in, George. Might as well remove your clothes."

Wearing a long nightshirt and his boots, George sat near the fireplace and ate supper.

"Did you have to cut my hair and beard so short?" he asked.

"You need to look respectable when we reach Wichita Falls," Murphy said.

"George, do you have any family?" Knoop said.

"Had me a son and daughter," George said. "If they are still alive, they'd be in their fifties by now, I expect."

"George, I work for Pinkerton's Detective Agency," Knoop said. "When we reach Wichita Falls, I can wire Mr. Pinkerton and ask to have the detectives locate your family."

"They can do that?" George asked.

"Nobody is better at finding people than Pinkerton's," Knoop said.

"Maybe going to town won't be so bad after all," George

said. "Course, it will take some getting used to."

"That's to be expected," Knoop said.

"What's a light bulb?" George asked.

"We're burning daylight," Silver Fox said.

George and Silver Fox sat in the buckboard of the wagon. Boyle and Silver Fox's horse were hitched to the wagon. Lexi was loosely tethered to a wheel. Supplies and George's chest of clothes and cashbox were in the back of the wagon.

"Melvin, let's go," Murphy shouted.

A few moments later, Knoop and a dapper-looking George emerged from inside the adobe hut and walked to the wagon.

"Well, look at you, George," Murphy said.

"Give an old man a hand," George said.

Murphy helped George into the buckboard.

Knoop mounted Lexi and looked at George.

"You're traveling in style, George," Knoop said.

Murphy yanked on the reins and the wagon moved forward.

"They got a place for me to live in Wichita Falls?" George said.

"I expect," Murphy said.

"Restaurants?"

"Most likely," Murphy said.

"Saloons?"

"Definitely."

"Dancing girls?"

Murphy looked at George.

"I'm old," George said. "But I ain't dead."

CHAPTER TWENTY-TWO

Four days and eighty miles later, Murphy drove the wagon along Main Street in the town of Wichita Falls. Along the trail, after two days, two of the four horses were cut loose by the criminals and just the two riders continued on. Silver Fox determined that they set the two captive horses free on the open Llano to prevent them from being found by anyone looking to follow them.

Wichita Falls was a booming town of two thousand people, thanks mostly to the construction of the Fort Worth and Denver City Railroad. Neighboring ranchers could easily move their herds to markets in boxcars instead of on extended cattle drives.

"The sheriff here is Beauregard Hardy, but call him Bo if you want to stay on his good side," Silver Fox said.

"I ain't seen so many people in one place since the second Apache War," George said.

They rode past the railroad station and several large saloons to the sheriff's office, which sat adjacent to a telegraph office.

"Let's go see the sheriff," Murphy said.

Sheriff Hardy was a grizzled veteran of law enforcement, having served as sheriff for several towns in Texas and Arkansas as well as Missouri. He employed six deputies, and every one of them was needed when cowboys drove their herds to town for transport on the railroad.

Murphy did most of the talking, with George answering an

occasional question or two.

Hardy had four of his deputies in the office and they were silent the entire time, fascinated with the old man's tale.

"So, Sheriff, what can you do to help out old George here?" Murphy asked when he finished the story.

Hardy looked at George.

"I have to say that is one amazing story, George," Hardy said. He turned to his deputies. "Fetch the widow Lang and Mr. Dobbs from the bank."

The widow Lang, a plump woman in her sixties took in boarders at her large house to supplement the life-insurance policy her husband left her when he died of natural causes almost a decade ago.

She charged twenty dollars a week for the room and ten dollars a week for two meals a day.

"I have a lovely room on the first floor that faces the sunrise," Lang said. "If you have special dietary requests, why you just let me know."

"Dietary requests?" George said. "I been living on snakes, lizards, and cactus stew."

"Well, no more snakes and lizards for you, Mr. Went," Lang said. "I pride myself on my home cooking."

"We'll bring him right over as soon as we finish with Mr. Dobbs," Murphy said.

Murphy set the heavy cashbox on Hardy's desk and looked at Dobbs.

"This is Mr. Went's life savings," Murphy said. "Forty thousand dollars. He wants to open an account at your bank for him to draw upon as needed."

Dobbs, a squirrely little man in a black suit, looked at the cashbox.

"My, oh my," Dobbs said.

Murphy pulled out his wallet and showed him his identification. "Mr. Dobbs, if I ever get wind that you cheated George, I will come to your bank and pin your ears back. Is that understood?"

"You're a mite testy, aren't you big fellow?" Dobbs said.

"You should see him when he's in a bad mood," Knoop said.

"Melvin, would you take George across the street to the bank and set up the account," Murphy said.

Knoop attempted to lift the cashbox, which weighed at least one hundred pounds.

"Better let me help you with that," Silver Fox said.

Once Murphy was alone with Hardy, he said, "Sheriff, can I buy you a cup of coffee?"

Murphy and Sheriff Hardy had a window table at the Wichita Falls Café across the street from Hardy's office.

"I did receive that blanket telegram from Washington about the killing of sporting women, but we don't have any in town," Hardy said.

"All the saloons in town, all the cowboys that pass through, and not one brothel?" Murphy said.

"It's the Woman's Temperance Organization," Hardy said. "They convinced the town council to ban brothels in town about a year ago. They want to ban the use of liquor inside the town limits, but so far the council won't go along with that. The town would go bankrupt inside a week if they had their way."

"That must dampen the cowboys who come to town after driving herds for a month," Murphy said.

"Not really," Hardy said. "Fred Roscoe, owner of the biggest saloon in town, he had the idea of operating a brothel outside the town limits where the new law doesn't apply. He bought the old Baker Ranch ten miles east of town and set up what he calls 'the Chicken Ranch.' Course the only chickens on the ranch are of the female persuasion."

"I want to see Roscoe and then take a ride out there," Murphy said. "Care to ride along?"

"It's inside the county, so that's still my jurisdiction," Hardy said. "Roscoe is out of town on business. He went to Houston to buy a saloon that came available."

"Then we'll go straight to the ranch."

Knoop and Silver Fox entered the café and went to their table.

"We're done at the bank," Knoop said. "I'm taking George over to the boarding house now."

"When you're done with that, find us a hotel and livery for tonight," Murphy said.

"Try the Brentwood on Elm. It's the best in town and has a private stable," Hardy said.

"Thanks," Knoop said.

Murphy reached into his jacket pocket for an envelope. "Drop this off at the post office for me," he said.

Knoop took the envelope. "Sure."

"Sam, stick around for a minute," Murphy said.

"I never heard of such a thing," Silver Fox said. "Why is it called the Chicken Ranch?"

"I asked Roscoe that, and he said it sounds better than the whorehouse ranch," Hardy said.

They road to the archway that separated two empty cattle-holding pens. It was a tenth of a mile to the main house from the arch.

"The woman who runs the ranch is an Italian lady named Florence, but nobody calls her anything but Mama, short for Mama Mia, some Italian phrase," Hardy said.

"It means Madonna, the Mother of Christ," Silver Fox said.

Hardy looked at Silver Fox. "Now how in the world do you know that?"

"Italian is one of the romance languages," Silver Fox said. "I'm fluent in French, so I understand a good deal of Italian."

"Well, hell, I've known you fifteen years and I thought you was just a noble savage," Hardy said.

"I hear that a lot," Silver Fox said. "You can make it up to me later by buying me a drink."

They neared the main house. It had been built to raise a large family in and had a wraparound deck with an awning. A bunkhouse for forty men was fifty yards behind the house on the right. A large barn sat behind the house to the left. A corral with six horses in it took up the grounds in front of the house.

A large, well-kept garden served to make guests feel welcome.

They dismounted at the corral and walked to the house.

Murphy knocked on an elaborate wood door with an etched glass center.

The door was answered by a handsome, middle-aged black man wearing a white dinner jacket.

"Sorry, gents, we don't open until four," he said.

Hardy stepped forward. "Tom, it's Sheriff Hardy. This isn't a social call."

"Sorry, Sheriff, I didn't see you behind the big fellow. Come in. I'll get Mama."

A maid served coffee in the parlor. Mama Mia was a large woman near sixty years old and dressed in a low-cut gown that displayed her ample breasts.

The coffee was served in fine china, and Murphy had some trouble fitting his fingers into the tiny handles.

"Of course I remember the two gentlemen in question," Mama Mia said. "It isn't often I hear my native language spoken these days, even if they did have a Swiss accent."

"Are you sure?" Hardy asked.

"Sheriff, how many Italian-speaking giants do you think visit us here at the ranch?" Mama Mia asked.

"How do you know their accent was Swiss?" Murphy asked.

"Have you ever been to Europe, Mr. Murphy?"

"I have not."

"Going from Italy to Switzerland is no more difficult than going from Texas to Arkansas," Mama Mia said. "There is a lot of back and forth between the two peoples, and Italian is spoken in Switzerland almost as much as German. If German is your first language, then your Italian will have a somewhat different accent to it. See?"

"I do," Murphy said. "Did they stay the night?"

"They did, after much arguing between themselves," Mama Mia said.

"What were they arguing about?" Murphy asked.

"Women, what else? The smaller man wanted blondes. The big one, he wanted black women. They finally settled on my two Negro girls."

"How many women do you employ?" Murphy asked.

"Sixteen, and every girl has her own room in what used to be the bunkhouse," Mama Mia said. "The bar has been reconstructed into private rooms where clients can stay the night if they wish and have the means to pay extra. Our establishment isn't cheap, but then neither is our service."

"The Negro girls aren't missing?" Murphy asked.

"Why, no."

"You're sure?"

"Let's go talk to them," Mama Mia said.

The bunkhouse had been divided into sixteen bedrooms, each with its own door. Centered down the middle aisle was a large table with chairs, a stocked pantry, and a bookcase filled with books and a large flat woodstove for cooking.

Several women were eating at the table.

"Where are Rhea and Chrissie?" Mama Mia asked.

"Taking a bath, getting ready for tonight," one woman at the table said.

"Tell them to come to the house right away, would you," Mama Mia said.

Rhea and Chrissie were beautiful Negro women in their mid-thirties. Both had been born slaves on a Georgia plantation and were freed in 'sixty-five. Neither had a formal education, but they had learned enough on their own throughout the years so they could read and write enough to get by.

They weren't related by blood, but as they had no notion of what their actual bloodline was, they considered themselves sisters, which they just might have been.

"Is something wrong, Mama?" Chrissie asked when they entered the living room of the house.

"No, dear," Mama said. "This is Mr. Murphy. He is a federal lawman, and he has some questions about some wanted men."

Chrissie and Rhea looked at Murphy.

"You can sit. Please," Murphy said.

They took seats on the plush sofa.

Hardy and Silver Fox stood in the background.

"What kinds of questions?" Rhea asked.

"About two Italian men," Murphy said. "One medium size, the other close to a giant."

Rhea nodded. "I had the small one," she said.

"Tell me about him," Murphy said.

"He was sort of handsome, about forty-five or so," Rhea said. "Dark hair with a little bald spot on the top of his head."

"He spoke English to you?" Murphy asked.

"Yes. In fact, that's all he wanted to do was talk."

"You mean he didn't want to bone?" Mama Mia asked.

"No, Mama, he didn't. He just wanted to talk is all."

"What did he want to talk about?" Murphy asked.

"He seemed real interested in me," Rhea said. "He asked a lot of questions about where I was raised and about my health."

"Your health?" Murphy said.

"Yes, sir. Asked a lot of questions about my health," Rhea said.

"And what did you tell him?"

"I told him I had some sickness as a child, but otherwise I've been very healthy."

"What kind of sickness?"

"Female kind," Rhea said.

"Could you elaborate a bit more?" Murphy asked.

"I don't . . . what does that word mean?"

"It means tell us more," Mama Mia said.

Rhea lowered her eyes. "I was thirteen when I come of female age," she said. "The plantation owner's son took me. I got pregnant. That happened a lot back then. Thing was, I started to bleed and it wouldn't stop. After days of bleeding, they sent for a doctor and he said I was going to die if he didn't operate. He said it was a new procedure and would save my life. He called it a hyster . . . something. After that, I got better, but the doctor said I could never have another baby."

"You told him this?" Murphy asked.

"I did."

"And after that?"

"He tipped me ten dollars and told me I could go."

"Did he tell you his name?"

"No, and I didn't ask. I'm not in the asking business."

"What about you, Chrissie?" Murphy asked.

"The giant just wanted to bone all night," Chrissie said. "A bigger man I never did see. He like to crush my bones to dust, he was so heavy."

"Did he talk to you at all?" Murphy said.

"He talked a lot in that Italian when we was doing it," Chrissie said. "He said very little in English except to say he wanted to go again. It was like being in bed with a rutting bull. In the morning he left, and I had to soak in a hot tub I was so sore."

"Did either of them say where they were going next?" Murphy said.

"Not to me," Rhea said.

"Dallas," Chrissie said.

"He said that?" Murphy asked.

Chrissie shook her head. "He took a bunch of stuff out of his pockets and put them on the dresser. I went to get some water from the pitcher and saw a train ticket on top of his folding wallet. I don't read big fancy words, but I could read the word Dallas on the ticket."

"Thank you, ladies," Murphy said.

"You can go, girls," Mama Mia said.

After Chrissie and Rhea left, Murphy said, "Thank you for the time and information, Mama."

"Anytime," Mama Mia said.

"Say, Mama, what time do you open for business?" Silver Fox asked.

Murphy looked at him. "Let's go," he said.

"What do you think it means?" Knoop asked.

Murphy, Knoop, Silver Fox, and Hardy were having dinner in the restaurant inside the Brentwood Hotel.

"I'm not sure," Murphy said. "But since they always kidnap two women for their rituals, I think they want them both to be healthy."

"Healthy for what?" Silver Fox asked. "They're just going to kill them. What do they care if one of them isn't healthy?"

"Maybe it's some kind of satanic thing?" Knoop said. "Where the sacrifices have to be in good health for the ceremony?"

"This doesn't make any sense to me at all," Hardy said.

"That makes all of us," Murphy said. "Sheriff, can you send a telegram to the sheriff and marshal in Dallas about this. Ask them to check for missing women, and also to check if any so-called giants have been in town the past few days."

"Are you going to Dallas?" Hardy asked.

"First train out in the morning," Murphy said.

"I'll be going with you," Silver Fox said. "I'll send a wire to the major and let him know I'll be gone awhile longer."

"Are you sure?" Murphy asked.

"I haven't scalped a paleface in years," Silver Fox said.

"Sam, you are so full of crap," Hardy said.

"Maybe so, but don't tell the palefaces that," Silver Fox said.

A waitress approached the table.

"Coffee and dessert?" she asked.

"What have you got tonight?" Hardy asked.

"Peach pie with fresh whipped cream," she said.

"Sounds good," Hardy said.

While Hardy and Silver Fox went to the telegraph office, Murphy and Knoop walked to the railroad station.

The hours posted on the chalkboard were ten a.m. to six p.m. except for Sunday hours of noon to six.

A lone clerk sat behind a gated booth. Otherwise, the depot was empty.

"We close in a few minutes," the clerk said. "One train tonight scheduled at eight. You have to wait outside on the platform if you want a ticket."

Murphy took out his wallet and showed it to the clerk.

"We're interested in two men who might have gone to Dallas," Murphy said. "They're wanted, so any information you can provide is vital."

"Two men? I need more information than just 'two men' if I'm to answer any questions," the clerk said.

"One man is about forty-five, slender with dark hair," Murphy said. "The other could be classified as a giant. As tall as or taller than me, but over three hundred pounds or more."

"I know exactly of who you speak," the clerk said. "The smaller man bought the tickets. Two to Dallas and paid extra for their horses. I didn't see the giant until afterward when they caught the ten a.m. train to Dallas two days ago."

"Just two days ago?" Murphy asked.

"I closed the office at nine forty-five for thirty minutes so I could pick up the mail, and on the platform were the two men you are inquiring about," the clerk said. "You can't miss the big fellow. Odd now that you mention it, but neither had horses with them. Just a couple of suitcases."

"How were they dressed?" Murphy asked.

"Tailored suits, although where the big fellow got a suit to fit him is anybody's guess," the clerk said.

"Did you happen to hear the talk?" Knoop asked.

"I did not. I'm not in the habit of eavesdropping on people."

"When the smaller man purchased the tickets, did he speak with an accent?" Knoop said.

"As a matter of fact, he did," the clerk said. "He spoke English just fine, but with some kind of foreign accent to be sure."

"I'll need three tickets to Dallas, and we'll be taking our horses," Murphy said. "How long is the ride?"

"The train leaves at ten and arrives in Dallas at six," the clerk said. "It's not an express run. That will be thirty-three dollars for three seats and board for three horses."

★ ★ ★ ★ ★

Murphy and Knoop met Silver Fox and Sheriff Hardy on the porch of the Brentwood Hotel, where they ordered coffee from the restaurant.

"I sent the telegrams to Dallas," Hardy said. "The town sheriff is Jason McCoy. He's a good man. Marshal Rourke has county jurisdiction. One or both will meet you at the station."

"Thank you," Murphy said.

"You got a Chinese laundry in town?" Silver Fox asked.

"No, but the hotel has a laundry service," Hardy said.

"I believe I'll have a bath in the morning," Silver Fox said. "I could do with some clean clothes."

"That's an excellent idea," Murphy said. "I'll reserve three baths for the morning."

"I have to get to the office," Hardy said. "I'll see you gents for breakfast."

After Hardy left, Knoop said, "They probably left Dallas by now."

"Most likely, but what choice do we have?" Murphy said.

Knoop nodded and sipped his coffee.

"We have no way of knowing at the moment, but I have to wonder if they have questioned all their victims the same way they did the two women at the Chicken Ranch."

"I think they have," Murphy said. "Judging by the way the smaller man questioned Rhea, it seemed very important to him."

"If we were in Chicago, I would visit the main library and check on books about ancient rituals," Knoop said.

"That's an idea, Melvin," Murphy said. "I don't know what kind of library system they have in Dallas, but it's worth looking into."

"There is an old Apache saying," Silver Fox said. "The only thing worse for a man's spirit than wanting something is knowing you will never have it."

"How does that apply to this?" Knoop asked.

"It doesn't, but I sure wish that chicken ranch was closer," Silver Fox said.

Knoop looked at him. "Jeeze," he said.

CHAPTER TWENTY-THREE

After a long and uneventful train ride to Dallas, Murphy, Knoop, and Silver Fox were met on the platform by Sheriff Mc-Coy and Marshal Rourke.

"I'm Marshal Rourke. This is Town Sheriff McCoy," Rourke said. "Hardy said you was a big man, so you must be Murphy," he said looking at Murphy.

"This is Pinkerton's Agent Melvin Knoop and Army scout Silver Fox, but call him Sam," Murphy said.

"I've booked you into the La Casa Dallas, a really fine hotel," McCoy said. "It has its own livery for your horses. We'll walk over there and if you'd like, get a bite to eat at the Café L'Amour. We have much to discuss, and I figure you'd rather do that on a full stomach."

The walk from the station to the center of town was about two-tenths of a mile. Dallas was a boom town of ten thousand residents that seemed to have grown overnight. With the Red River as a northern border and the railroad as its central focus, it had enjoyed a large economic growth over the past decade.

The La Casa Dallas was centered right on Main Street, a wide, congested boulevard. Women wore the latest fashions, businessmen wore fine suits, and the cowboys went unarmed due to an ordinance against openly carrying firearms inside the city limits.

"Stables are out back," Rourke said. "Take your rifles and saddlebags in with you, and McCoy and I will walk your horses to the livery and board them for you."

"We'll meet you in the lobby and walk over to the L'Amour for supper," McCoy said.

"Sounds good," Murphy said. "And I'll pick up the tab."

"That sounds even better," McCoy said.

Murphy, Knoop, and Silver Fox entered the large, very plush lobby and immediately drew stares from patrons on sofas and chairs.

A slight man with spectacles at the check-in desk seemed slightly taken aback when Murphy, Knoop, and Silver Fox approached him.

"Name is Murphy. We have a reservation for three rooms," Murphy said.

"Two. Two rooms I'm afraid," the clerk said.

"The reservation is for three," Murphy said.

"I'm afraid you don't understand," the clerk said. "This is a high-class hotel for gentlemen and ladies only. There is a hotel on the other side of town that takes his kind," the clerk said and looked at Silver Fox.

"By his kind, you mean exactly what?" Murphy said.

"You know perfectly well what I mean," the clerk said. "Now you and your associate can stay, but I'm afraid the Indian has to go."

Every eye in the lobby was now on the desk.

"Why?" Murphy asked.

"Why? Why? Well because, that's why," the clerk said.

"*Why* is a question, and the word *because* is generally followed with an explanation and not another question," Murphy said.

"Now see here . . ." the clerk said.

"This man has fought in more wars than you have fingers and toes, starting with the Civil War, and against dozens of Apache, Sioux, Crow, and too many others to count so pipsqueak assholes like you can sleep safe in their beds at night," Murphy said.

"I'm calling the sheriff," the clerk said.

"You do that. In the meantime, we'll take three keys for three rooms preferably with balconies," Murphy said.

The clerk stared at Murphy.

"Mister, on all that is holy and all that isn't, I wasn't asking," Murphy said.

"How are the rooms?" Rourke asked when Murphy, Silver Fox, and Knoop appeared in the lobby.

"Fine," Silver Fox said. "Mine has a nice big balcony."

"While you were checking in, I reserved a table for five at the Café L'Amour," McCoy said.

"Wait one second. I forgot something," Silver Fox said and dashed back to the desk.

The clerk glared at him. "Yes?"

"When we return from dinner, if anything in my room is disturbed, anything at all, I will go to your home tonight and take your scalp," Silver Fox said. "And that is one thing I know a great deal about."

"Thank you, Louis, that will be all," Rourke said to the waiter.

"I shall be back in about twenty minutes with your steaks. If you wish more coffee, I will bring a fresh pot," Louis said and walked away.

The Café L'Amour was a reservation-only establishment open for dinner from five to nine p.m. except for Sunday, when they served what was quickly becoming known as brunch. It was a European custom, Louis had explained.

"Let's get down to it," Rourke said. "We knew from the original telegrams from a month ago there was a manhunt on for the two described in the telegram we received yesterday afternoon. I have four deputies and McCoy has twelve, and sometimes that doesn't seem near enough."

Rourke looked across the table at McCoy.

"We set up an immediate manhunt," McCoy said. "There are at least a dozen or more saloons that offer sporting women and two regular brothels on the bad side of town, so to speak. I assigned my deputies to work in teams of four to check each one."

McCoy paused to take a sip from his coffee cup. "Four of my men caught up with them when they were leaving a brothel around midnight on Ash Street in the so-called bad side of town. They had two women with them from the brothel. My men were armed with .44 Schofields and shotguns. The two men were unarmed, but that didn't matter. My men surrounded them and told the women to step aside. My men had handcuffs, and two of them went to cuff the suspects. According to what they told me from their hospital beds, the giant moved so fast they never had a chance."

"He attacked them?" Murphy asked.

"That's one way of putting it," McCoy said. "One man has a broken back. He said the giant picked him up as if he were a child and smashed him into the ground. It will be a miracle if he ever walks again. Another man has a broken neck and probably will die from it. The other two have broken arms and legs. The two women said that if they had to guess, the entire skirmish took six or seven seconds, no more than that."

"The two men?" Murphy said.

"They were seen riding south out of town by several witnesses," Rourke said. "Two of my deputies and two of McCoy's men left this morning to try and pick up their trail."

Silver Fox looked at Murphy. "We'll leave at first light," he said.

"Shouldn't you wait for our men to return?" Rourke said.

"They won't return," Silver Fox said.

Rourke and McCoy looked at Silver Fox.

"You can count on that," Silver Fox said.

"How about I buy you gents a drink after we eat?" Murphy said.

"When you said buy us a drink, I assumed you meant at a saloon," McCoy said.

They were in the parlor of Miss Marla's Gentlemen's Club, the brothel where the suspects were approached by the deputies.

Marla, an experienced madam of around forty, served rye whiskey over ice and smoked a thin cigar.

"Outcalls are allowed," Marla said as she took a chair. "I don't own the place, just run it, or they wouldn't be."

"Where are the two ladies?" Murphy asked.

"I'll send for them," Marla said.

Faye was barely in her twenties, had little to no formal education, and couldn't read or write. She was beautiful to look at with blond hair, blue eyes, and a petite frame, and she was one of the most popular girls in town. She regularly received proposals of marriage from a dozen cowboys a week that she rejected. "A smelly cowboy is a smelly cowboy, married to him or not. If I'm to bone a smelly cowboy, it's better to get paid for the work and not have to cook him supper afterward," she was fond of saying.

Murphy questioned her first.

"That man is an animal," Faye said in a Texas drawl. "He damn near crushed me with his weight, he was so big. I asked him if I could get on top, but he ignored me and kept pumping away like he was some kind of steam piston on a train. The second time I told him I couldn't stand his weight, so he flipped me over and we did it from behind."

"I'm not interested in that," Murphy said. "Did he make conversation and ask you any questions?"

"Questions? Wait, he did," Faye said. "He asked me if I was healthy. He said he didn't want to catch no whore's pox. I told him I never been sick a day in my life."

Murphy looked at Marla. "The other girl?"

Jolie was in her late twenties, but looked so much like Faye they could pass for sisters. "All that man wanted to do was talk," she said.

"Talk or ask questions?" Murphy said.

"Now that you mention it, he did ask a lot of questions," Jolie said. "I had me some cowboys ask questions about catching a pox, but this guy was asking like he was some kind of doctor or something."

"Obviously you're in good health," Murphy said.

"Perfect," Jolie said.

"I inspect each and every cowboy's bean when they walk in the door," Marla said. "If there's anything leaking that shouldn't be, they are rejected. My girls will not catch a pox from some cowboy off the trail and spread it around town."

"What did they offer you for an outcall?" Murphy said.

"Fifty dollars each to go with them to their hotel," Jolie said.

"Did they pay you in advance?"

"Yes."

"You were lucky," Murphy said. "Very lucky."

"If there was any doubt those are our men, there isn't anymore," Murphy said as they walked to the hotel.

"You'll pull out in the morning?" McCoy said.

"At first light."

"I can't risk losing any more men," McCoy said. "Why not wait until my men return."

Murphy sighed. "Sam said it true when he said they won't be

coming back," he said. "Best get used to that idea."

"I'll see you before you go," McCoy said.

"The café opens at seven," Rourke said. "Let's meet for breakfast. The general store doesn't open until eight, so you'll have to wait anyway to get supplies."

"All right," Murphy said.

After McCoy and Rourke left, Murphy, Knoop, and Silver Fox took chairs on the long front porch of the hotel.

Murphy stuffed and lit his pipe.

"They know we're after them now," Knoop said.

"They know somebody is, and probably suspected it anyway," Murphy said.

Silver Fox sighed. "Well hell, if I might get kilt myself chasing these assholes, I ain't going to spend my last night on earth in the company of you two dandies," he said, then stood and left the porch.

"Sam? Where are you going, Sam?" Knoop asked.

Silver Fox didn't respond and vanished on the dark street.

"He's going to get his bean inspected, Melvin," Murphy said.

"His . . . oh," Knoop said. "Oh."

CHAPTER TWENTY-FOUR

Silver Fox was last to the breakfast table at the café located in the hotel lobby.

"Enjoy yourself?" Murphy asked as he munched on a piece of toast.

"Those two girls are crazy," Silver Fox said. "Plumb crazy."

"Two girls?" Knoop said.

"Best twenty dollars I ever spent," Silver Fox said.

"Never mind that now," Murphy said. "Right after breakfast I'll pick up supplies. Sam, I'll meet you and Melvin by the livery."

"Don't forget oranges and chocolate," Knoop said.

"I won't."

McCoy and Rourke looked at Murphy.

"He has . . . it's for . . . never mind," Murphy said.

Murphy carried fifty pounds of supplies in two large sacks to the hotel where Silver Fox and Knoop waited with the horses. Standing with them were Rourke and McCoy.

Murphy loaded the supplies onto Boyle's saddle, and then shook hands with McCoy and Rourke.

"I'll send word back about your men," Murphy said and mounted the saddle.

It took until late afternoon for Silver Fox to be certain they were following the right trail left behind by the two men. What finally confirmed it was that the tracks made by the giant were much deeper in soft ground than that of his companion. A side-by-side comparison of the two prints told the story.

Murphy dismounted and stood beside Silver Fox, who knelt on the ground beside two sets of tracks.

"No sign of the posse?" Murphy said.

"No."

"What do you want to do?"

"There's an hour of daylight left," Silver Fox said. "Make camp. I'll scout ahead and be back by dark."

Steaks were sizzling in a large pan, beans were bubbling, and coffee was ready when Silver Fox entered camp.

"I picked up the posse's trail about a mile ahead," Silver Fox said as he dismounted. "They're on a collision course to intersect sometime tomorrow afternoon."

"Any chance we'll catch them tomorrow?" Knoop asked.

"No," Silver Fox said.

"Best eat and grab some sleep," Murphy said. "We'll need to be in the saddle before sunrise."

"Murphy?" Knoop said from inside his bedroll.

Murphy turned over and looked at him. "What is it, Melvin?"

"When we started this in New York, I never dreamed we'd be out this long," Knoop said. "Doing what we're doing."

"You've come far, Melvin," Murphy said. "The baby fat around your middle is gone, and your hands have toughened up considerably."

"I'd like to ask you a question," Knoop said. "I've been carrying around a letter from Scotland Yard for months. They want me to take a position with them as an investigator. The thing of it is, I quite like America. I'm not sure I want to go back."

"I can't tell you what to do, Melvin. You have to decide that for yourself," Murphy said. "I can tell you this though. A man should do and be what he is best at. Farmer, lawman, banker, it's all the same if you're true to your nature. I've seen many a man lose his way because he was hell-bent on being a farmer when he was meant to be a store clerk. Whatever you do in your life, don't cheat yourself out of opportunity."

"Thanks for the advice," Knoop said. "I'll really give it some serious thought."

"Goodnight, Melvin," Murphy said.

"They intersected the trail here," Silver Fox said. "South and slightly east."

"How far to the Pecos River?" Murphy asked.

"Not far. If they cross it, we can pick up their trail," Silver Fox said. "If they travel in the shallow bed, we'll lose them for a while."

"How far behind is the posse?" Murphy asked.

"A day, maybe less."

"We've made up some time," Murphy said.

"We have," Silver Fox said.

"Take us across the river, Sam," Murphy said.

Silver Fox guided them to a shallow crossing at the Pecos River. He dismounted and spent considerable time inspecting the area.

"Wait here," Silver Fox said.

He mounted his horse and entered the shallow riverbed. He followed signs left behind in the stones and pebbles, then crossed the river in water that touched the heels of his boots and emerged on the other side and dismounted.

He turned and waved to Murphy and Knoop to cross.

"Lexi isn't a tall horse," Murphy said as he reached for the rope on his saddle. "The water will reach the top of your boots and she won't like it." He looped the lasso end around Lexi's neck and tied the other end to Boyle's saddle horn. "She might panic a bit. Keep her calm and let Boyle do the work."

Murphy guided Boyle into the river and Lexi followed. She was calm until they reached midpoint where the water level was above Knoop's boots, and she began to panic.

"Rub her neck, keep her calm," Murphy said.

Lexi froze in place and tried to buck, but Murphy yanked on the reins and Boyle all but towed her to a shallower point in the water. Then she calmed down and crossed to the other side without incident.

Murphy removed the rope and replaced it.

"That wasn't so bad, was it girl?" Knoop said as he rubbed Lexi's neck.

"It's as if they want the posse to catch them," Silver Fox said.

"They probably do, Sam," Murphy said.

Silver Fox got back in the saddle. "We'll ride until noon and rest the horses then," he said.

"A pot of coffee would be good," Silver Fox said.

"I'll make it," Murphy said.

"Be back in a bit," Silver Fox said and rode away to scout ahead.

While Knoop removed the saddles from Lexi and Boyle, Murphy built a fire and put on a pot of coffee.

"Do you think it's true what Sam said, that they want the posse to catch them?" Knoop asked as he brushed Lexi.

"Yes," Murphy said. "The best way to get rid of a posse is to let them catch you."

"You mean an ambush?" Knoop said.

As he stuffed his pipe, Murphy nodded.

"I feel like some fresh meat tonight," Murphy said. "Keep your eye out for any game."

"You don't want to talk about it," Knoop said.

"No."

Kai made a quick trip to town for supplies and to pick up the mail. She was pleasantly surprised to find another letter from Murphy. It was posted in Wichita Falls, a town she had never heard of before.

She rushed the carriage home and left the groceries unattended in the kitchen, sat at the table, and tore open the letter.

My Dear Kai, I am posting this letter from Wichita Falls in north Texas after crossing the Llano. The trail led to the ghost town of Adobe Walls and the only way there was across the Llano. Surprisingly, we came across an old hermit named George who has been living there since the Apache Wars in 'seventy-four. We took him to Wichita Falls where he will live out his days in a boarding house. I wanted to write the things that are in my mind, but I am having a difficult time finding the right words. During the many months I didn't see you I have to confess it was deliberate on my part. I've never been able to figure out how a woman feels inside. I didn't want to show up and be a nuisance to you if the feelings were one sided. It was stupid on my part to deny the feelings I've had for you since we met so many months ago and I am glad I corrected the situation. I can't say for sure when I will return to Fort Smith, but I have the feeling it won't be much longer. Yours, Murphy.

"Corrected the situation?" Kai said aloud. "Yours, Murphy? How, how can a man be so intelligent and sure of himself in one way and such a complete fool and idiot in another."

Kai folded the letter and tucked it into the pocket of her skirt. As she put away the groceries, she sighed and said, "I'll keep him, though."

Late in the afternoon, while Silver Fox was riding point about a mile ahead of Murphy and Knoop, rifle shots echoed ahead of them. Five or six shots in quick succession.

Murphy yanked Boyle's reins and said to Knoop, "Let's go."

They raced after Silver Fox's tracks. After a quarter of a mile, Murphy brought Boyle to a sudden stop.

"What?" Knoop asked as he stopped Lexi.

"Look at the sky," Murphy said.

Knoop looked at the circling dots in the sky. "Buzzards," he said.

Several more shots rang out and two dots fell from the sky.

"We better get there," Murphy said.

He raced Boyle and within minutes, Murphy arrived at the site where Silver Fox was bashing dead buzzards with the butt of his rifle.

"Filthy . . . stinking . . . bloodsuckers," Silver Fox screamed in a rage.

Murphy dismounted and grabbed Silver Fox by the arm.

"Look what they did, these filthy creatures," Silver Fox said.

Knoop arrived and dismounted. "My good Lord," Knoop said.

The buzzards had picked away at the four dead lawmen's flesh clear to the bone in some places.

Silver Fox yanked his arm free and smashed at a dead buzzard with the butt of his rifle. "Sons a bitches," he snapped.

"Enough, Sam," Murphy said. "There's enough daylight to scout ahead while I bury them."

Silver Fox looked at Murphy.

"Go on," Murphy said.

Silver Fox mounted his horse, held the rifle in his left hand, the reins in his right, and rode away.

Murphy removed his jacket and placed it over Boyle's saddle. He removed the folding shovel and turned to Knoop.

"Find a spot to make camp up ahead while I bury these men," Murphy said.

After dark, Silver Fox returned. He dismounted at the campfire, and Murphy filled a cup with coffee and added some bourbon to it.

Silver Fox took the cup and nodded. "Thanks."

Murphy stirred the bacon and beans cooking in fry pans.

Silver Fox sat on the ground and sipped from the cup. "I found their horses a few miles ahead and set them free. I left the saddles for anyone who might come along to find."

"And the trail?" Murphy said.

"You won't like this, but five miles from here, they split up and went separate ways," Silver Fox said.

"Split up? Why?" Knoop asked.

"They split up means we have to split up," Murphy said. "Divide and conquer, Melvin. They don't know how many are on their trail, but by splitting us up, it weakens us as an effective tracking force."

"I'm liking these two less each day," Silver Fox said.

"What direction did they take?" Murphy asked.

"The big man headed south toward the Brazos," Silver Fox said. "The small man rode southeast along the Pecos River. It was too dark by then to continue, so I turned around."

"As far as we know, these two have been together since New York, but it's my opinion they have been together much longer than that," Murphy said. "My guess is they will look to team up again at a designated place."

"Where?" Knoop asked.

"What's along the Brazos?" Murphy asked.

"Waco and then Houston," Silver Fox said.

"The Pecos?"

"Nothing. It ends at Galveston," Silver Fox said.

"My guess is they'll meet up somewhere along the line," Murphy said.

"Where?" Knoop asked.

"We'll figure that out as we go along," Murphy said. "Right now let's eat and get some sleep."

CHAPTER TWENTY-FIVE

"Here is where they split up," Silver Fox said.

Murphy dismounted and knelt beside Silver Fox.

"No doubt the big man is headed south," Murphy said.

"What do you want to do, Murphy?" Silver Fox said.

"I'll trail the big man, you and Melvin follow the small man along the Pecos," Murphy said.

"Are you sure?" Silver Fox asked.

"I'm sure."

"We might be riding into a trap?" Silver Fox said.

"That's a good possibility," Murphy said. "How many days' lead do they have on us from here?"

"Two and a bit," Silver Fox said. "They lost a whole day ambushing the four lawmen."

"Our choices are to push hard and try to catch them, or ride to the nearest town and recruit a posse. By the time we're on the road again, they will have a week on us," Murphy said.

"Agreed," Silver Fox said.

Murphy looked at Knoop.

"Agreed," Knoop said.

"Let's divide up the supplies," Murphy said.

Murphy gave two-thirds of the supplies to Silver Fox and Knoop. They shook hands and mounted up.

"Watch out for an ambush," Murphy said. "If something doesn't look right, feel right, it probably isn't."

"Good advice," Silver Fox said. "I hope you follow it."

"Murphy, I . . . I have no words," Knoop said.

"Well, when you think of something, you can tell me when we meet up again," Murphy said.

By noon, Murphy followed the big man's trail close to the Brazos River. His deep-set tracks and narrow gait said he was in no particular hurry. He might be planning an ambush and wanted to give time for a posse to catch up with him. More likely, the horse couldn't handle his weight if he opted for speed.

He gave Boyle a thirty-minute rest. He used the time to study his maps. The Brazos went on for hundreds of twisted and winding miles. It was at least a three days' ride to Waco, but Murphy doubted the big man was headed there. He and the smaller man knew they'd been posted and they would avoid cities and towns with law enforcement in them.

Murphy nibbled on some cornbread with sips of water, then packed away the maps and continued following the trail. Late in the afternoon, he spotted a large herd of cattle a quarter mile in the distance.

The herd was stagnant. They were grazing and probably wouldn't move on until they cleared the land of grass.

Murphy rode until close to sundown. He filled his canteen with fresh water from a stream offshoot of the Brazos and then found a spot to make camp.

He cooked bacon and beans for supper and ate them with a hunk of cornbread. Afterward, he sat against his saddle to drink coffee and smoke his pipe.

"Tomorrow we will need to make up some ground," Silver Fox said. "The smaller man is riding in a hurry."

"Lexi can keep up," Knoop said.

"She will have to," Silver Fox said. "I can't afford to wait on her if we're to catch him."

"She'll keep up," Knoop said.

"Best get some sleep," Silver Fox said. "We'll leave at day-break."

"Do you suppose Murphy is correct, that they plan to meet up on the trail?"

"Possible," Silver Fox said. "A lot of things can happen on the trail."

"I was thinking that if Murphy does catch up with the giant, he'll be alone," Knoop said.

"Believe me," Silver Fox said as he got under his blanket. "From what I've learned about Murphy, you don't want to be on the wrong end of him."

Close to noon, Murphy thought about hunting some wild prairie chickens or a hare, but didn't want to wander too far away from the trail.

He stopped to rest Boyle for thirty minutes and ate some jerky strips with water. Murphy had some sugar cubes in the saddlebags and he gave Boyle a few to munch on between blades of grass.

Midafternoon, he spotted a wagon a hundred yards to his right and Murphy paused to check it out.

A woman alone was standing beside the wagon, looking at the rear wheel. A team of horses were hitched in front.

"Let's go see," Murphy told Boyle and trotted over to the wagon.

"Hello," Murphy said.

"Hello yourself," the woman said.

She wore pants and a man's shirt, a Stetson hat, and boots. Her chestnut-colored hair hung past her shoulders.

"Something wrong?" Murphy said.

"Got a bad wheel here in back," the woman said.

Murphy dismounted and approached the wheel.

"What are you doing out here alone?" Murphy asked.

"Who said I'm alone?" she said.

An old man hiding inside the wagon poked up with a single-barrel scattergun aimed directly at Murphy.

"Twitch, and I blow you straight to hell," the old man said.

Murphy looked at the old man.

"Go ahead, daughter," the old man said.

She pulled a knife from behind her back and stabbed at Murphy. Boyle rose up on his hind legs and smashed the woman with his front legs. The woman hit the wagon and knocked the old man over.

Murphy quickly grabbed the scattergun from the old man.

"Your daughter is unconscious," Murphy said. "I suggest you tend to her and then find a new trade. Robbing people doesn't suit you very well."

Holding the scattergun, Murphy mounted the saddle and galloped Boyle back to the trail. After a hundred or so yards, he tossed the gun into some tall grass.

Rubbing Boyle's neck, Murphy said, "Thanks for the help, boy."

Boyle snorted.

"Yes, you can have more sugar cubes," Murphy said.

"His horse is fast," Silver Fox said as he inspected tracks late in the afternoon. "As fast as mine, maybe faster."

"What are you saying? We won't catch him?" Knoop asked.

"Probably not until we reach Galveston," Silver Fox said. "Unless you want to kill that little bay you're sitting on."

"What if . . . what if you left me behind?" Knoop asked.

"I still wouldn't catch him," Silver Fox said. "In Galveston, he has nowhere to go, if that's where he's headed. He still might plan to meet up with the giant at some point."

"If Murphy doesn't meet up with him first," Knoop said.

"Something on your mind?" Silver Fox said.

"If we turned south, how far to the Brazos River?" Knoop asked.

"If we pushed hard, a day and a half."

"Maybe one of us should follow Murphy and the other ride to Galveston?" Knoop said.

"We're three days from Galveston," Silver Fox said. "It would take five days to catch Murphy. Whatever is going to happen will have happened by then. Let's push on until nightfall."

An hour before sunset, Murphy dismounted to inspect tracks. The giant's horse was faltering, close to stumbling. He felt the dirt and estimated the tracks were less than twenty-four hours old.

"Let's walk a bit, boy," he told Boyle and took the reins.

They walked about a mile to the point where the giant dismounted and walked his horse. Murphy inspected the tracks.

"Tomorrow," he said. "We'll catch him tomorrow."

Murphy awoke a little before sunrise and made a fire and put on some coffee. Supplies were low and he ate some cornbread and jerky with the coffee.

Anticipating a long ride ahead of them, he gave Boyle some grain for the extra source of energy he might need.

As he saddled Boyle, Murphy rubbed his neck and said, "We'll catch him today. One way or the other."

"I'm riding south, Sam," Knoop said. "To find Murphy. You go on to Galveston if you want to, but I'm going after Murphy."

About to mount his horse, Silver Fox paused. "I can't let you do that, Melvin."

Knoop mounted Lexi and looked at Silver Fox. "My mind is made up, Sam."

"So is mine," Silver Fox said, and as Knoop turned Lexi, Silver Fox grabbed Knoop by the leg and pulled him to the ground.

"Goddammit, Sam," Knoop said as he stood up. "I'm going."

Silver Fox punched Knoop in the face and Knoop hit the ground.

"No, you are not," Silver Fox said.

Knoop rolled around on the ground in pain for a few moments and then he sat up and looked at Silver Fox. Blood from Knoop's nose and mouth ran down his chin.

Slowly, Knoop stood and reached for Lexi.

Silver Fox grabbed Knoop and punched him again and Knoop fell to the ground.

"I'll hog-tie you to the saddle and tow you to Galveston," Silver Fox said.

Knoop spat blood, sat up, and looked at Silver Fox. "I'm sorry, Sam," he said.

"Okay, now let's go," Silver Fox said.

"No, for this," Knoop said. He reached inside his jacket and pulled Murphy's .38 revolver, cocked it, and aimed it at Silver Fox.

"You're going to shoot me?" Silver Fox said.

"If you leave me no choice," Knoop said. "Now back off, Sam. Please."

Silver Fox backed up until he touched Lexi's stomach. He turned and patted Lexi's chest and said, "Okay, go on then. We'll meet up later."

Knoop stood and said, "Move away from Lexi, Sam."

Silver Fox turned and walked to his horse.

Knoop mounted Lexi, put the .38 away, and looked at Silver Fox. "I'll see you in a week, Sam."

Silver Fox touched the rim of his hat.

Knoop yanked the reins and Lexi took off running. After

thirty feet or so, the saddle slipped off Lexi, and it and Knoop fell hard to the ground.

Silver Fox walked to Knoop, who was slightly dazed.

"You loosened the saddle when your back was to me, didn't you, Sam?" Knoop said.

"Hey, you were going to shoot me," Silver Fox said.

"Shit," Knoop said.

Close to noon, Murphy spotted a dead horse about three hundred yards in the distance. He galloped Boyle to the dead horse and dismounted. The horse had been ridden to the point of exhaustion and had collapsed.

The giant left the saddle on him, but took the saddlebags and set out on foot.

Murphy touched the neck and felt around its chest. The corpse was still warm to the touch. He looked up and spotted the buzzards as they started to gather.

"Looks like you'll feast on this one for a month," Murphy said as he watched the buzzards.

"I'm sorry I struck you," Silver Fox said.

"I'm sorry I pointed the gun at you," Knoop said.

"Hold up," Silver Fox said.

"What?"

Silver Fox dismounted and inspected the tracks.

"What?" Knoop asked.

"The left rear shoe is cracked," Silver Fox said. "We're two days from Galveston. If his horse goes lame, we can catch him before he reaches it."

Silver Fox mounted the saddle and looked at Knoop.

"Lexi will keep up," Knoop said.

★ ★ ★ ★ ★

"Whoa, boy," Murphy said and brought Boyle from a gallop to a stop.

Five hundred yards ahead of them, the giant sat in a clearing beside a small campfire.

Murphy got the binoculars from the saddlebags and zoomed in on the giant. He was calmly drinking from a cup.

"He's waiting for us," Murphy said. He tucked away the binoculars and tugged on the reins. "Let's go take him up on the invitation."

Silver Fox raced his horse at full stride and Lexi, not to be undone, stayed very close to him.

Silver Fox was determined to catch the man, and if he had to ride his horse to exhaustion that is what he would do.

He glanced to his right. To the smaller horse's credit, she was only ten or twelve feet behind him.

It happened so fast Knoop was stunned into disbelief as Silver Fox fell from the saddle and a shot rang out so close together, it was almost one and the same.

Silver Fox hit the ground and his horse came to a stop.

Knoop yanked hard on the reins and brought Lexi to a stop. He dismounted and ran to Silver Fox. A huge hole in his left shoulder was bleeding a river.

"It's a through and through," Silver Fox said. "The worst kind of gunshot. It bleeds from both sides."

The man came from the tall grass behind Knoop. "Toss your guns," he said with an accent. "I don't want to kill you. I just want his horse."

Silver Fox looked at Knoop and nodded.

Knoop pulled the .38 and tossed it away. Then he removed the Colt from Silver Fox's holster and threw it near the .38.

"Now stand up," the man said.

Knoop stood.

"Turn around."

Knoop turned and looked at the man.

He was about twenty feet away and holding a rifle. He fit the description perfectly. "Hands in the air," he said.

Knoop put his hands above his head.

"That was a pretty good shot," Silver Fox said.

The man walked toward Knoop. When they were just feet apart, the man swung the rifle and struck Knoop in the jaw with the butt, and Knoop fell unconscious to the ground.

"I don't know who you are or if you're even following me, but I'm borrowing your horse," the man said and took Silver Fox's horse by the reins. "You'll find him in Galveston. I'll leave you your supplies."

He mounted the saddle, tossed down the saddlebags, and galloped away.

Silver Fox strained to sit up and nearly passed out, but he managed to reach Knoop and checked to see if his jaw was broken. It wasn't. Slowly, Knoop opened his eyes and looked at Silver Fox.

"Make a fire," Silver Fox said. "You have some work to do."

CHAPTER TWENTY-SIX

Murphy stopped Boyle about fifteen feet from the giant. He sat there beside a campfire and drank coffee from a cup. A pot rested in the flames.

"My horse died," the giant said. His voice was deep and thick with an accent.

"I came across it a quarter mile back," Murphy said.

"Where are my manners," the giant said. "Would you like a cup of coffee? It's fresh made."

"I would, actually."

The giant picked up the pot and filled a second cup and placed it three feet in front of him.

Murphy slid down from the saddle. As he walked toward the giant, he pulled and cocked his Colt and aimed it at him.

"I have no weapon," the giant said. "I have no need of one."

"I believe you," Murphy said.

Up close, the giant was massive the way a bull in his prime was massive. He had a large head that was attached to his shoulders by a neck as wide as his ears were far apart. His chest was barrel-like; his hands were bear claws. Murphy put his weight at over three hundred pounds.

Murphy held the Colt on the giant as he squatted to pick up the cup, then he stood and backed away.

"Who are you? Are you the law?" the giant asked.

"I am. My name is Murphy."

The giant sipped from his cup and said, "I am Aldo Zutter."

"Swiss?" Murphy asked.

"That's a matter of opinion," Zutter said. "My mother is Italian, my father from Switzerland. I was born in Switzerland and have lived in both countries. I speak Italian, German, English, and some Romansh."

"Would you mind telling me why you are running around murdering women?" Murphy asked.

"Women? You mean filthy prostitutes?"

"Call them what you will, the question is why."

Zutter reached for the pot and added some coffee to the cup.

"Murder is a harsh word," he said.

"What would you call it?" Murphy asked.

"I came to America six months ago to help my brother," Aldo said. "His name is Klaus. He is the greatest surgeon in the world."

"Your brother is a doctor?"

"No. A doctor wipes the snot from a child's nose and gives you medicine for a tummy ache," Aldo said. "My brother is a surgeon."

"I ask again, why are you and your brother murdering prostitutes?" Murphy asked.

"Please, put the gun away," Aldo said. "It doesn't frighten me, and after a while your hand will get tired."

Murphy de-cocked the Colt and replaced it into the holster. He sipped from the cup and said, "You make good coffee."

"Thank you."

"So tell me about your brother—what was his name?" Murphy said.

"Klaus."

"Right, Klaus. Tell me about him."

"What would you like to know?"

"Everything."

Aldo shrugged his massive shoulders. "He came to America

in eighteen sixty-two after graduating medical school in Geneva. To Boston, to your Harvard. After one year of study, the Union put out a cry for help for doctors for the war. My brother volunteered to join the army as a doctor, as a surgeon. They gave him the rank of captain, but he quickly rose to colonel. He traveled all over with the army and at every battle, he treated the wounded. Sometimes twenty amputations a day. Have you ever seen a man's leg amputated without morphine?"

"I have," Murphy said. "Many times."

"You served?"

"Under Grant for three years."

"Then you are familiar with the horror of war?"

"Yes."

"It was during these years on the battlefront that my brother began to develop his ideas about surgery," Aldo said. "After the war, he returned to Harvard and graduated, and then returned to our country in 'seventy-one where he continued to develop his ideas."

"What ideas?" Murphy asked.

"Organ transplant," Aldo said. "During the war, he removed hundreds of organs destroyed by bullets and mortars, and he used to write me letters about how powerless he felt when soldiers would die when they didn't have to."

"Men die in war," Murphy said. "It's simply the nature of things."

"Yes, but many died needlessly," Aldo said. "My brother deduced that a diseased or destroyed organ can be replaced with a healthy one if one was available. A person with kidney failure, for instance, could continue to live if someone gave him a healthy kidney and there was a surgeon skilled enough to replace one with the other."

"Transplanting organs, that's your brother's idea?" Murphy said. "Does your brother think he's God?"

"Go ahead and laugh, that's what his colleagues did all across Europe," Aldo said.

"I'm not laughing," Murphy said. "So he decided to return to America and . . . continue his experiments on prostitutes?"

"Who really misses prostitutes if they don't show up?" Aldo said.

"That's why he tried to match them up as closely as possible?"

Aldo nodded.

"And that's why he insisted they be healthy?"

"Yes."

"And how did these experiments fare?"

"Most of the donors died within an hour, but some of the recipients lived for as long as six or seven hours," Aldo said.

"But they didn't live?" Murphy said.

"Greatness comes at a cost," Aldo said.

"Explain to the dead women the cost of his greatness," Murphy said.

"They are worth more as laboratory experiments than as people," Aldo said.

"And where do you fit into all this?" Murphy asked.

"My money finances my brother's work," Aldo said. "I am quite wealthy, you see. Perhaps you've heard of me as Aldo the Giant, heavyweight wrestling champion of Europe."

"I'm afraid I'm not all that familiar with European wrestling," Murphy said. "But from looking at you, I'll take your word. So where is your brother now?"

"That is the wrong question."

"What is the right question?"

"Not where is he now, but where is he going?"

"Okay, where?"

"It's not going to be that easy," Aldo said and slowly stood up. He easily topped six foot five and weighed even more than

Murphy first thought. "However, I will tell you where he is going and what name he will be using to travel under if you can best me man to man."

"You mean fight you?" Murphy said.

"You could shoot me, but then you will not gain the information," Aldo said. "Or you could arrest me at gunpoint and by the time we reach Houston, my brother will be well on his way and I won't tell you where anyway."

"I think you might have a slight advantage at hand fighting," Murphy said.

"I give you my solemn word I will tell you," Aldo said.

"If I lose?"

"Then you'll be dead and have no use for your horse," Aldo said. "And a fine horse he is."

Murphy tossed the coffee cup to the ground.

Aldo smiled.

Murphy opened his gun belt and placed the holster on Boyle's saddle.

Aldo opened the buttons of his shirt and said, "It is a fine beautiful afternoon."

"Yes, it is," Murphy said.

Aldo removed his shirt and tossed it aside.

Murphy looked at him. Aldo was a solid wall of muscle.

Aldo watched as Murphy removed his shirt. "You are strong. Good," Aldo said.

Murphy took a few steps forward and held up his hands to show Aldo they were empty. Aldo did the same.

They stopped with six feet separating them.

"Begin," Aldo said.

Murphy clenched his fists, danced in, jabbed Aldo three times in the nose, followed up with a right hook, and then danced backward.

"Very good, Murphy," Aldo said.

Murphy rushed in, jabbed twice, hit Aldo in the jaw with an uppercut, and danced backward out of range.

Aldo looked at Murphy, spat blood, and grinned. "I see you've had some training," he said. "Good. I hate to kill the helpless."

Murphy pushed off his left leg, caught Aldo by surprise, and kicked him in the jaw with his right boot.

Aldo actually took several steps backward. He spat blood and looked at Murphy with mild surprise. Then, moving with a quickness that seemed impossible for a man his size, Aldo reached Murphy, grabbed his legs, lifted him over his shoulders, and flipped Murphy to the ground.

Aldo turned and looked down at Murphy. "I will end this quickly for . . ." Aldo said as Murphy hooked Aldo's right leg in his, turned on the ground, and tripped the giant onto his back.

Aldo slammed his hand against the ground. "Good. Very good," he yelled.

Murphy rolled over and kicked Aldo in the face with his right boot, then jumped to his feet.

Aldo looked at Murphy and then spat out a piece of a tooth. "You are pretty good," he said and quickly stood up.

For a moment neither man moved, and then Aldo rushed Murphy and as Murphy moved to his right Aldo cut left and slammed Murphy with a massive right arm. The brunt of Aldo's forearm caught Murphy just below the neck and sent him flying backward to the ground.

"But not good enough," Aldo said.

Before Murphy could recover, Aldo grabbed him around the waist and lifted him off the ground and slammed Murphy's back into his right knee.

As he released Murphy, Murphy moaned and fell limp.

Aldo grabbed Murphy again and lifted him to his feet, then encircled Murphy's neck in his bear-claw hands and actually lifted him off the ground.

"It will all be over in a minute," Aldo said and applied more pressure.

Murphy felt his throat close. Aldo had the strength of a bull.

"I promise I will not harm your horse," Aldo said.

Murphy felt as if would pass out and used his last bit of strength to grab Aldo's shoulders and delivered a world-class head butt directly into Aldo's face. As blood squirted onto Murphy, Aldo released him, and Murphy collapsed to the ground and gasped for air.

Aldo wiped blood from his eyes and grunted loudly. "Son of a bitch."

Murphy rolled away and stood up, gasping for air.

"I am going to kill you for that," Aldo said.

"Are there rules in European wrestling?" Murphy asked.

"Rules? Yes, of course."

Murphy opened his belt and slid it free and wrapped the leather end around his right hand.

"Well, we're not in Europe at the moment, and there are no rules in survival," Murphy said and lashed out with the belt like a whip and cut Aldo in the face with the heavy buckle.

Stunned for a moment, Aldo blinked and then felt blood trickle down from the fresh cut.

Enraged, Aldo charged Murphy, and again Murphy lashed out with the belt and cut Aldo's face.

Aldo screamed and charged again and Murphy cut him under the left eye.

Undeterred, Aldo charged a dozen more times, and each time he was cut and had to back off. His face was a mask of cuts and blood.

Then there was a moment of calm. Aldo lowered his hands and Murphy lowered the belt. After several seconds, Aldo nodded as if he approved of Murphy.

Then Aldo raised his hands and Murphy the belt, but instead of charging, Aldo reached down and grabbed a burning log from the campfire and threw it at Murphy's face.

As Murphy stumbled backward, Aldo seized the moment, charged Murphy, and flipped him over his shoulder.

Murphy hit the ground hard. Aldo scooped him up and flipped him again and then a third time.

Exhausted, Aldo stepped backward and gasped for air. "You are a great deal of trouble," he said.

Murphy looked up at Aldo.

"But, as much as I hate to kill a man like you, I must," Aldo said. He lifted his right leg and held it above Murphy's neck.

Just as Aldo brought the leg down, Murphy brought his right foot up and delivered a powerful kick to Aldo's testicles.

It took a second for the pain to register, and then Aldo held his testicles and sank to the ground and fell into a fetal position.

Murphy looked up at the blue sky and waited for some strength to return to his body. Then he rolled over and got to his knees.

Aldo had recovered enough by then to do the same.

Not three feet separated them.

"What is that poem you have in America?" Aldo said as he reached into his right boot and produced an eight-inch-long dagger. "Oh, yes. One if by land, two if by sea."

Murphy looked at the knife.

Aldo brought his hand back readying to thrust.

Murphy whistled three times.

Boyle charged forward and as Aldo turned to look at him, Boyle rose up and delivered a deadly kick to Aldo's skull.

Skull split nearly open, the giant fell dead to the ground.

Murphy took a deep breath as he looked at Aldo. Then he looked at Boyle.

"Help me up, boy," Murphy said.

Boyle lowered his head and Murphy took the reins. As Boyle brought his head up and took a few steps backward, Murphy was lifted to his feet.

Murphy rubbed Boyle's neck. "I think we're getting too old for this kind of work, don't you, boy?" he said.

Boyle nuzzled Murphy's face.

"I know, you're never going to let me hear the end of it," Murphy said.

Boyle snorted and pushed against Murphy's chest.

Murphy reached for his holster and strapped it on. He was about to mount the saddle when he paused and looked at Aldo.

"What did he say?" Murphy said aloud. "One if by land, two if by sea."

He put his left foot in the stirrup, ignored the aches and pains, and mounted the saddle.

"Two if by sea," Murphy said. "Galveston is a port town, isn't it, Boyle?"

Boyle snorted.

"Let's go to Galveston," Murphy said.

CHAPTER TWENTY-SEVEN

Silver Fox was asleep in the saddle. Knoop had tied his hands to the saddle horn to keep him from falling off Lexi, which he would have otherwise.

Holding Lexi by the reins as they walked close to the Pecos River, Knoop thought about the events of the day before.

Silver Fox instructed him to build a fire and then gave him his long Bowie knife to put in the fire until it was hot enough to melt flesh.

Silver Fox had a pint bottle of whiskey in his saddlebags and he instructed Knoop to pour some on both wounds. Then, while the knife heated up, Silver Fox drank the rest of the whiskey.

"Slap the knife on the chest wound first," Silver Fox instructed. "I'll probably pass out and you can put me on my stomach and do the back."

He didn't scream when Knoop put the hot knife to the open wound. Silver Fox gritted his teeth and sucked down the pain as the heated metal melted his flesh and closed the wound.

As predicted, Silver Fox passed out, and Knoop was able to quickly close the wound on his back without Silver Fox being aware of it.

Knoop made camp after that and kept a close eye on Silver Fox the rest of the day and night. During the night, Silver Fox developed a fever and Knoop kept him cool with a wet cloth that he placed over his forehead.

By morning, Silver Fox was awake, but weak.

Even now, twenty-four hours later, Knoop could still smell the burning flesh in his nose.

"Hey, Melvin?" Silver Fox said.

Knoop stopped and turned around.

"You're awake, good," Knoop said.

"I'm hungry and my ass hurts from being tied up like this," Silver Fox said.

After crossing the Pecos, Murphy didn't bother to try and find tracks. There was no need. He knew the final destination was Galveston.

He pushed Boyle hard, and the massive horse delivered thirty miles before sunset. He rewarded Boyle with a healthy dose of grain and a handful of sugar cubes. While some beans and bacon cooked, Murphy gave Boyle a good brushing and checked his shoes.

"I must look a sight," Murphy told Boyle as he sat against the saddle to eat. "We're just about a half-day's ride to Galveston. What say in the morning I take a bath in the Pecos and change into my clean shirt."

Boyle looked at Murphy and snorted.

"I agree, I don't exactly smell like roses," Murphy said.

"How do you feel, Sam?" Knoop asked as they ate supper close to the campfire.

"Better," Silver Fox said. "We're probably seven hours' ride from Galveston. Can Lexi hold both of us?"

"I don't know, Sam," Knoop said. "She's very game, but small."

Silver Fox looked at Lexi. "I've grown quite fond of that horse," he said. "It would be a shame to break her spirit."

"Or her back," Knoop said.

"Or her back," Silver Fox agreed.

★ ★ ★ ★ ★

"I can walk some, Melvin," Silver Fox said.

"The walking doesn't bother me much, Sam," Knoop said. "Besides, I don't want you . . ."

"Want me to what?" Silver Fox asked.

"By the river up ahead, see that tall horse?" Knoop said.

Silver Fox peered into the sun and shielded his eyes. "It looks like Murphy's horse," he said.

Murphy was soaking in the cool water of the Pecos when Knoop and Silver Fox arrived on Lexi and stopped next to Boyle.

"Is it Saturday?" Silver Fox asked. "Or are you just partial to baths?"

"That must have been some fight, judging from your face and the bruises on your body," Silver Fox said as he sipped coffee.

"A doctor? I can't believe it," Knoop said.

"What's important right now is we reach Galveston before he sets sail," Murphy said. "We don't know the name he's traveling under, so if we don't physically identify him, he's gone. Melvin, you can ride with me. Sam, you'll have to keep up."

Silver Fox looked at Lexi.

"She'll keep up," he said.

Galveston, Texas, was a huge city of nearly twenty-five thousand residents. Its size and economic growth came from being one of the largest and busiest port cities on the gulf coast.

Citizens on the streets looked at Murphy as he rode into town with Knoop and Silver Fox on Lexi right behind him.

They ignored the stares from people and the clogged streets and raced toward the large harbor.

They dismounted at a portside office marked *Harbormaster.*

★ ★ ★ ★ ★

"At least a half-dozen ships have set sail in the past thirty-six hours," the harbormaster said. "Four-mast schooners carrying cargo and some passengers and passenger ships bound for Europe and South America. I can't check registers for a name if you haven't got one."

"I doubt he'll go to South America," Murphy said. "Where in Europe?"

The harbormaster checked his registry book. "One cargo ship with one hundred passengers and one passenger ship with three hundred aboard bound for England," he said. "One cargo ship without passengers bound for Spain, and one cargo ship with fifty passengers bound for Portugal."

"He wouldn't go to Spain or Portugal," Murphy said. "He's bound for England."

"That's four hundred souls, and you haven't got the name he's traveling under," the harbormaster said.

"No, we don't," Murphy said.

Having dinner at the Galveston Harborside Hotel, Murphy said, "What did the doctor say about your wounds, Sam?"

"He said Melvin saved my life," Silver Fox said. "I'll heal with scars, but I'll be fine in a few months."

"Good," Murphy said.

Knoop sighed.

"What?" Murphy asked.

"He got away," Knoop said. "After all this, he got away."

"One of them did," Murphy said. "Besides, I have the feeling we haven't heard the last of him by a long shot."

"What a crazy idea, transplanting human organs," Silver Fox said.

"I'm not so sure it's all that crazy, even if he was," Murphy said.

"Sam, I wonder if I may ask a favor of you?" Knoop said.

"The least I can do," Silver Fox.

"Would you keep Lexi for me?" Knoop asked.

"As I've been unable to locate my own horse, Melvin, I'd be happy to," Silver Fox said.

"Decided to return to Scotland?" Murphy said.

"Yes, to Scotland Yard to take that job," Knoop said. "I'll wire my bank in Chicago to send me all my funds and book passage on the first ship sailing to England. Who knows, maybe I will get to meet up with this . . . this ripper once again."

"Stranger things have happened," Murphy said.

"What about you?" Knoop asked.

"There's a ten o'clock train leaving tonight that will get me into Fort Smith by ten tomorrow morning," Murphy said.

"I believe I'll catch that train and switch out for home," Silver Fox said.

Murphy pushed his plate away. "Right now I'm going to have my clothes cleaned and soak in a hot tub," he said.

"Is this Saturday?" Silver Fox asked.

After Murphy and Silver Fox boarded Boyle and Lexi into the boxcar, they shook hands with Knoop on the platform.

"Murphy, I . . . I have no words," Knoop said with mist in his eyes.

"None needed, Melvin," Murphy said. "Send me a letter when you get settled in Scotland in care of my farm in Tennessee."

"I will. Take care of Lexi for me, Sam," Knoop said.

"She's a fine horse," Silver Fox said.

"She is," Knoop said. "Murphy, in all likelihood we will never meet again. I was wondering if you would care to share your first name with me."

Murphy leaned in close to whisper in Knoop's ear. "No,

Melvin, I surely wouldn't."

Murphy and Silver Fox boarded the train. Knoop stood on the platform and watched it slowly roll away from the station.

"I believe I'll go have me a drink," Knoop said.

Chapter Twenty-Eight

Kai was hanging linen to dry on the clothesline on the side of her house when she heard a horse snort from behind her.

She turned around and looked at Murphy, who was standing just outside the picket fence with his horse.

She dropped the linen and, like a schoolgirl, Kai ran across the yard and stepped over the fence and then froze in place when she saw the bumps, bruises, welts, and cuts on Murphy's face.

Kai put one hand over her mouth and gasped.

"Well hell, it's me," Murphy said.

"More like what's left of you," Kai said.

"I know I must look a . . ." Murphy said.

Kai threw her arms around Murphy, kissed him, and then hugged him tight. "If you are going to come home looking like this every time, we need to make some adjustments in our relationship," she said.

"Adjustments?"

"Be quiet, you fool," Kai said and kissed him again.

As a dozen guests filed into the dining room for supper, they found it dark, cold, and quiet.

There was a note and a one hundred dollar bill on the table.

One of the guests picked up the note and read it aloud. "Dear guests, I won't be making supper tonight as I am preoccupied.

Please use the hundred dollars to buy yourselves dinner at the café in town. Kai"

Kai nestled her head into Murphy's chest and said, "I don't think my guests will be very happy with me right now."

"Speaking of your guests, don't take any new ones until we get back," Murphy said.

"Are we going somewhere?"

"Yes."

"Where?"

"New York City to visit an old friend," Murphy said.

Kai sat up. "I can't go to New York City."

"Why not?"

"I'm half Navajo. The people in New York will . . ."

"Will think you're as beautiful as I do," Murphy said.

"What about clothes? I don't own the fashionable clothing women wear in places like New York," Kai said.

"We'll go shopping tomorrow morning," Murphy said.

"Who is the old friend?" Kai asked.

"Nobody important," Murphy said. "Just an old friend I'd like to see before we go meet my parents."

"It's hard for me to imagine you with parents," Kai said.

"Well, I have them you know."

"I can't wait to talk to your mother," Kai said.

They heard the front door close and Murphy said, "Sounds like your guests have gone to dinner."

"Good," Kai said. "Maybe you wouldn't mind preoccupying me one more time then. If you're not too tired and beat up, that is."

"I think I can find the energy," Murphy said.

"Good," Kai said. "We'll talk about your letter-writing skills later."

"My what?"

CHAPTER TWENTY-NINE

"President Ulysses S. Grant? That's your old friend we're going to see?" Kai said as the train arrived in New York City.

"He prefers to be called General," Murphy said.

"You ass. You are such a total ass," Kai said. "Why didn't you say something before we reached New York?"

"I didn't want you to think it was too big a deal and back out," Murphy said.

"Too big a . . . Grant only won the war. He was President of the . . . Murphy, what the hell is wrong with you?"

"A lot, probably," Murphy said. "I'll get our bags. We have a long carriage ride to Mount McGregor."

"My clothes, my hair, I need to . . ."

"Relax," Murphy said. "Grant is not that kind of man."

"What kind of man is he?"

"The kind who likes good cigars and whiskey and a good cuss word or two," Murphy said.

Kai sighed. "I wonder who he reminds me of," she said.

Julia Grant opened the door of the cottage and looked at Murphy. She was a handsome, dark-haired woman in her late fifties.

"When Hiram received your telegram that you were coming for a visit, it brought a tear to his eye," Julia said.

"Are you sure that wasn't the bourbon?" Murphy said.

Julia looked at Murphy for a moment and then her lips formed a big smile. "Maybe a little bit of both," she said. "And who is this lovely woman on your arm, Murphy?"

"Kai, I'd like to present former First Lady Julia Grant," Murphy said. "Julia, this is Kai."

"I do believe I have never seen such beautiful green eyes, Kai," Julia said.

"Thank you, ma'am," Kai said.

"Why don't you and I have a cup of tea while Murphy visits Hiram in the study," Julia said. "You'll have plenty of time to talk with Hiram over supper."

"Yes, ma'am," Kai said.

Julia took Kai's arm and looked at Murphy. "Second door on the right in the hallway is the study," she said.

Murphy walked down the hallway and knocked on the second door on the right.

Grant's gravelly voice said, "Come in."

Murphy opened the door and entered the study. Grant, behind his desk, stood up as Murphy walked to him.

"How are you, General?" Murphy asked.

They shook hands across the desk. Even though Murphy towered over Grant, it was Grant that was in command of the room.

"Not as spry as I once was," Grant said. "Want a drink?"

"I could use one."

Grant turned to the liquor cabinet against the wall and removed a bottle of bourbon and two glasses. He filled each glass with an ounce of the whiskey and handed one to Murphy.

"Your health, Murphy," Grant said.

"To yours, General," Murphy said.

They tossed back the shots and set the glasses on the table.

"Sit," Grant said as he took his chair behind the desk.

Murphy took a chair and looked at the stack of handwritten pages on the desk.

"What are you doing, General?" Murphy asked.

"Writing my memoirs," Grant said. "Boring, tedious task that it is. Don't worry. I won't use your name. No one would believe it anyway. Enough of that. I hear you've been called back into action by that pipsqueak in the White House."

"On occasion."

"I hear you did some big deal investigation for the pipsqueak in New York."

"I did."

"I hear that you found yourself a new woman."

"You hear a lot, General."

"We're old soldiers, Murphy," Grant said. "Our job is to win the wars and then fade away into the background."

"I'm starting to understand that, General," Murphy said.

"Judging from the look on your face, I'm not so sure," Grant said. "Get out while you can, marry that woman, and make a life for yourself before it's too late, Murphy."

"I'm considering it, General," Murphy said.

Grant poured another ounce of bourbon and tossed it back as if it were cold tea. He set the glass down and looked at Murphy.

"I wasn't asking," Grant said.

ABOUT THE AUTHOR

Ethan J. Wolfe is the author of the western novels *The Last Ride, The Regulator, The Range War of '82, Murphy's Law, Silver Moon Rising,* and *All the Queen's Men.*

The employees of Five Star Publishing hope you have enjoyed this book.

Our Five Star novels explore little-known chapters from America's history, stories told from unique perspectives that will entertain a broad range of readers.

Other Five Star books are available at your local library, bookstore, all major book distributors, and directly from Five Star/Gale.

Connect with Five Star Publishing

Visit us on Facebook:
https://www.facebook.com/FiveStarCengage

Email:
FiveStar@cengage.com

For information about titles and placing orders:
(800) 223-1244
gale.orders@cengage.com

To share your comments, write to us:
Five Star Publishing
Attn: Publisher
10 Water St., Suite 310
Waterville, ME 04901